SCHOOLING SYLVIA

by

ROXANE BEAUFORT

CHIMERA

Schooling Sylvia published by
Chimera Publishing Ltd
PO Box 152
Waterlooville
Hants
PO8 9FS

Printed and bound in Great Britain by
Omnia Books Ltd, Glasgow

SCHOOLING SYLVIA

Roxane Beaufort

Sylvia stood at the top of a staircase with shallow, carpeted treads. There was nowhere to hide, every head turned towards her, but she was hardly aware of anyone except Theo who lounged in a carved throne on a dais.

He fixed her with his tiger's eyes and rose to his feet, his deep purple cloak swirling around him. Sylvia advanced down the stairs like steel drawn to the magnet. Her dress displayed her body rather than concealed it. She had nowhere to run, nowhere to hide, prey to the eyes feeding on her from all sides.

She reached the bottom of the steps and Theo loomed over her. His robe parted with the sibilant whisper of silk and he pulled her into its darkness. He was naked, his phallus already hard, pressing into her belly.

He looked down at her and smiled grimly, 'Welcome to the Brimstone Club… welcome to the holy place where your virgin knot will be untied.'

Chapter One

The coach careered over the rutted road, every jolt vibrating painfully through the slender body of the young woman seated by the window. She clenched her hands in her lap, head lowered, face shadowed by her bonnet.

Flushing hotly, she was all too aware of the gentleman opposite, a good looking man in a high collared tail coat, exceedingly form fitting breeches and shining black Hessian boots. Her blush deepened as the pain in her buttocks increased, pressed into the upholstery beneath her. It was padded, but even so, nothing could ease those crimson welts.

What would he think of her, that quiet man who appeared to be absorbed in his book, if he had any idea of the event that had taken place that morning? The heat within her mounted as she visualised him witnessing her humiliation.

It seemed she was back in that long, comfortably furnished room where pupils, servants and staff had gathered for breakfast. The meal was over, and as she went to leave, mind preoccupied with the journey ahead, her way was blocked by the headmistress, Mrs Dawson.

'And where do you think you're going, Sylvia Parnell?' she enquired in her quiet, smooth voice, always perfectly controlled.

'To collect my coat and hand luggage, ma'am,' Sylvia replied, head held at a haughty angle, confident she had nothing to fear now. She was about to embark on the new life that awaited her once she had left The Academy For Young Gentlewomen where she had undergone education for five years.

'Your part of the dormitory is in a disgraceful muddle. Do you imagine you can walk out of here and have someone else clean up after you? Lady High and Mighty, too superior to soil you hands, I suppose,' Mrs Dawson continued, her tone light, yet with a threatening undertone.

Her black taffeta skirt rustled as she came closer, staring down at Sylvia with cold eyes. Her face was stern, greying hair confined beneath a snowy white mob-cap that matched the apron fastened below the chatelaine hanging on slender chains from her belt. This was the symbol of her authority, carrying a money purse, scissors and keys to every room.

'That's not true,' Sylvia protested, despite the terror that was making her shake. 'I've packed my trunk and cleared out the tallboy. I'll strip the bed before I go.'

'Are you arguing with me?' Mrs Dawson asked, her thin brows drawn down, the two hectic spots of colour appearing on her cheeks betraying her inner turmoil.

'No, ma'am. Simply telling the truth.'

'The truth, is it? I think not, girl. You wouldn't know the truth if it upped and bit you,' Mrs Dawson declared and grabbed her by the arm, jerking her around. Then she gave her a hard slap across the face with her open palm.

Sylvia yelped, her cheek stinging, her fear replaced by raging indignation. Instead of cringing, she shook Mrs Dawson off and stepped back. The watching pupils gasped. No one dared defy the headmistress.

Mrs Dawson turned pale, her breasts rising and falling beneath her cream lace fichu, then, 'Take off your dress,' she ordered, still using that quiet tone. 'If you refuse, Eliza shall do it for you.'

Eliza was Mrs Dawson's maid, a raw-boned, ugly creature who resented anyone with a claim to beauty, forever subjecting Sylvia to her spite. She stood by her mistress's side, her small eyes gleaming as they roved over the girl's body, her tongue creeping out from the cave of her mouth to lick her lips in greedy anticipation.

Aware of all eyes on her, Sylvia reluctantly unbuttoned her high-waisted muslin dress. It dropped down, clinging to her rounded hips till she stepped out of it and kicked it aside. Now she wore nothing but her lace-trimmed chemise and thin lawn petticoat.

It was chilly and her nipples bunched, red as cherries pressing against the flimsy fabric, embarrassing her by their pert ripeness.

She crossed her hands over those full breasts to conceal them, but Mrs Dawson would not tolerate this, commanding, 'Put your arms down. Stand straight. Back stiff. That's right. I'll not have my girls slumping.'

Her eyes narrowed as she examined Sylvia, pacing slowly round her, looking her up and down from toe to crown.

Clara Dawson was no dowdy schoolmarm, a well-preserved person who appreciated good living and indulged her appetites to the full. Her occupation provided her with ample means. The girls were mostly orphans, but not poor ones. Indeed, most came from the nobility, handed over to the care of godparents or relatives who could not really be bothered with them.

Mrs Dawson freed them from responsibility for a substantial fee and, in return, assured the girls' guardians that they need not trouble their heads about their wards, need not even see them until they reached eighteen.

The girls were taught to read and write, embroider, paint watercolours, learn a smattering of French, play the pianoforte and sing prettily. More important still, they were instructed on how to comport themselves so they could net a wealthy suitor when the time came to put them on the marriage market.

They were smartly dressed, chaperoned at all times, and given plain though nourishing food. Mrs Dawson and her staff were strict and the pupils caned for the slightest misdemeanour. Not that their relatives ever knew this. On their infrequent visits, Mrs Dawson was the very soul of respectability and the girls too scared to complain.

It did not occur to them to question this harsh treatment. They accepted that they would be whipped and publicly humiliated. Mrs Dawson's indoctrination had been thorough and they fully believed that wilfulness and lack of submission were undesirable qualities in a female and that their future husbands would expect obedience at all times, using the birch if necessary.

But there was one who rebelled against this, and that was Sylvia. Proud, fiery tempered and hotheaded, she had always presented a challenge which the headmistress had enjoyed meeting. As Sylvia had ripened into womanhood, so her beauty had increased. Mrs Dawson lusted after lovely women, needed to subjugate them, became heated at the sight of their naked helplessness – found satisfaction in so doing.

Now she propelled Sylvia to the refectory table and pushed her, face down, across it. Eliza leaped forward and seized her wrists, binding them with thick hempen ropes. Then she spread her arms up and over the shiny oak surface, fastening them securely, and rucking Sylvia's petticoat to the waist and beyond.

Sylvia shivered though her face burned with shame. She could feel the cold air playing over her naked thighs and caressing the rosy hillocks of her buttocks. Further rope was fastened round her ankles and her legs splayed and tethered, displaying the deep amber cleft between, and the plumpness of her pouting pudenda crowned by curly fair floss.

She was aware of dampness there, and a curious, pleasurable spasm in her loins. She trembled, remembering nights in the dormitory when similar feelings had flooded her inner core at the touch of soft fingers exploring her. Clever little fingers that opened her, dabbled in the honeydew seeping from her vulva and wooed that tiny nub of tissue that crowned her slit, playing with it till she exploded in exquisite pleasure.

She wanted it now, wriggling against the cold, hard wood, trying to bring pressure to bear on her clitoris and, in that moment, Mrs Dawson brought the cane down with a whistling crack.

Sylvia yelped and jerked against her bonds, scalding pain shooting through her bared backside, leaving an awful, throbbing sensation. The cane rose and lashed her again – once – twice – thrice. Mrs Dawson, a past master at flogging, handled the rod expertly. No blow fell on the same place twice.

She laid on the strokes with cruel accuracy, leaving a half-inch gap between each, the former one already swelling and purpling, the agony of it reaching its crest as the next cut deep.

Tears ran from Sylvia's eyes and fell to the tabletop. She bit her lower lip till it bled to restrain her moans, twisting and threshing to no avail. All this did was chafe her wrists and ankles, bright red weals appearing, matching the long, livid marks on her bottom – crimson roses blossoming where the cane had seared those fleshy mounds.

Mrs Dawson left that reddened area and concentrated on the backs of Sylvia's thighs, slashing her from bottom crease to knee. Then, an equally skilled practitioner in the paradox of pain/pleasure, she ran her hands over the stinging flesh. Her fingers were cool, bringing instant relief, and Sylvia hoped against all hope that her ordeal was over.

Mrs Dawson removed her touch. There was a split second pause and then the cane attacked Sylvia's rump, falling everywhere without cessation, till not an iota of skin remained un-flayed, all a glowing, throbbing scarlet.

Sylvia could not restrain a sob. Her bladder was uncomfortably full, adding to her distress, but there was no way she intended to void its contents, refusing to add to her embarrassment by this lack of control over her water. She had seen girls do this under the harsh kiss of Mrs Dawson's lash, drenching the table and floor beneath with a stream of urine. Everyone had witnessed it – staring, even laughing.

Sylvia gritted her teeth and hung on, though every time the rod sliced into her buttocks the pressure on her bladder was almost unendurable. She could feel sticky liquid trickling between her pussy-lips to stain the oak, shamed to know this came from her secret entrance, her pubis scorching hot, echoing the heat radiating from the stripes that seared her derriere.

Her belly ached, her bladder yearned for release, her clitoris throbbed from the pressure and Mrs Dawson leaned over to whisper in her ear, 'You're ripe and ready. I wish I could be the fortunate man who will penetrate your sweet, juicy, tight little cunt with his hard cock.'

Sylvia started, unable to believe what she was hearing. The words were unfamiliar and coarse, yet she guessed their meaning. Could this be Mrs Dawson speaking, that correct lady who led a sedate crocodile of pupils to church every Sunday, who entertained the vicar to luncheon and had the town worthies to tea?

All thought was wiped away by the next onslaught of that thin, whippy cane.

Sylvia shut her eyes and clenched her teeth, refusing to cry out or wet herself, refusing to let go of her modesty and subject herself to this ultimate humiliation. It was nigh impossible, the torment of her tingling clit, the urging of her bladder very nearly causing disaster as she lay there with spread legs and haunches raised, receiving six more savage blows.

Unable to make her scream for mercy, Mrs Dawson grew tired of the game and threw the cane aside, gesturing impatiently to Eliza. She stood watching, hands on her hips, as the maid released Sylvia.

Smothering her groans, she eased herself from the table, gathered up her garments and, hardly able to walk straight with the need to pass water, managed to reach the privy. There, settling gingerly on the mahogany seat, she gasped in relief as the urine gushed from her.

Her back was one pulsing area of pain from waist to knee, but she limped to her room, washed her tear-stained face and dressed, coldly and deliberately feeding her rage. Her wrists were bruised, her ankles, too, but she refused to be deterred from donning those garments prepared for her release. After tidying her tawny-blonde curls, she fastened her green velvet pelisse over a new gown, and then put on a matching bonnet with a shovel brim, tying the ribbons under her chin.

She stared at herself in the pier-glass, critical of her appearance, but her face showed no sign of her torment, heart-shaped and delicate as a cameo, the heightened colour bathing her cheeks adding to this delightful picture of fresh, unsullied young womanhood. Her mouth, like her nipples, was deep pink, its shape slightly too generous for the fashion of the time, hinting at sensuality and passion. It was a face to inspire desire in every man she met – and women, too, if they were of the persuasion that preferred their own sex.

She was slim of waist, and her hips were rounded, wide enough to accommodate the most well developed male member. Her breasts were full and firm, rising proudly, with ultra-sensitive nipples that puckered tightly at the smallest breeze or lightest touch.

Only her unusual green eyes betrayed her force of character, wide-spaced and brilliant, shaded by lashes that were dark at the base and fair at the tips. They shone with a fierce light, frightening in their intensity, a challenge to anyone who thought to tame her.

She teased a few wispy curls across her forehead, and then turned from the mirror, ready to undertake her journey from Bath to London, shaking the dust of the academy from her feet forever.

She was just eighteen, young and resilient, filled with hope for the future, but even so, every movement was agonising. Proud though she was, she could not avoid being constantly reminded of her beating by the soreness of the raised welts on her behind.

'Are you all right, my dear young lady?' enquired a deep, masculine voice, bringing her back to reality. It was the gentleman on the opposite seat of the stagecoach.

'Yes, sir, thank you, sir,' she answered, unaware that her cheeks were wet with tears.

'You seem upset,' he said, adding nervously as he laid his book aside. 'I hope you'll forgive the presumption.'

'She is perfectly well, sir,' said the finely dressed woman seated next to Sylvia. 'I am her chaperon.'

'My most humble apologies, madam,' he answered, giving an ingratiating smile as he lifted his roll-brimmed topper in deference to her. 'I deduced this to be the case. Such a genteel young lady would hardly be travelling alone.'

Sylvia's companion inclined her head, the yellow plumes adorning her extremely fashionable hat nodding in agreement. 'You are correct in your assumption, sir, and I'm surprised, nay, astonished, that you should so far forget the proprieties as to address her when you've not even been introduced,' she admonished, yet with a hint of coquetry.

'I am so sorry and meant no harm. I swear it,' he vowed and placed one hand on his heart in a charming gesture. 'Dear madam, I trust I am forgiven.'

Sylvia's spirits rose and her tears dried. This was indeed a personable man. Were all the gentleman in London equally handsome and, here she took a quick peep to where his thighs rested, slightly apart on the seat, so generously endowed?

She knew next to nothing about male genitalia, but was impressed by the fullness nestling beneath his elegantly cut fawn breeches. He seemed genuinely concerned that he had caused offence and she hoped her companion's manner would not make him withdraw into silence again.

Mary Standish had been a surprise to Sylvia when she arrived at the academy and announced that she would be accompanying Miss Parnell to her aunt's house in Mayfair. She had introduced herself as Lady Rowena Bancroft's personal maid and confidante and whisked Sylvia away to the waiting coach – not Lady Rowena's private vehicle but one used for public transport.

Now Mary, too, was considering the gentleman closely. Though able to ape the grand lady, she had always been a servant, rising through the ranks to the privileged position of personal maid to a famous society beauty like Lady Rowena. Sylvia couldn't wait to meet her aunt, though knew little about her. Lady Rowena had never condescended to visit the school, content to let Mrs Dawson bring up her niece.

Mary gave the gentleman a calculating stare, a little smile playing about her red lips, as she said, 'I believe my charge is tired, sir. Perhaps I should take the seat beside you, then she can lay down and sleep.'

'Whatever pleases you, madam,' he replied, eyes sparkling as he continued. 'May I rectify my earlier omission by introducing myself. I am the Honourable Mr Henry Lanston.'

'And my name is Miss Standish,' she answered, equally formally, though Sylvia could not fail to notice that her dimpled hand, placed so close to her own, was shaking and her large breasts heaving in response to her quickened breathing.

Mary stood up and while attempting to negotiate the coach's sway ended up in Henry's lap, knocking his hat off. He made no attempt to dislodge her or reclaim his headgear, his arm tightening about her ample waist, pressing those big, soft breasts against the frills rising above the gold watch-chain and fobs spanning his brocade waistcoat.

Sylvia watched this performance with round eyes. She was avid to learn everything she could about the strange, mysterious act that took place between a man and a woman, a scandalous mode of conduct that the girls had whispered about after the candles had been extinguished in the dormitory.

She could hardly believe that such tales were true. Alarmed and intensely curious, she was so arouse and excited that the fluffy hair coating her secret lower lips became dampened with honeydew.

Her nipples crimped against her chemise, two points of passion aching to be touched. She pressed her thighs tightly together, that odd, aching sensation spreading from her womb to her cleft. She wished it was herself sprawled across Henry Lanston, her arms wound round his neck, fingers buried in his brown hair, face pressed to his shirt front, hips nudging that area hidden in his breeches which she was so curious to explore.

Mary caught her looking at them and said sharply, 'Lie along the seat, my dear. That's right. Put my reticule under your head and try to have a nap. Close your eyes. We've a way to go yet. I'll wake you when we get there.'

Sylvia did as she was bid though the stripes hurt, buttocks stiff and sore. Lifting her legs, she stretched out, the bag making a soft pillow. An imp of perversity made her open her long, fitted coat, and her limbs gleamed under the sprigged cotton gown, girded by a pink ribbon just beneath the breasts. This, together with the low oval neckline, emphasised those swelling globes, succulent as fresh apples. Even with a petticoat, this modish attire was revealing, no more substantial than a nightdress.

Glancing across before lowering her lids in feigned sleep, she saw Henry admiring her over Mary's shoulder. The expression in his fine dark eyes sent a spasm of longing through her, making her juices flow even more. She could feel it soaking her inner thighs, and slipped her hand down to cup her mound, very casually as if simply resting it there, but in reality allowing her middle finger to press into her warm, wet crease.

'Sleep, Miss Sylvia,' Mary commanded, squirming on Henry's lap and making no attempt to leave this cherished position.

'Yes, Mary,' Sylvia answered obediently, but in reality she was peeking beneath her lashes.

Confident that her charge was asleep, Mary shifted from Henry's knee to his side, then, turning, she deftly unfastened the buttoned flap of his breeches, letting it fall open.

Sylvia almost betrayed herself by a gasp but managed to suppress it, feasting her eyes on the large, pink snakelike organ that Mary drew out from its nest of sepia curls. It was long and thick and upward pointing, the stem knotted with veins, the cap red and shiny smooth, a clear drop of dew seeping from its single eye. Beneath this proud staff she could see a pair of balls, bulging potently in their velvety sac.

It was true, then. The other girls had not been wrong. This was the aroused male equipment they had giggled about. But how could one possibly permit such a huge object to be inserted into one's tender hole? Wouldn't it split one apart?

Sylvia's caned buttocks stung; her vulva clenched; a further trickle of wetness soaked into her petticoat; her bud swelled from its tiny hood and her finger pressed down on it involuntarily.

Mary worked her fingers over Henry's weapon and it jerked in her hand as she pulled back the foreskin and lowered her head. Slowly, lecherously, and with infinite care, she took the tip between her lips. Her tongue furled around it, and her mouth glided back and forth, gradually taking in the whole thickness and length of his shaft until her face was buried in his dark, wiry thatch.

She purred, deep in her throat, sucking enthusiastically.

Sylvia was bewildered, excited, disgusted. How could Mary do such a thing? Yet, even as she was aware of the coach's jouncing along the highway, the rumble of wheels, the passing hedgerows heavy with blossom, so she seemed to be encapsulated in a sensual dream.

Her eyes fed on the sight of Mary sucking the gentleman's cock. She could smell it, salty and strong, different to her own seashell washed emanations wafting from between her legs, and the more powerful odour of Mary, too. The forceful aroma of a mature, experienced woman fully aroused and about to take her pleasure.

Henry was pressing upwards, forcing his penis further into Mary's mouth, but she withdrew teasingly and lifted her skirts. Sylvia watched intently, no longer careful, for the couple were too absorbed to notice her.

Mary was wearing flat-heeled white kid boots and pink silk stockings fastened with buckles just above her knees, but as the skirt rode higher, an extraordinary spectacle was revealed. Her fleshy thighs and big, dimpled buttocks were bare and as marked with red stripes as Sylvia's own. Someone had been whipping her, and recently, too, drawing blood to the surface.

From where she lay, Sylvia looked straight into the vast, deep crease dividing those massive haunches. As Mary spread her legs wide, she could see the crinkled mouth of her anus, the darkly furred outer labia, the wet red inner lips and the pulsing clitoris that swelled like a miniature penis between them.

Henry had pushed Mary's brief bodice down over her voluptuous breasts and was tweaking the long, brown teats. She reared above him and thrust one breast against his lips. He sucked the hard nipple into his mouth with the avidity of an infant, while she rolled her head from side to side, breathing in great gulps.

With her fist clamped round his phallus again, moving up and down, he buried his fingers between her legs, plunging two into her slick-wet channel and rubbing her clitoris with his thumb. Mary moaned, a light sweat beading her upper lip. Sylvia's excitement mounted as she watched him circling Mary's nub, pressing each side of it, flicking and tormenting it, while his fingers imitated the movement of coition.

Mary's palm was slippery with his pre-come juice, his prick standing hard and ready to explode. Then she gave a strangled cry and jerked against his hand, head flung back, eyes closed.

'It's coming… it's coming,' she whispered hoarsely. 'Oh, my God… yes… yes!'

Henry let her spasm round his fingers for a second, and then raised her so she straddled him, legs wide open, the bruises on her posterior glowing with renewed colour. Sylvia saw how he thrust his turgid prick into Mary's love tunnel while she moaned and worked herself along its length.

'Good girl. That's right. Do it. Harder. Harder!' he gasped, and his face was like that of a tortured saint. He gripped her buttocks in his strong hands, aiding the rapid rise and fall.

Mary increased her speed, pumping frantically. He gave a great cry and then slumped back in the seat with Mary milking him of every last drop of semen before collapsing over him with a long, groaning sigh of satisfaction.

Sylvia's heart was pounding, her cleft soaking wet, lower lips swollen and aching. She needed most desperately to raise her skirt and rub herself, but did not quite dare. They might come to their senses and see her. She must pretend to have witnessed nothing, lost in sleep.

Mary was the first to stir. As she lifted her hips away from Henry, Sylvia was amazed by the amount of creamy white fluid that smeared his phallus and dribbled from her vulva. She knew this carried his seed and wondered why Mary was not afraid that he might make her pregnant. Was it possible to perform this weird and wonderful act and not get with child? She realised she had much to learn and was impatient to start her lessons, sadly realising that this would probably not happen until her wedding night. Till then, she resolved to watch and make notes of other people's courtships and, as Henry wiped his flaccid organ on a monogrammed handkerchief drawn from an inner pocket, she observed that it was not quite subdued as yet. It was half erect, and the movement of the linen over its bulbous head caused it to thicken again.

Mary, meanwhile, was attending to her sex valley, dabbing it dry with her own kerchief, then smoothing down her skirts as best she could in that rocky and confined space, and finally adjusting her hat. Within moments, she and Henry were seated chastely side by side, books to hand, and no one would have been any the wiser.

The Fox and Hounds was the most prestigious coaching inn the market town of Marlborough possessed. Dusk was drawing a veil over redbrick Queen Anne houses, impressive civic buildings and the wide central street as the carriage bowled under the tavern's stone arch and into its cobbled yard at the back.

It was a hive of activity, ostlers shouting, horses being taken from between the shafts and led away to hay filled stables, the coachmen alighting, groaning and stretching before stamping off in the direction of the tap-room. Those who could only afford seats on the open tops of the carriages climbed stiffly down from these uncomfortable perches, while more affluent passengers left the interiors by way of little iron steps unfolded by grooms.

The mouth-watering smell of roasting meat and game drifted from the inn's kitchens. It was a fine old place, a gallery running round the four walls of the yard, attained by stairs which, in turn, connected with the bedrooms, giving guests the opportunity to observe the comings and goings below, if they so desired. Mary had broken her journey there on the way from London to fetch Sylvia.

'It's a splendid inn, recommended by all the very best people,' she declared, resting her fingertips on Henry's arm as he handed her down.

'I, too, have a room here for the night,' he answered, smiling at her. 'Perchance we might sup together?'

'La, sir… I'm not sure this would be quite proper,' Mary simpered, with a vain attempt to control the purple cashmere shawl that kept slipping out of place, drawing attention to her swelling bosom.

'Surely there could be no harm to your reputation,' he said earnestly. 'I'm not suggesting that it be served privately, but in the parlour. Besides which, Miss Sylvia will be with us throughout.'

How false they are, Sylvia thought as she trailed behind them into the tavern. Why, Mary's fanny is running with the copious liquid of her own arousal and his spunk, yet she is behaving with all the piety of a Sunday school teacher.

The tavern was not the first at which they had changed horses since leaving Bath. A team of four could barely cover ten miles without being winded, particularly in hilly country. There were always fresh animals waiting to draw the heavy coaches onward. These pauses provided not only stopping off and picking up points, but welcome respite where passengers could slake their thirst, satisfy their hunger and answer the call of nature.

Now, the Fox and Hounds would house Sylvia and her companion overnight and the journey be completed on the morrow.

The landlord was expecting Lady Rowena's niece and her

chaperon, rooms having been booked in advance, and he ushered them inside, bowing almost to the ground. He was a bumptious individual, wearing a green wool coat and breeches, a canary coloured waistcoat, a black cravat, black hose and buckled shoes. Short of stature and given to corpulence, he had heavy jowls, a balding head and beady eyes peering out above sagging pouches.

'Miss Parnell, welcome to my humble hostelry,' he began obsequiously. 'And Miss Standish… such a pleasure to serve you again so soon.'

'Good evening, Rawley,' Mary answered loftily, addressing him without the dignity of a title, as she did all tradesmen and servants. 'I trust you've ensured that the beds are warm and dry.'

'Of course, ma'am. You'll find naught to complain about here. Our service is beyond question. We are famed for our excellent food, clean rooms and carefully aired beds spread with fresh linen.'

He clapped his hands and summoned a boy to carry their smaller bags upstairs, the rest remaining strapped to the coach roof with a watchman standing guard, hefting a blunderbuss. It was Rawley's proud boast that clients' belongings were perfectly safe while on his premises.

Mary entered the bar parlour and went straight to the inglenook fireplace, holding her hands to the crackling logs. Spring it might be, but the evenings were still chilly. 'I want fires in our bedrooms,' she ordered crisply.

'Certainly. I'll see to it at once,' Rawley replied, and bustled away, but not without a lingering glance in Sylvia's direction.

A few locals and other travellers looked up from their pints and cards, acknowledging the entrance of gentry before settling back to drink and gamble. They were mostly men, female guests and children already tucked away upstairs.

Henry had taken it upon himself to order supper, accompanying the ladies to a table not far from the fire. 'I'm so glad you've done me the honour of permitting me to escort you,' he said, placing his hat on a spare chair and loosening his impeccably tailored coat. 'Ladies travelling alone… well, anything can happen.'

It already has, Sylvia thought wryly, though keeping this opinion to herself. I've seen your cock, Mr Lanston, and a fine specimen it is to be sure. There you sit, dignified and controlled, yet what will take place later when Mary imagines I'm safely ensconced in my maidenly bed? Will you creep into her room and repeat this afternoon's performance?

She envied her duenna, longing to have him lavish those sensual caresses on her, to take his plum between her lips and suck it, and feel his mighty weapon plunging through the sealed gateway of her virginity. The notion made her scorch with shame from the ribbons in her bonnet to the soles of her satin pumps.

The conversation was light, but Sylvia contributed little, only speaking when addressed directly, occupied with the difficult task of restraining herself from grimacing as her buttocks came into contact with the wooden chair.

She cursed Mrs Dawson silently for leaving this reminder of the academy imprinted on her tender flesh. At a time when she wished to appear calm and well behaved in order to impress her aunt, this was made doubly hard by the pain she found it hard to conceal.

She needed to reach the seclusion of her bedchamber, there to strip, twist round to view her posterior in the mirror and ascertain the damage sustained during the beating. From experience she guessed this would be extensive, the finger thick stripes turning purple. The arrival of covered dishes of hot food put this from her mind temporarily. She was ravenously hungry, and the menu lived up to the tavern's reputation. There were roast capons, stuffed with herbs and sausage meat and dripping with butter, a selection of vegetables, followed by tansy pudding and syllabub, each dish accompanied by fine wine. Even Henry and Mary stopped gazing meaningfully into each other's eyes and concentrated on eating.

Sylvia, used to drinking wine mixed with water, felt slightly tipsy by the time a waiter took away their used plates and brought cheese and dry biscuits to the table.

The tavern was noisier now, tongues loosening as the ale, wine and sack circulated. There was laughter and loud talk between customers and the buxom barmaid who, arch and flirtatious, tossed her dark locks and leaned forward so that her breasts rose above her bodice, bare to the nipples.

Rawley caught her doing this and though he made no comment, his small mouth set grimly even as his eyes roamed over those treasures so shamelessly revealed. He came across to the table where Sylvia sat, saying to Henry, 'Is everything satisfactory, your Honour?'

'It is indeed, landlord. I think we'll finish with a bumper of your best brandy. What do you say, Miss Standish?'

'Thank you, sir,' she answered, her face already flushed with wine and the excitement of his presence.

'And you, Miss Parnell?' Henry fixed Sylvia with his sparkling dark eyes, and she was certain that he knew she had not been asleep while he rogered her companion in the coach.

'A small glass, if it please you,' she murmured shyly.

The landlord slid away to fetch their order and Sylvia, feeling increasingly dizzy, inadvertently dropped her napkin to the floor. She bent to retrieve it and, in so doing, happened to glance beneath the edge of the white damask cloth.

She had fully intended to rise, but what she saw delayed her. It was dark there, but her eyes became accustomed to the gloom and she was astonished to see Mary's leg, her skirt slipped back above her knee as she stretched it out, her fashionably shod foot connecting with the mass between Henry's thighs. Even as they carried on a perfectly normal conversation, so she wriggled her toes, working them against the cods and prick concealed within his breeches.

Up and down she stroked him with that nimble foot and the bulge grew bigger, harder, pressing against the restricting fabric.

Sylvia sat up, spreading her napkin over her lap, feeling the light fabric of her bodice rubbing against her breasts which felt larger, fuller, the nipples protruding like the upturned noses of hopeful pets. She swayed a little, the parlour blurring, the sounds rising and falling, drifting and dipping.

'I'd like to retire now,' she said, tripping over the words, her tongue suddenly too big for her mouth.

'A good idea. I, too, am tired,' Mary agreed, smiling across the table at Henry. He lifted one eyebrow and rose, taking her hand in his, bowing from the waist and brushing her wrist with his lips.

'Very wise. An early night, ladies. We shall be off on the last leg of our journey at daybreak,' he said. 'For my part, I'll linger here a while. Finish my brandy before I seek my bed.'

Your bed or hers? Sylvia wondered, and followed Mary out.

Chapter Two

A maidservant led Sylvia and her chaperon up the central staircase with its wide, shallow treads and carved handrail, and along a candlelit passage.

She paused at a door, opened it with a key and stood aside to let them pass. The room was illumined only by the glow of firelight, till the maid went round, taking a taper to the candles in branched sconces.

She then crossed to a further door and flung it wide, 'Your room, Miss Standish,' she announced. 'It leads from the young lady's, but also connects with the corridor and gallery, should you desire to take the evening air. I've already had hot water sent up for your ablutions.'

When the maid had gone, Mary examined their lodgings and found them in order. Then she gave a prodigious yawn and said, 'Mercy on me, but I'm weary. Can you manage, my dear? I really must seek my bed.'

'Don't fret. I'm perfectly capable of washing and getting into my nightgown alone,' Sylvia replied, almost pushing her through the door that linked their rooms. She would hardly school her impatience to find out if Henry Lanston intended to share Mary's couch.

'Good night, dear, and sleep well,' Mary carolled as she disappeared into the adjoining apartment. 'Call me if you need anything, and don't forget to keep the passage door locked. One never knows what vile seducer may be creeping about at the dead of night, intent on having his wicked way with a helpless female.'

How true, Sylvia mused, and we both know who that is likely to be.

The dizziness was receding, replaced by restlessness. It was all too strange, new and exhilarating. No longer a schoolgirl, she was a lady adventurer on the road to London, that legendary city where, so it was said, the streets were paved with gold. Not that she believed this, but her heart thumped as she tried to imagine what kind of man might propose to her once her aunt had launched her into society.

She walked around her room, noting the solid oak furniture and panelled walls. The firelight danced over it, casting shadows on the plasterwork cornice edging the ceiling. The bed was a four-poster, big enough for more than one person, draped in cretonne curtains patterned all over with flowers.

Sylvia took off her pelisse and lifted her skirt, backing up to the cheval mirror on its stand. It gave her a full-length view of herself and her anger against Mrs Dawson rose up in a torrent as she saw the condition of her buttocks and thighs.

'Damn the woman!' she cursed aloud. 'How could she have dared treat me thus?' The better to see, she stripped off her gown, chemise and petticoat and stood there naked, save for her stockings and shoes. The candle and firelight played over her slender body, turning the skin to pale gold, and highlighting the fair triangle covering her mons. Sylvia raised her arms and sucked in her ribs, thrusting her breasts high. No one could have faulted this perfection, until she turned, presenting her back to the looking-glass.

Her fury returned tenfold.

A ladder of red rungs covered her rump, and further scarlet tracks lay across her thighs to the knees. She reached round and touched them, her anger increasing. Far from making her submissive, each beating she had ever received had only served to fire her rebellion.

Going to her bag, she took out a soothing unguent and applied it to the bruises. This always helped, she had found, and she continued to rub in the soothing balm, sighing with relief as it went about its healing work.

Feeling a little less stiff and sore, but no easier in her mind, she took up her discarded garments and, naked, walked to the armoire built into the wall that separated her room from Mary's. It was empty and smelled faintly of mothballs and lavender. As she reached for a hanger on the clothes rail, she became aware of a tiny chink of light striking the interior from somewhere at the back. Wondering, she ducked under the rail and applied her eye to this opening once blocked by a knot of wood.

To her amazement, she found this gave her an uninterrupted view of Mary's chamber, focusing directly on the bed. It was ablaze with light. She must have ignited the wick of every available candle in the chamber, with the exception of the one she held in her hand.

Mary wore nothing but a negligee, her opulent breasts poking almost aggressively from the opening down the front. The silken material parted, flowing back over her thighs to display her rotund belly and the wedge of thick black pubic hair beneath it.

She was sitting on the edge of the mattress, her thighs apart, one hand holding open the plump petals of her labia, the other working the candle over the pink slit between and frigging the engorged head of her large clitoris. She moaned as she moved it, gazing down to glimpse the fulcrum of her pleasure as the tissues darkened and the pearly tip of her prominent organ gleamed. Her hips gyrating, she slipped the candle into her vagina, the fleshy lips sucking at it eagerly till it all put disappeared.

As Sylvia watched her, fascinated, she lifted her hands to her own breasts, cupping their roundness and circling the nipples with her thumb pads. Sweet, suffocating anguish passed through them and down to her bud that swelled between her lower lips.

Mary withdrew the candle from her vagina and started to rub herself with its tip. Sylvia could hear her harsh, panting breaths as the candle moved faster, flashing creamy white in Mary's hand. But before she could bring herself off, someone tapped on the gallery door.

Mary threw the makeshift phallus aside and sprang up, amazingly agile for so solid a woman. At first Sylvia could not see the visitor, but he soon came within sight. It was Henry, his breeches already open, one hand fondling his erection.

He moved close to the spy-hole, quite unaware, and Sylvia had an uninterrupted view of his penis as the glans appeared and retreated, sheathed by his fist. When he took his hand away that tumescent prick remained upright, firm as a lance, needing no support.

Now, standing by the bed, Henry started to peel off his clothing, first the cravat, then the jacket, his wide shoulders outlined by the waistcoat beneath before this, too, was removed. Mary sprawled on the bed, her legs and arms open to welcome him, her negligee an abandoned silky puddle on the floor at his feet.

Henry unbuttoned his shirt and slid his arms free. He was strongly built, his torso rippling with muscle, and Sylvia's hand strayed down to her delta as she yearned to run her fingers over that firm flesh. Her impatience mounted. She longed to see what further delights he would soon display.

She did not have to wait long. Leaning with one hand on the bedpost, he thrust a booted leg at Mary and had her tug if off, then repeat it with the other and inch down his hose. Barefoot now, he eased himself out of his breeches. Sylvia very nearly gave herself away in her excitement as she drank in the sight of his lean buttocks sharply divided by a dark crease, and the iron-hard thighs deeply indented at the hips. His calves were worthy of admiration, the entire length of his legs upholding him in a manner that would have delighted the most fastidious sculptor.

Oh, please turn round, Sylvia begged him silently. Don't deny me the sight of your cock and testicles. I need to see them… to see it all!

As if in answer to this prayer, Henry half turned and she was granted a magnificent spectacle. His penis was fully erect, pointing skywards, the candlelight glittering on the tear weeping from its lone eye. Beneath this impressive column hung his weighty balls, swinging as he moved, though the skin was taut around them, ready to discharge a stream of seed-filled libation.

He turned his back on his unseen audience and Sylvia almost cried out in protest, the hunger in her womb like a raging fire. His attention was focused on Mary, blind to all save the need to release the pressure building in his groin.

She lay back with a moan, offering her sumptuous sex to him, her legs dangling over the side of the bed. Henry sank between them, spreading her open with his two hands, then sinking his face into her moist crack as if he would drown in the essences seeping from that splendid vulva. His tongue was long and agile, penetrating her there, diving into her hole, then retreating to lick over her bud.

Sylvia was as if hypnotised, glued to the spot.

She did not want to miss a moment of this blissfully exciting show, yet became aware of tormenting thirst, wishing she had not drunk so much wine. Even so, she could not drag herself away from the peep-hole that afforded her a glimpse of heaven.

Henry towered over Mary and carefully rolled her so that she lay on her stomach. He paused for an instance as he saw the telltale lines left by a cane. 'Who's been beating you, madam?' he asked, his voice thick with excitement.

'Lady Rowena chastises me when she thinks fit,' she answered huskily, wriggling her bottom as he caressed the weals.

'Does she, by God! And would you like me to do the same?'

'Whatever pleases you, sir. I'm putty in your hands,' Mary averred.

'This pleases me at the moment,' he cried, and parted her flesh, leaning over and kissing the deep fissure. Then he slipped his hands round her body and grasped her hanging breasts, lifting her up towards him, his blunt-nosed phallus finding her gaping vagina. He thrust into her, swinging his tool in and out for a moment, and then stopping.

She whimpered in protest, but he turned her over, muttering, 'I want to watch myself taking you from the front.' He straddled her body, raising himself so that his penis found refuge in the massive cleavage of her bosom. His hands pushed the two globes together, making a tighter passage for his prick and Sylvia, entranced, saw how his taut arse moved, rising and falling rapidly as his passion mounted.

With a cry, he quickly slipped down Mary's heaving body and thrust his weapon violently into her cunt. She screamed as if it was too large for her, hurting her with its force and length, but her cries were soon transformed into whimpers of ecstasy as the base of his phallus massaged her nubbin at each thrust and withdrawal. Sylvia was suffering acute distress, her clitoris at the point of explosion at the sight of the lovers straining towards fulfilment, her throat dry as grave dust. She knew that she must satisfy this thirst before she could fully enjoy pleasuring herself to climax.

She left the armoire and searched the bedside table for a carafe but could find none. Someone had neglected to place it there. The water in the jug was too hot to drink, scalding her lips when she tried.

Torn between the need to watch Mary and Henry reach their apogee and the burning in her throat that was threatening to make her cough and thus betray her presence, she slipped on her silk nightgown and peignoir and opened the passage door.

Moonlight flooded through a latticed window at the end of the corridor, but Sylvia had little idea of the direction in which the kitchen lay. She padded along in her light slippers, making no sound. The inn was sunk in silence and darkness, but she persevered, reaching a lower floor. Then she became aware of a sound somewhere ahead, one whose familiarity struck her blood with cold.

It was the noise made by a lash meeting bare flesh.

Sylvia forced her trembling legs to carry her on, following the sound that was now accompanied by heart-rending moans and sobs. She guessed she had reached the landlord's private quarters, light piercing the gloom from a half opened door, forming a sharp triangle on the stone flagging.

Now, above the whistling of the whip and the cries of its victim she heard Rawley's voice, growling hoarsely, 'Stop that bloody row! Do you want to wake my customers? If a single one of them complains, then you'll get fifty strokes next time, slut!'

Unable to help herself, Sylvia crept nearer and peered round the door. A doleful sight met her horrified gaze.

The barmaid who had been making merry with the clientele earlier was strung by her wrists from a metal ring set in a beam. This position forced her to stretch up, only able to touch the ground with the tips of her toes. She was nude, a big built, well formed girl with heavy breasts and buttocks, both areas now fiery red.

Her ankles were secured, too, legs spread wide, Rawley's tawse curling round her thick haunches, laying a zigzag track across that once white flesh.

'You dirty bitch!' he hissed, in his shirt-sleeves the better to free his arm to whip her, an evil expression twisting his features. 'Flaunting your dugs at my customers... indulging in filthy talk! If I find you've let a man push his cock into you, making your belly swell with child, you'll be cast out into the street, I promise you! The magistrate shall be told and you'll be flogged as a whore, branded moreover, and driven from this place.'

'I've done nothing, master,' the unfortunate girl sobbed piteously. 'No man's laid a finger on me, I swear.'

'Ha! Trying to convince me that you're a maiden, are you?' he bellowed, augmenting his words with another slashing blow of the many thonged tawse. 'We'll see about that.'

He lunged for the helpless girl and jabbed his finger up between her vulnerable cleft, forcing it past her vulva, plunging deep into her female opening.

'Mercy... mercy!' she shrieked, fighting against her bonds in her vain struggle to escape that brutal invasion.

He withdrew his finger, lifted it to his nostrils and inhaled deeply of her secretions. 'You're a liar,' he declared. 'No virgin, but a woman whose been well used, by the feel and smell of it.'

'I was raped,' she protested. 'But there's been no one since that... I've been too scared and my fear of men has made me cold.'

'So why encourage them?' he demanded, and flexed the tawse in his stubby-fingered hand. 'You're nothing but a prick-tease, if that be the case.'

'You've told me to be pleasant to customers, beaten me if I wasn't. I can't win,' she moaned.

'You never will win. You're a female, aren't you? Men will always be your master, and this is a reminder of our power,' he growled and raised his arm, then brought it down with so much force his feet nearly left the ground. The leather strap bit into her flesh, attacking several points at once, but she suppressed her cries though obviously in great distress. Sylvia's heart went out to her, and she longed to throw herself on the heartless landlord, but feared to make things worse for the poor girl.

He laid three strokes across her from one side, and then passed to the other, laying on three more. He reached further over this time, so the leather strips wrapped round her ribs and caught the swell of her breast. She gasped, muffled a scream and he proceeded to the other side, repeating this punishment.

She hung limply in her bonds, half fainting, and it was then that he served the final blow. He stood behind her and directed the tawse at her crotch. It came winging between her legs and cut the pouting, hairy lips exposed by her open-legged stance. She screamed then, a hellish shriek that rang through the room.

'Be silent!' he ordered, and lashed her again in the same place. He released her after this, and she collapsed on the floor, writhing and clasping her hands about her wounded cleft, the agonising pain of which made her forget her bruised back and breasts.

Sylvia watched helplessly, seeing how Rawley handled the girl with coarse familiarity, an enormous erection distending the front of his breeches.

'That'll teach you,' he chuckled wickedly. 'You'll not have anyone touching you there for days to come, nor will you even be able to frig yourself.'

Still laughing deep in his chest, he made towards the door, so swiftly that Sylvia had no time to dart away. He saw her at once and his smile deepened, a sly look appearing in his eyes. 'Miss Parnell,' he exclaimed, coming so close that she could smell the rancid, unwashed odour of his body. 'And what might you be doing down here?'

'I require a drink of water,' she answered coldly.

'All you had to do was ring the hand bell in your room, young lady,' he said slowly, and his eyes went over her, noting her state of undress. The semi-transparent nightgown and over-robe did little to conceal the shadowy 'V' at the apex of the thighs.

'I was not aware of that,' she said, edging away along the passage, back pressed to the wall. 'If you will fill a carafe for me, I'll return upstairs.'

'Will you indeed? Leaving me so soon?' he said mockingly. 'Will you tell Miss Standish and the Honourable Mr Lanston all that you have just witnessed?'

'No, sir… though I consider you have treated that girl with undue severity,' she protested, almost tripping over her hem in her eagerness to get away from this nasty individual.

If Rawley had not been drinking heavily he would never had dared treat a lady so rudely, but his low grade lust roused by the torture he had just inflicted, he was only aware of satisfying it as speedily as possible. He reached down and opened his breeches, displaying his large, curved, brown skinned phallus. Lust increasing as he watched Sylvia retreat in disgust, he stroked and caressed his uplifted member. Facing her front on, he did not spare her as he masturbated, his cock-tip slippery wet between his fingers.

She was unable to move a muscle, as mesmerised as a rabbit before a stoat. He breathed in panting gasps, the fingers of his right hand curled around his shaft, working it with fast, eager strokes, jerking and pulling at it in his frantic need to attain his crisis.

Suddenly he grunted as a jet of creamy fluid shot from his helm, spattering Sylvia's nightdress. She awoke then, leaping back in revulsion, then turning tail and fleeing to her room.

There she slammed the door and threw the bolt, leaning against the wood with her heart racing and his emission soaking through the silk of her robe to besmirch her skin. She shuddered and tore the garment off, sickness rising in her throat. Running to the washstand she poured water into the china bowl. It was lukewarm, but this did not matter as long as she could wash away Rawley's slime. In that dreadful moment, she felt that all the perfumes of Araby would not suffice to cleanse her from the smell of his pollution.

'So, she's arriving today,' said the tall, dark man as he ran the thongs of the whip lovingly between his slender, aristocratic hands.

He was slim and strong as a rapier, and exuded the same steely threat. Blue-black hair sprang back from his brow, and curled low at his nape. His skirt was open over a muscular, darkly furred chest, the billowing sleeves ending in deep ruffles of lace. Black leather breeches fitted his flanks like a second skin, the bough of his penis clearly outlined as it rested against the inside of his left thigh.

'She is. Your bride-to-be... a beauty, they tell me, and with a generous fortune,' whispered Lady Rowena, feeding on the sight of his bulge, her loins yearning for him.

'It will be mine, of course.'

'Of course. All yours, once the knot is tied.'

'There won't be any difficulties?' he murmured, moving across to where she was bound to a wooden crosspiece.

Irons embraced her ankles, forcing her legs far apart. She

was naked, exposed, secured there for his pleasure. Her nipples were hard, pierced by little gold hoops with chains attached. These symbols of bondage connected with rings passing through the rosy wings of her labia majora.

'None that I anticipate,' she answered, her eyes slitting in ecstasy as he trailed the silver mounted stock of his whip over the tips of her breasts. They hardened instantly at the touch.

It travelled down her flat belly, past her navel and slipped between the depilated lips of her pussy. He wriggled it experimentally, then found her vulva and inserted it.

The metal warmed, heated by the velvety walls, and Rowena pressed down on it, seeking a closer invasion till it contacted her cervix. Her eyelids drooped languidly and she sighed. The sensation was glorious, stretching and filling her, but she hungered for his even larger instrument to take its place. That massive organ, the biggest cock she had ever taken into herself, and her experiences had been legion.

'She must be mine, Rowena,' he murmured, menace in every word that dropped, fresh-chilled, from his lips. 'You know what I'll do to you if you fail me, don't you?'

'I shall be punished,' she breathed, every muscle, each nerve and sinew responding to him.

'You will, madam,' he promised. 'Severely punished.'

He twisted the stock and jabbed her painfully. Rowena tried to withdraw from this implement, which had now become one of torture, but he simply increased his hold, impaling her helpless body.

'Oh... stop... stop, please!' she begged, her blue eyes swimming with tears.

'Very well, my dear,' he said with a saturnine smile. 'Do as I command and I shall reward you.'

He stroked her gently now, his fingers replacing the whip.

A whirlpool of heat swirled in Rowena's cunt, his slightest movement thrilling low into her clitoris. If it could be said that she loved anyone, then it had to be Lord Theo Aubrey, her mentor and master.

33

It had been so ever since she met him in Venice last summer. Having once come under the sombre, amber-eyed scrutiny of this beautiful, sinister, narrow-hipped man, she had joyfully delivered herself up to him.

A friend of Lord Byron, the poet who was reputed to be mad, bad and dangerous to know, Theo enjoyed a hedonistic lifestyle, doing what he willed when he willed it. Europe was his now that the war with Napoleon was over – the Mediterranean his playground – Greece, Italy, France, Spain and Morocco. And each place he visited gave up its secret vices to him, ones that he absorbed into himself and shared with his favourites.

But luxurious, decadent living cost money, and Theo had squandered most of his inheritance. He needed a rich, pliant, meek little wife.

Rowena knew precisely who this should be. Her niece, Sylvia Parnell.

But just for the moment, she was freed from thinking about the girl. Nothing was of importance except this magical, pain and pleasure racked hour orchestrated by Theo. He was an enigma. She never knew whether to expect a blow or caress. He would ignore her for weeks, then arrive unannounced, seeming unable to bear being parted from her, demanding that she be constantly at his side.

This was one of those times. Rowena would have liked to believe he wanted her for herself but, cynical and worldly wise, knew it to be the expected arrival of the heiress that was drawing him like a magnet.

She had gone to him that day with the express purpose of fornication, driving her high-flying phaeton with reckless speed beneath the yawning arch of his lair, Burbank Abbey, which lay on the outskirts of London.

Now she was tethered in the vaulted cellar, lit by the lurid glow of torches in iron cressets. It flickered over the manacles and chains dangling from the walls, along with bullwhips and riding crops, switches and paddles, gags, restraints and leather blindfolds.

Merely to step over the threshold was enough to make excitement flicker through Rowena's body and send urgent messages to her clitoris, hindquarters and thighs.

Theo withdrew the stock from her slippery vagina and, bracing himself on straight arms each side of her, leaned forward and nibbled at the hard cone of one nipple, his tongue tangling with the gold ring, twisting it painfully. She held her breath and his teeth closed tighter on the reddened teat till a bright drop of blood smeared his lips. Slowly, he slackened his bite, his tongue lapping over the darkened tip, caressing it before he straightened up.

Rowena arched her hips, rubbing her hairless pubis against the erection distorting his breeches. High and rock hard it rose, almost to his waist. She yearned to touch it, her manacled hands clenching with desire. Theo smiled, a tigerish look in his eyes.

'You are hot today, milady… a wanton whore. Isn't that so?'

'Yes…'

'Yes what?' He picked up the whip and made a few practised sweeps. The air crackled. Rowena shivered.

'Yes, master,' she whimpered.

'I've never met a more disobedient slave,' he observed. 'You need a severe thrashing to bring you to order. A dozen lashes, I think.'

'Yes, master.'

'You must take every blow without a sound. Do you understand? Any screaming and I'll increase the strokes to two dozen.'

Rowena bowed her head in assent, her mane of ringleted auburn hair obscuring her face. She quivered and tried to clench her buttock muscles, but this was impossible to do with her legs so far apart. If she took her punishment without flinching, then he might reward her by allowing her yearning cunt to sheath his spear of power.

He revolved the wooden structure to which she was chained, exposing her naked back, bottom and thighs. Rowena tensed, regretting this dark skein of wanting that caused her so much angst. She was proud of her flawless white skin. Only her lustful, obsessive cravings would have permitted it to be damaged.

She waited, shivering in anticipation of the excruciating agony she knew was coming. All was silent.

Then she heard the song of the whip.

The first blow caught her low, where the fatty tissue protected the underside of her rump. The pain was like a lightening shock and she pulled on her bonds, biting back a cry. Her spine arched, the second lash coming before she had time to recover from the first, laying another scarlet trail across the ivory skin. Rowena ground her teeth and rode the pain, keeping silent.

Hot tears streamed down her face and her breath became ragged sobs as she heard the whip whistle again. The next blow was higher, cutting a burning swathe across her back. The fourth and fifth were a blur of sensation, part of her rebelling against such degradation, the other, stronger, darker side, responding to the heightened heat and awareness that spread to her genitals.

Each lash cutting into her rear sent fiery shocks through her loins, till pain became pleasure and pleasure pain. She no longer knew where one ended and the other began. She could smell Theo as he sweated with exertion, her own body odour mingled with it – the flowering of perspiration and sexual juices.

She knew he was naked beneath the tailored breeches and full-sleeved shirt, and could picture him in her mind's eye, every muscle, each duelling scar, the hollows in his tight flanks, the plain of his flat belly, the scribble of black hair that thickened where his penis sprang, rampant and eager.

Now there was silence, a cool, dark silence. Her arse and back were on fire. She stilled her sobbing breath to listen, and then felt him behind her, his breath cooling her burning skin. She braced herself for another blow, but instead felt his fingers sliding into the copious flow of liquid pooling at her vulva, spreading it between her nether cheeks. He sank one finger to the knuckle into her tight anal ring, then added a second and a third, preparing the way for something larger. Rowena stilled, hardly daring to breathe lest he change his mind. She did not even attempt to look round, but could feel his shirt against her wounded back and was rewarded by the brush of his erect cock.

He was breathing against her ear, his tongue exploring the rim, even as his fingers withdrew from her delta to be replaced by the head of his penis nudging against her – not her vagina but her forbidden hole. He pushed forcefully, penetrating her ultimate darkness till the entire length and thickness of his phallus was lodged within her.

Rowena thrust her pelvis down, taking it deep into her rectum till she was filled to the utmost. His hands snaked round between her legs, one fastening on her cleft and holding the slippery lips apart, the other stroking her aroused clit head, overloading her with pleasure.

The pain of her thrashing mingled with the growing ecstasy, his penis pulsing in her anus as he rode her in furious frenzy. She could feel herself peaking, gaining the acme of release, while he gave a sudden, final thrust, spending himself deep within her.

Then, as swiftly as he had taken her, so he withdrew. Libation dripped from his cock on her nether cheeks, that stalwart weapon still firm and curving. He raised himself and seized a handful of the coppery hair that cascaded down her back, wiping himself in it, the pearly drops shining against the rich, vibrant colour.

Rowena moved languorously, her sigh like the deep, satisfied purr of a cat. 'Theo…' she murmured, her eyes still closed. 'Theo, darling… let me stay here a while longer. I can never get enough of you.'

He untied her bonds and she swung round as she fell against him, nipples rising as they chafed against his shirtfront. She breathed deeply of the exotic smell that symbolised Theo to her. Fragrance of incense, a hint of brandy and tobacco, the sweet, insidious odour of the opium he mixed with his wine.

He put her from him, saying brusquely, 'Not today, madam. I am otherwise engaged. I've arranged to attend a main with Balty. Two of my best game chickens are contending, fierce fighters both. And you must go home, there to await the arrival of my heiress.'

Chapter Three

Sylvia gazed from the carriage windows in awed wonder as the coachman carefully negotiated his vehicle through the snarl of traffic. Horsemen, brewers' drays, private calashes and tradesmen's' carts jostled for passage, the acrid smell of trampled dung and animal urine rising on the warm air.

The uproar was deafening. Street vendors cried their wares, apprentices stood in shop doorways bawling the merits of their masters' merchandise, hackney carriage drivers argued and swore, declaring their right of way, and goodwives nagged their children while attempting to haggle for bargains.

People thronged the pavements. Not only sober citizens going about their business but a sprinkling of beggars, too, and ladies with exposed bosoms and gaudy hats, their cheeks daubed with rouge.

'Are they a part of polite society?' Sylvia asked Mary innocently.

'Good heavens, no!' the duenna snapped sharply. 'They're brazen hussies who are no better than they should be.'

'I've no idea what you mean,' Sylvia continued, baffled by this answer. 'Could you please elaborate?'

'No, Miss Sylvia, that I could not,' Mary said grumpily. 'You'll have to ask your aunt. It's not my place to enlighten you about such matters.'

She was in a bad mood as Henry had bidden them farewell at Chelsea without making any definite arrangement to call on her. Sylvia refused to let her spirits be dampened. They had reached London and that was all that mattered. She could even forget the unpleasant incident concerning the landlord of the Fox and Hounds. He was a worm and of no importance. Nothing was of significance but her meeting with her aunt who would surely throw open the doors of elegant people for her. There would be galas and fetes, balls and visits to the opera – maybe they would even be invited to Carlton House, the palace of the Prince Regent himself.

The salve had worked wonders on her welts, and she was borne on a wave of optimism about her future. This good feeling grew when they left the tangle of streets and emerged into the broad avenues of Mayfair, with its magnificent houses facing squares planted with trees and shrubs.

'Are we nearly there?' she cried eagerly, nose pressed to the window glass.

'Yes, Miss Sylvia. Calm down do! Your bonnet is askew. Here, let me straighten it for you,' Mary said with a smile, getting over her disappointment, having come to the conclusion that men were rats. 'I think it best we forbear mentioning Mr Lanston to her ladyship. She might not approve.'

'Very well, Mary.'

Sylvia was willing to agree to anything as the coach drew up outside Laurel Mansion, the largest and most impressive of the houses. Hardly able to contain herself, she almost jumped from the carriage with Mary puffing behind her.

When her feet touched the ground it was as if it burned through the thin soles of her pumps, a frisson darting up her legs, into her loins, belly and straight to her heart. One of her ambitions had been achieved. She was actually standing on London soil.

She goggled at the mansion's stately facade, with its long narrow windows and marble pillars, the row of gleaming steps leading up a front door with leaded lights, protected by a shell-shaped arch. This was now opened by a footman in splendid livery, a fine figure of a man wearing a white powered wig. He bowed and stood back that they might enter, then gave a crisp command to a younger servant who immediately set about hefting in the luggage.

'Milady awaits you in her boudoir,' the footman proclaimed in a stentorian voice. 'Please follow me.'

Walking as if in a dream, Sylvia was barely conscious of the immense black and white tiled hall, the statues in alcoves, the little gilt chairs and paintings in elaborate frames. Light poured down from a central dome, and the staircase was a miracle of stone suspended from a delicate ironwork frame. It curved upwards to a broad landing, and Sylvia kept her eyes fixed on the footman's upright back, her feet sinking into deep-piled carpet.

They passed closed doors with ornate architraves, and tall sashed windows that gave a view over a well-tended garden with lawns and flowerbeds, further stone statues and a quaint summerhouse like a ruined temple. Everywhere was evidence of wealth and luxury.

The footman paused before a pair of cedarwood doors with brass fittings. He knocked discreetly and a maid opened them.

Sylvia could not believe the evidence of her own eyes.

The woman's breasts were bare, nipples rising over the edge of an exceedingly tight black satin basque. Her skirt was tucked high over buttocks and belly, displaying the fat cheeks of her arse and the curve of her stomach.

Not knowing where to look, Sylvia could not help seeing the thick dark pubic bush that shielded the maid's pudenda, and the crimson stripes on her buttocks.

'Good day, Cora,' Mary said, and bustled into the room.

'Miss Standish, ma'am,' the girl replied and dipped a curtsey, keeping her eyes down, her entire attitude one of servitude.

Neither Mary nor the footman showed the slightest sign of surprise at Cora's attire. It was as if it were an every day event. Some of Sylvia's confidence began to drain away, replaced by trepidation. She had thought to escape corporal punishment now she had left the academy, but the state of both Cora's and Mary's hindquarters caused her to have serious doubts.

They are servants, she consoled herself. Even Mary is an employee whom her mistress may chastise whenever she thinks fit. Is this why Mary was so anxious we keep quiet about Henry Lanston?

She had no further time for speculation for now she found herself in an even more impressive room. It was furnished with theatrical gusto, the pillars disguised as palm trees, the purple silk hangings imported from China and the inlaid wall panels from Italy. Immense mirrors in rococo frames reflected the scene over and over, and the centrepiece was a scroll-backed sofa on which reclined a stunning vision in a silver and green gown.

A monkey in an embroidered bolero and felt fez was tormenting a miniature spaniel curled up in a ball at the vision's feet. The ape's shrill chatter was punctuated by squawks from a large white cockatoo who glared around as it moved along its gilded perch.

'Ah, there you are. Sylvia, is it not?' said a mellifluent voice as the vision turned a pair of azure eyes in her direction.

'It is indeed, milady,' Mary put in unsteadily. 'I've brought her to you, safe and sound.'

The blue eyes flashed and the upper lip curled as Rowena Bancroft said haughtily, 'Did I give you permission to speak?'

'No, mistress,' Mary replied, cringing.

'Have you your notebook there?'

'Yes, mistress,' Mary said, fumbling in her reticule.

'Then take a memo. At once, do you hear?'

'I'm ready, mistress,' the unfortunate chaperon stuttered, and dropped her pencil in her eagerness to obey.

'Careless slummock!' Rowena shouted. 'That will cost you dear. Now, add this to your list of misdemeanours: For speaking out of turn, twelve lashes. For being clumsy, six lashes. That's eighteen in all, plus the score that remain from the other day. I did not give you your full quota, if you recall, feeling particularly merciful as you were about to fetch my niece.'

'You were generous, mistress, but I'm not worthy,' Mary began, standing before the couch, never daring to look at Rowena's face.

'I know that, but is there more? Have you something to confess?' Rowena asked, her eyes cold as the Arctic sea.

42

She rose from the couch, a strikingly beautiful woman in her late twenties. Her flaming russet hair was swept up into a coronet, with a mass of ringlets cascading from the crown, little kiss-curls touching her brow and covering her ears. Her limbs gleamed through the diaphanous gown. It clasped her breasts close, their curves swelling above her décolleté, squeezed high by the tiny basque worn beneath, designed to separate and divide each alabaster globe.

Sylvia was dumbstruck, both by this conversation and the extreme elegance of her aunt's person. The lack of modesty surprised her, too, for Rowena's nipples were clearly defined, and the dark smudge at her fork where those long thighs joined.

Mary, unable to keep her secret, sank to her knees, her big body quivering, tears trickling down her fat cheeks. 'I have, mistress... I have,' she sobbed.

Rowena stood over her, an inscrutable expression on her cat-like face. 'And what, Miss Mary Standish, have you been doing?' she enquired slowly.

'I'm guilty of lecherous behaviour and indulging in sins of the flesh,' Mary whimpered. 'There was a gentleman on the coach, and I permitted him to use me with gross indecency, not only there but in my bed later.'

'Tell me about it,' Rowena encouraged, and her gaze suddenly cut to Sylvia, gauging her reaction.

Sylvia felt her face flaming. Could this worldly lady read her mind? Did she know the lustful feelings Sylvia had experienced while watching Mary and her lover? And why had Mary felt compelled to confess?

Her welts throbbed as heat coursed through her. To her dismay, her female juices oozed, and she suddenly longed to have her aunt caress her, to become aware of her as a sexual being, not a naive girl fresh from school.

Cora stood quietly to one side, her hands linked above her head, obviously obeying a command that condemned her to this vulnerable position. The action caused her heavy, coral-tipped breasts to rise from the basque, while her high heels made her calves bunch and the muscles of her buttocks clench. She was fully exposed to view, her bare parts inviting the touch of inquisitive fingers.

The noises made by the animals were irritating Rowena.

'Take them away, Farid,' she commanded, addressing the page lounging on the window seat.

His face was like polished ebony, teeth gleaming as he gave her a cheeky grin. He wore a suit of blue satin, a turban of gold tissue on his inky hair. She returned his smile, fond of this privileged youth who she treated in much the same way as she did the other members of her private zoo. He retired, the monkey on one shoulder, the parrot on the other, leading the dog on a jewelled leash.

Mary had collapsed, grovelling at Rowena's sandaled feet. 'Forgive me, mistress,' she implored, and placed her lips on the superbly turned ankle peeping from beneath the flimsy gown.

'Did he pleasure you? Drive his prong into your cunt and make you come? Did he rub your love-bud and finger your teats?' Rowena asked calmly, though an expression of distaste flickered over her perfect features as Mary's wet, blubbering lips contacted her skin.

'Yes, mistress, he did.'

'And you allowed this without asking my permission?'

'You were miles away. How could I ask you?'

'That's no excuse. You should have controlled your base desires,' Rowena chided, and lifting one foot, she pressed it down hard on Mary's head, grinding her face into the carpet.

'I'm sorry,' came Mary's muffled cries.

'You will be,' Rowena promised, and released her. 'Now get up. It is time we gave Miss Sylvia a demonstration of what happens to disobedient females.'

Mary dragged herself to her feet, wiping her streaming eyes and nose with the back of her hand. She was still sobbing, her breasts shaking with emotion. Rowena strolled towards Sylvia, who had not dared to move.

'My dear child, it is such a joy to have you with me,' Rowena said, and took her warmly by the hand, then placed a pink, oval-nailed finger under her chin as she scrutinised her face. 'So pretty, too. So fresh and innocent. The gentleman who already seeks your hand in marriage will be delighted.'

'Someone wants me? But I've not been introduced to any suitors,' Sylvia exclaimed.

Rowena gave a bell-like laugh. 'Silly goose, of course there is someone. I'm making provision for you, my pet. Every girl wants to be married, doesn't she?'

'But I thought… imagined, that I'd be given time to look around… enjoy London… perhaps find a man of my choice who I could love,' Sylvia protested.

Rowena's hand gripped her firmly by the jaw, her touch turning to steel as those brilliant blue eyes bored into Sylvia's green ones. 'Love?' she said with a little laugh. 'How sentimental. Love has nothing to do with marriage, I can assure you. An overrated emotion and totally impractical. Ladies in our position do not marry for love.'

'But…' Sylvia stammered, with the sudden unpleasant awareness of being taken over and controlled.

'No buts, my sweet. Come now, you must not argue. Rebelliousness does not become a genteel girl. No man wants a troublesome wife. Men are our masters and when they command we obey. Didn't Mrs Dawson teach you to be meek and humble in their company?'

'We rarely saw any men,' Sylvia answered crisply, and drew herself up to her full height. 'Yes, she did try to instil this notion into us, but I have no intention of becoming any man's slave.'

'This is foolish talk,' Rowena said. 'Even I am submissive to my lord.'

'Your husband?'

'Oh, no. I am a widow. I was married at sixteen to a man old enough to be my grandfather. He ruled me till the day he died, but even now, when I am free and rich in my own right,

I obey he who is my master.'

Sylvia's chin lifted mulishly. 'That I shall never do,' she declared.

'Is that so?' Rowena murmured, and her eyes raked over Sylvia thoughtfully. 'Stubborn, eh? And of an independent spirit. It is time I took you in hand, my dear. Your training shall begin forthwith.'

'Training? But I thought we'd be shopping, calling on people... that you would want to introduce me to your acquaintances,' Sylvia said, disappointment sending the tears to her eyes, ones she was too proud to shed.

Rowena smiled again, saying, 'And so we shall, darling. I can't wait to take my lovely niece to the Ranelagh Rotuna and Vauxhall Gardens, while my friends are dying to meet you, but your schooling shall take place, nevertheless. We'll begin at once.'

She turned and snapped her fingers at Cora who sprang to attention, then came over and sank to her knees.

'What do you wish, mistress?' she asked, her eyes cast down.

'A cane, Cora. The Malacca, I think,' Rowena said, pointing to where a collection of rods and sticks stood in a large porcelain jardinière in one corner.

Cora returned carrying a long, thick black rod. Mary gave a despairing cry as her eyes alighted on it. Rowena took it in her right hand and tapped it on her left palm. Even the sound of this lightest of blows gave Sylvia goose bumps.

'Kiss the rod,' Rowena commanded Mary. 'Kiss it with as much devotion as when you sucked your lover's cock. Kiss it and weep, and may its brand burn into your flesh to remind you never, never to disobey me. I shall choose the time and place for your vile couplings, and the person who shall be your partner and the audience who will watch you. Never forget this.'

'No, mistress, I won't,' Mary choked through her tears.

'Now, step over here, bend and clasp your ankles,' Rowena said, a vibrant note in her voice.

46

Mary did as she was bidden, throwing up her skirts, her huge buttocks parted as she leaned over from the waist. This was no skinny, girlish bottom offering itself to the cane, but the mature flesh of a thirty-year-old woman, well nourished and abundant. Sylvia kept seeing Henry Lanston taking possession of the split-fig of her pudenda that protruded between her legs, fully displayed by her posture, the glossy mat of hair giving scant protection. The light shone on the silvery trail of moisture that seeped from the entrance to her vagina.

As Mary waited in dreadful anticipation, her thighs shook and her massive butt clenched. A small, whining noise escaped from her throat. Cora watched impassively, but Sylvia's own posterior glowed in sympathy. The stripes already scoring Mary's white flesh were still inflamed, and those to come would but add to the agony.

Rowena kept her waiting, as cool as ice. She was magnificent, her body perfectly proportioned. Her waist was delicate, her hips just full enough to make her truly feminine in appearance, complimenting the ripe breasts crowned by rose-pink nipples surrounded by deeper hued aureole. These were larger now, and hard, as if engorged with excitement, though she appeared absolutely calm.

She seemed almost too frail to wield a cane, but this was an illusion. It hissed through the air with a mighty force, and landed to cut into Mary's fleshy rump like a knife through butter. Sylvia felt the impact as if it was herself on the receiving end. The cane sprang back, leaving a red track in its wake that darkened and swelled as she watched.

Mary howled as the surging agony flowed into life after the first numbness. The black wand descended again, almost too fast to see. Rowena's strength was astounding. She had acquired it breaking and handling thoroughbreds, a renowned horsewoman. Now she drove that fearsome cane into Mary's cringing rear, its bite burning and bruising, leaving bright red lines across the thick dark welts of former beatings.

Mary's body wobbled like jelly under the force of the blows, the weight of the cane and the power of Rowena's wrist. She writhed as she tried to absorb the atrocious pain, her hands clenched round her ankles, the tears streaming down her face to drip from her chin to the floor. She did not scream, but mewled like a kitten.

A dozen blows rained down, and now her grunts of pain rang with anguish. She swayed, could hardly stand, and Rowena gave her a moment's respite. She was allowed to straighten, her hands flying to her discoloured rump.

'Surely she has suffered enough?' Sylvia shouted, unable to hold her tongue.

Those crystal blue eyes switched to her and Rowena's hand gripped the rod's handle even more firmly.

'What do you know about suffering?' she asked, her voice low and husky. 'You are young… untutored. How can you know the cleansing fire of the lash? How appreciate the peace that laps at the heart of the pain? You shall learn, girl, in time… learn to accept your frailty and thank your master for his clemency.'

'I would expect compassion from a woman,' Sylvia began, and then remembered that Mrs Dawson had shown none.

Rowena gave her a look that should have blasted her where she stood. 'This is indeed a foolish chit,' she said conversationally, addressing the tearful Mary. 'There is much work ahead to make her change her tune. Perhaps we should concentrate on this. Your punishment is over, for now. Report to me later for a further thrashing.'

She handed the cane to Cora who replaced it among its fellows.

Mary, hands clasped about her throbbing backside, stood there shaking, unable to believe her good fortune.

Sylvia was casting about desperately in her mind for some means of escape from this terrible household. Her aunt was cruel, no better than Mrs Dawson, and she a helpless prisoner in her hands. Then, with a mercurial change of mood, Rowena clasped her round the waist affectionately and said,

'You need a completely new wardrobe. We shall drive to Bond Street this very afternoon and visit a modiste, a shoemaker and glover. I'll not have my niece appearing in public looking so dowdy.'

Pressed close to those glorious breasts, inhaling the mingled aromas of expensive perfume and Rowena's own magical elixir, Sylvia's fear dissipated. Perhaps it would not be so bad, after all. New clothes had been promised and she never could resist the lure of shopping, and somewhere in London lived the man whom her aunt had mentioned – a man who already wanted to marry her, though they had never met.

'I'll put ten guineas on the brunette,' Theo Aubrey said, throwing his lithe body into a brocade upholstered chair and crossing one knee over the other as he eyed the two Amazons stalking through the vestibule and flexing their muscles.

One of the contenders, wearing a flowing burgundy cloak over her scanty costume, saw him looking. She stuck out her pierced tongue, jiggled her blue-veined breasts and cocked one leg, giving him a flash of her shaven pussy.

'You're on! Ten guineas it is. I'll wager the blonde doxy beats her,' declared his companion, Sir Balty Stebbings, sweating with excitement as he rubbed his palm over the erection straining the front of his breeches.

He was a rubicund, overweight man, already tipsy, his bleary eyes moving from the female wrestlers to feast on the voluptuous charms of half a dozen painted whores touting for trade in this high-class bordello.

'It'll be a night to remember, gentleman,' put in the proprietress from where she sat at a table counting money. It was a case of business first, fun later, each client telling her what he wanted and how much he was prepared to pay. The house catered for all tastes, from straightforward coupling to any number of deviations.

'It had better be, Mrs Jones,' Theo said with his sinister, mocking smile. 'You've charged enough for the tickets, dammit!'

'Would I disappoint a fine gentleman like yourself?' she asked, rolling her eyes. 'First the fight, then there's a virgin on show…'

'A virgin? Here?' Theo said with a sneer. 'That I find hard to believe.'

'It's true, my lord. I've been saving her for tonight. She's going to get a whipping and then sold to the highest bidder. Will you be in the running?' she asked, her avaricious eyes sharp as gimlets.

'Maybe,' he replied carelessly. 'Though I prefer my field already ploughed. A virgin can be mighty hard work.'

'But worth it, sir,' she chortled, leering at him. 'At least you'll be assured that you won't get a dose of Cupid's Measles.'

'True, but I thought you vowed your girls were clean.'

'Oh, they are, sir. I have the doctor in to examine them once a month, regular like. Any that's been working on the sly and caught something nasty is chucked out. You won't find a healthier bunch of ladybirds this side of the Thames. But first there are the famous fighters, Lightning Bolt and Cruncher. They've performed before the Prince, and he gave them a purse full of gold.'

Of large build, Mrs Jones had a shadowy upper lip, rouged cheeks and a ginger wig. Her gown, cut extremely low, displayed a broad expanse of brawn-like skin and a cleavage that resembled a canyon. Theo suspected that, like all pimps, she was greedy, grasping and a born liar, willing to sell her grandmother for sixpence.

He was in a sombre mood and needed stimulation. Rowena had been quite specific when she said that he was not to call at Laurel Mansion until much later that night. They had arranged that he should use the secret staircase leading to the little room where he might view his prospective bride through a trick mirror.

Theo was not accustomed to waiting for anything, an aristocrat who fully expected to ride roughshod over everyone. His good looks and louche sexuality, his reputation as a whoremaster, even possibly a Satanist, which he carefully fostered, stood him in good stead. Few could resist him – men or women.

Now, superbly attired in black velvet with snowy Mechlin lace at throat and wrists, he stretched his long legs before him and prepared to hone his appetites.

A steady flow of well-heeled gentlemen was arriving, mostly coming directly from their clubs, Whites or Almack's. There were a sprinkling of military uniforms, a priest or two and an elderly duke accompanied by his entourage. There was much bowing and scraping as he was ushered in, an obese man with a massive belly, and several chins nestling above the folds of his voluminous cravat.

Some of those present had come to sample the wares. Some, like the duke, to witness the show. Mrs Jones had not stinted on advertising, expecting a large response. She was not disappointed.

She rose and clapped her hands, 'Are we all here? Good. Then let us begin. Come, your Grace, and the rest of my sporting gentleman.'

So saying, she gathered her jewel-spangled train in one hand and her ostrich feather fan in the other and moved across the gilded, scarlet hung foyer to a large salon.

The furniture was expensive yet succeeded in looking as overblown and tawdry as its owner. There were candles in floor-standing girandoles and a central chandelier with cut glass drops. The prints on the walls were of couples spending themselves in the throes of passion, and included several of nuns and monks indulging in flagellation.

The whores wandered about in various stages of undress, their breasts exposed, nipples gilded, tight stays nipping in their waists and making their buttocks bulge. Each wore an expression of acute ennui.

The duke was settled in the finest chair placed where it would give him an uninterrupted view of the proceedings, and the rest occupied couches facing a platform at one end of the room. At a signal from Mrs Jones, the plush curtains parted, as she cried,

'I give you Lightning Bolt and Cruncher!'

There was an appreciative roar from the audience as the girl warriors launched themselves on to the stage and twirled round a central pillar. Cruncher gripped it between her thighs, humping it, her head thrown back, dark hair flying. Then they prowled the floor like lionesses, arrogant, powerful, expressing disdain for the men who drooled as they watched them.

Lighting Bolt dived a finger into her vulva, withdrawing it wet with juice, then leaned from the stage, breasts dangling, and thrust it under the nose of the duke. His tongue came out, lapping at it eagerly, savouring the strong, piscine flavour.

The crowd whooped with joy.

The girls were Junoesque in build, with huge breasts and tiny waists, their white skin contrasting with the leather straps that emphasised those monumental mammaries, the nipples jutting like organ stops. The minute suede cache-sexe they wore were split-crotched, blatantly revealing their high cleft, denuded pudenda.

They strutted in thigh length boots, Lightning Bolt wearing crimson leather, Cruncher black. The men stacked around the stage leaned in so close there was a danger of the structure giving way. The wrestlers fell to the floor and, wrapping their long limbs around each other, squirmed in mock ecstasy as they gave a display of lesbian love, hands and lips working on nipples and salmon pink fissures. Then Cruncher switched to a dominating role.

She took up a candle and advanced it towards her partner's raised behind. Lightning Bolt snarled, whipped round, raised her clenched fist and punched her opponent viciously on one swinging breast. This was the cue for the contest proper to begin.

Punching, clawing, they writhed on the mat, each movement of those athletic legs fully exposing their female parts, the tiny leather pouches torn away. The men fought to grab these trophies, the successful ones shouting with glee as they buried their noses in the triangular scraps that had been pressed close to the girls' pubises.

Now the gladiators were on their feet, circling each other in professional style, and then jabbing ferociously at breasts and faces, trading punches in equal measure. Fiery red patches began to spring up on the tender flesh of the heavy breasts and muscular buttocks that had taken punishing blows.

A kick to the stomach had Cruncher doubled up and winded.

Lightning Bolt raised triumphant arms over her head, a triumph that was short-lived. With a savage yell, Cruncher recovered, sprang up and landed her a vicious upper cut to the jaw. Lightning Bolt went down like a felled tree.

Mayhem broke out round the stage.

'Gentlemen! Gentlemen! That will do!' Mrs Jones commanded, standing over them, every bit as stern as any nanny who had taken a switch to their bottoms when they were young. 'I give you the winner! Our champion... Cruncher!'

'I told you she'd win,' Theo said to Balty amidst the thunderous applause, shouts and catcalls. 'That's ten guineas you owe me.'

'I know, old chap. Damned fine show she put up. What a spirited filly!' Balty answered good naturedly, diving in his pocket and producing a handful of gold coins. 'But dammit, you always win. How d'you do it?'

Theo raised his velvet clad shoulders in a shrug, saying, 'Luck? Judgement? Experience counts the most, I think.'

'Are you going to roger the winner?' Balty asked, his grey eyes alight with lust. 'Can I watch you do it?'

Theo gave his reptilian smile and said caustically, 'She's a votary of Sappho, the great Greek lyrical poetess who lived on the Isle of Lesbos. She'd not have a man within a mile of her cunt.'

Lightning Bolt was carried off, blood bubbling from her nose. Cruncher received her prize money and the gamblers settled their scores. Wine was passed round by naked nymphets, and trays of delicacies, too. A string orchestra struck up light music and Mrs Jones stood, arms akimbo, a satisfied expression on her coarse features.

The curtains had been drawn across the platform during the interval. Now, appetite for food, drink and money satisfied, the audience were impatient for the next entertainment. The atmosphere was electric, men reaching into their breeches and fingering their cocks. Even the duke had his equerry release his elongated penis from the confines of his clothing.

Mrs Jones came over herself to pay attention to the royal equipment, which was thick but still flexible. She circled the glans with teasing deliberation. It already gleamed with jism, half out of its shrouding foreskin. Mrs Jones tweaked it playfully, murmuring, 'I've a treat in store, your Grace. Just you wait and watch.' She withdrew her hand, wiping it surreptitiously down the side of her skirt, then swung round and gave an order.

There was a drum roll, and the crimson drapes parted. As if with one voice, a sigh rose from the spectators.

Centre stage stood a bemused girl. She was blushing and trembling. Beneath her small firm bust, a criss-crossed pattern of laces held in the stiffened waist of a lilac satin corset. The crotch was cut away to reveal the top of her thighs, her hipbones and the fresh bloom of her sparsely furred mound. Her legs were bare, feet in cream calfskin boots.

'This is boring,' Theo complained, yawning behind his hand.

'Give it time,' suggested Balty, watching eagerly. 'I think that old bawd was telling the truth for once. The girl looks for all the world like a shrinking virgin, stab me if she don't.'

Now two women crossed the stage wearing a parody of soldiers' apparel, except that their breasts stuck out through holes cut in the jackets and the breeches were split from pubic mound to the dark furrow of their arses. They seized the girl's arms and snapped wide bracelets over her wrists. She squealed and struggled to no avail. A length of chain dangled from one of the manacles. Her arms were lifted, hands clasped behind her neck, the chain linked securely to the other metal cuff.

'Ah, this looks more interesting,' Theo said, sitting up and leaning forward.

The audience started to cheer and fidget, the atmosphere thick with the feral odour of masculine arousal. Mrs Jones climbed to the platform, shouting above the noise, 'I'd like to present Violet, a new recruit to my Temple of Venus. We'll give her warm welcome… a very warm welcome, especially round the arse.'

There were gasps and laughter, and whistles of approval. Mrs Jones reached into a basket on a side table and took out a pair of little bells. Each one was fixed to a spring clamp. As the women held Violet still, the procuress grasped one rosy nipple, tweaked it till it hardened and then set a clamp to grip it near the base. Violet yelped as the small sharp teeth bit into her tender teat. Ignoring her, Mrs Jones fixed the other in place, the delicate nipples reddening under the pressure.

The bells tinkled at Violet's every movement, causing a further uproar in the audience.

Mrs Jones nodded to the bigger of the women who turned the girl round so that her rear was visible to all. She had fair, mousy hair that fell about her face, and her thin shoulders heaved as she sobbed.

'No! Don't! Please!' she cried. 'Take the clamps off. They hurt!'

'Don't worry, deary. You'll get used to it,' said Mrs Jones.

'When you brought me here you told me I was going to be an actress,' her victim shouted.

Mrs Jones chuckled. 'So you are. You're on the bloody stage, ain't you? What more do you want? Give her a taste of the lash, Meg.'

The tall girl approached her, holding a whip, saying to the

other one, 'Ready, Amy?'

'Ready, Meg,' she replied, standing on Violet's left side, a birch in hand.

Meg struck first, the impact of leather on skin sounding through the room. Violet screamed, her hips twitched, her knees lifted and she did a dance of agony that delighted the watchers, the bells on her teats resonating with a clear, jangling sound.

Amy caught her a resounding thwack across the lower buttocks with the switch, the sharp tips of its twigs marking her woefully. Tears wetted Violet's cheeks as she howled, red-striped about the flanks, thighs and hips. Meg alternated Amy's blows with the slashing whip.

Violet dashed to the side of the stage, seeking to escape, but was immediately hauled back by one of the hulking, brute-faced bodyguards Mrs Jones employed to keep order.

Meg pretended to be a sergeant major, shouting,' March, wench! March on the spot! That's right! One… two… one… two. Higher, faster!'

Under the relentless rain of blows Violet did as commanded, her knees coming up high, the bells clamped to her nipples giving off a carillon that was almost eclipsed by her cries.

Her fair skin was blotched now with a bright pattern of red weals and scratches. Suddenly her knees buckled and she fell to the floor, unable to save herself, arms still chained at the back of her neck.

She lay there, curled on her side, moaning and sobbing. Meg and Amy, flushed with exertion and arousal, continued to beat her mercilessly, then flung her over, spreading her legs and exploring her virgin depths with their fingers, opening the furled labial petals and displaying the rose-pink interior to those who rimmed the perimeter of the stage.

'A virgin without any doubt,' declared Mrs Jones triumphantly, her own fingers wet with Violet's juices. 'Who will be man enough to take her? Who has enough gold to pay for the privilege? She's yours, gentleman… for a price. What say you, your Grace?'

The duke snorted down his patrician nose, a notorious roué, despite his blue blood and noble ancestry. He kept a harem in his castle in the country, beautiful slaves who obeyed his slightest whim. He nodded and beckoned to his equerry, little eyes set between fleshy rolls of fat running over the naked, helpless girl.

The bidding came, fast and furious, with the equerry in the lead, following the duke's orders. Theo was not one of the contenders. In his mind he was picturing Sylvia Parnell, the girl he had never yet seen, the heiress Rowena had acquired to be his wife.

Would she be dark or fair, slim or plump, willing or reluctant? It was a fascinating conundrum. He had never yet been a husband, and the prospect of owning a woman, controlling her money and making her his chattel had enormous appeal. The beast that slumbered between his thighs stirred and lifted its head.

'My lord, may I serve you?' whispered a voice, and he looked down to see a yellow-haired tart kneeling at his feet.

She was small bosomed and fully clothed, save for the holes in her bodice where her nipples stuck out. Her parted lips were red and moist, her fingers working on the buttons fastening his breeches. Theo watched her with heavy-lidded eyes, easing forward a little, lifting his hips to give her access to his genitals.

And all the while he was letting his imagination paint pictures of his future bride. He conjured up the scenes that would take place on the wedding night. He would open the girl, stretch her with a dildo in vagina and anus, make her ready to receive his phallus. She would probably scream, beg and cry, and the thought of this aroused him more than the skilled attentions of a dozen houris.

His prick rose from the wiry bush that coated his underbelly, the hood of his foreskin sliding back, the fiery helm jutting forth. The whore's fingers encircled the throbbing stem and tickled the satin underside of his scrotum. His member enlarged further, giving a vigorous thrust upwards to meet the warmth of her lips. They slid round the glans, drew him into her sucking, caressing mouth until he felt the pressure of her throat against his helm.

With an appalling violence, he was swept up in the unstoppable rush of ejaculation, the terrible serpent fire scorching and cleansing him as he spurted into her mouth.

'I say, old man, you came off like a cannon,' Balty exclaimed, admiringly. 'But don't you want to put in a bid for Violet?'

'No,' Theo stated flatly, recovering control with remarkable speed. His body was like a machine: he ate, drank, slept, eliminated and fucked, and rarely permitted his emotions to cloud his judgement. 'The duke will have her,' he went on. 'She'll be taken to his stable of women, caged for a while, chained up in her own filth, then lashed before he attempts to insert his cock into her.'

Business concluded, the whore sat up and spat out Theo's emission. He drew a coin from his pocket and tossed it to her. She caught it expertly, bit down on it to ensure herself of its validity, tucked it into her bodice and sashayed off.

Theo adjusted his clothing, said goodnight to Balty, picked up his cloak and hat, and went outside to where his carriage waited. He ordered the coachman to drive him to Laurel Mansion.

Chapter Four

It seemed to Sylvia that she had packed a lifetime's experience into the few hours since leaving the academy. Not only had she travelled further than ever before, but had watched a couple making love, nearly fallen prey to a satyr in the hideous form of Mr Rawley, had seen her chaperon being chastised and met her aunt, that stunningly beautiful and awesome lady.

Now, true to her word, Rowena took her shopping.

Bath was a fashionable spa, playground for the rich, but it was as nothing compared to the dressmakers, furriers, jewellers and other luxury establishments in London's centre, catering for those wealthy enough to change their entire wardrobe as fashion dictated.

Pink-cheeked and round-eyed, Sylvia allowed her aunt to lead her through the complicated byways of *haute couture*. She discovered that everything and anything could be purchased, though not with loose change. Great personages like Lady Rowena carried very little in the way of coins, simply signing bankers' drafts.

Mary had gone along, detailed to carry parcels, though her face was still tear-blotched and she walked stiffly, suffering the effects of the black rod's relentless attention.

'You may not realise this, Sylvia, but you are well provided for,' Rowena explained as they alighted from her bottle-green lacquered carriage, picked out in yellow and with her escutcheon emblazoned on the doors.

'I had not thought about it,' Sylvia said, following her into an exclusive shop with bow-windows facing Bond Street, Mary bringing up the rear.

'Yes, indeed. You're an heiress, my sweet. We must protect you from fortune hunters,' her aunt said decisively, half turning to snap over her shoulder. 'Don't dawdle, Mary.'

An exquisite being welcomed them in. He was dressed in the last extreme of fashion, wearing narrow trousers that strapped beneath his instep, his hair styled in the latest Brutus cut, brushed forward to curl over his brow like a Roman emperor's.

'Monsieur Andre, may I present my niece, Miss Sylvia Parnell,' Rowena said as he bowed over her hand. 'We're about to spend a great deal of money with you, providing you have what we require.'

'Yes, madame. Certainly, madame. Charmed, I'm sure, Miss Sylvia,' he gushed.

He snapped his beringed white fingers imperiously at his downtrodden female assistants who immediately scurried about, lifting heavy bolts of silk, velvet and chiffon from the shelves and unrolling them on the counter for Rowena's inspection.

'Can I afford such grandeur? I didn't know I was rich,' Sylvia demurred, perching on the edge of a small gilt chair, impressions crowding in on her with confusing speed.

Mary stood in the background, head down, hands folded, reduced to the servile position of Rowena's dog's-body. Sylvia had once looked up to her, but her ideas had undergone a rapid turnabout. How could you respect someone when you had just witnessed them being severely castigated?

'La, yes,' Rowena continued, while casting an acquisitive eye over a stunning hat consisting of a spray of purple and white feathers attached to a sequinned band. 'When my poor, dear sister Elizabeth died and left you in my care, the manager of Coutts Bank deposited the deeds to the estate in his strongbox, and every paper concerning your late Papa's investments, too. Your affairs are in the hands of Mr Middleton, a most competent solicitor, and I, of course, am your adviser.'

'I see,' Sylvia said, though she did not understand all the complicated ramifications entailed by her inheritance.

'As you will be aware, both your parents died of cholera in

India when you were twelve years old,' Rowena went on. 'Your Papa had been attaché to the Viceroy, a most important position. You did not travel with them, always left at Monk's Park, the Parnell family seat in Hampshire.'

'I remember it,' Sylvia murmured, little vignettes of earlier days flashing across her brain – happy, carefree days when she had run barefoot through the grounds or ridden her pony over rolling downs.

Memories of her parents were vague. They had been dim, misty figures whom she had seen but rarely, brought up by Nanny Talbot in the nursery wing of the great house. She had not mourned their passing.

'I was three and twenty when the tragedy occurred, and already a widow,' Rowena sighed, fingering a length of shimmering shot-silk faille. 'Though I had been devoted to Elizabeth, the care of her motherless daughter was too much for me. Your old nurse looked after you till we could arrange your admittance to the academy in Bath. My health, you see… it was vital that I spent much of the year in warmer climes.'

Sylvia thought this strange for Rowena looked far from frail and had demonstrated a steely strength when flogging Mary, but nevertheless she said, 'I understand, Aunt.'

Too late she realise that the use of this title in public did not please Rowena.

'Don't call me that,' she said sharply, and her tone sent a quiver of terror along Sylvia's nerves and into her still tender behind. 'It makes me feel elderly. You may address me by my Christian name. That will be quite in order.'

'Yes, Rowena,' Sylvia muttered, embarrassed because Monsieur Andre was listening.

'The young lady needs to be fitted out entirely,' Rowena said, while he hovered attentively. 'You had better take her measurements, Monsieur, and after that you may show us gowns that are already made. Possibly they may fit her, if taken in here and there. Her present clothing is just too terribly plain, and I need to show her off.'

'Certainly, milady. We'll see what we can do, shall we? Stand quite still, if you please, Miss Sylvia,' Andre said, and there was not a trace of a French accent. In fact he sounded suspiciously like a Londoner.

Sylvia was curious about him, unable to avoid noticing that whereas Rowena treated her menservants with a curious mixture of familiarity and contempt, shocking Sylvia when she saw her slip a hand down and jiggle the groom's balls as he was helping her into the carriage, there seemed to be no such tension between herself and Andre.

But there were other, more important issues on her mind. 'What happened to Monk's Park?' she enquired as Andre ran a tape measure around her curves. A thrill shivered over her skin at the accidental brushing of his fingers. He smelled of jasmine water, his clean-shaven face pleasingly formed, but she sensed that he was not interested in her, viewing her impersonally, as if she was one of the dressmakers' dummies on which his creations were displayed.

'It's there, darling… waiting to be opened up. A caretaker has been left in charge,' Rowena answered airily, taking off her bonnet and placing the feathered band on her Titian curls, turning her head this way and that as she admired her image in the mirror.

'So I could go and live there,' Sylvia said eagerly. How wonderful it would be to find that Nanny Talbot was still alive. Though a strict women who had not hesitated to pull down Sylvia's drawers and spank her bottom if she was naughty, she had been unstinting in her affection toward the lonely little girl.

Rowena shook her head. 'It wouldn't be practical or proper for an unmarried woman to run the estate alone,' she replied crisply. 'You will have to wait until your husband decides to take over.'

'But it's mine, isn't it?' Sylvia objected.

Andre raised a supercilious eyebrow at Rowena as if to say: Young girls! Whatever are they coming to these days?

'Yes, it is yours,' Rowena conceded. 'But you can't go there until you're married. It's quite out of the question.'

'Why?' Sylvia demanded, moving impatiently under Andre's ministrations.

Rowena frowned. 'It is not for you to question the decisions of your elders,' she remarked frostily. 'This is the way of the world. Now then, never mind about that. What do you think of that beautiful gown on the stand over there? The very thing for you to wear to your first ball.'

Sylvia was left with the feeling that she had come up against a brick wall. Mr Middleton would be under Rowena's thumb, no doubt. Between them, they had carefully arranged her future. She would marry the man they had chosen. Her fortune would belong to him as soon as the settlement had been signed, her freedom snatched away.

Who was this man? She feared to know, yet longed to meet him.

'This faille is marvellous, Monsieur,' Rowena said, changing the subject as she wrapped a swathe of it around her body.

'Freshly shipped from Paris. Isn't it superb? I'm about to have a dressing robe made of it for myself,' he simpered, jotting down details of Sylvia's measurements on a pad.

'Wonderful… make me a ball gown,' Rowena commanded, adding with a chuckle, 'We always like the same fabrics, it seems… and the same men.'

'You have impeccable taste, madame. Speaking of which, how is that handsome savage, Lord Theo?' Andre asked with a smirk.

'In excellent spirits, now that his fiancée has arrived in town,' Rowena said, concentrating on the way the fabric deepened the blue of her eyes and gave an added lustre to her skin.

'He's engaged? Who is it? Oh, milady, do tell! I won't breathe a word,' he cried, forgetting Sylvia and the tape measure momentarily.

Rowena gave a tinkling laugh, tossed the fabric aside and paced towards him, saying, 'My dear sir, she is here. Miss

Sylvia is to marry Lord Theo.'

'Good heavens! What a shock!' he exclaimed, and the look that passed between them was charged with meaning. 'This innocent young creature? Is that wise, milady?'

Rowena tapped him on the cheek with her closed fan, then did it again with vicious force as she murmured, 'Have you ever known me make an error of judgement, Monsieur?'

His cheek reddened where the ivory sticks had slashed it, and he answered meekly, 'Would I dare question your motives, Lady Rowena?'

'Not if you know what's good for you. Behave yourself, and I may permit you to make her wedding gown and trousseau.'

'Strip, Sylvia,' Rowena commanded as she swept into the boudoir.

Behind her came a procession of footmen, led by Mary and Cora, all weighed down with long dress boxes tied with big bows of ribbon, parcels in crisp wrappings and round containers in which hats nestled, cocooned in tissue paper. Farid followed, bearing a silver salver on which stood two porcelain cups of hot chocolate and a plate of fancy cakes.

Soon the room resembled a shop as one treasure after another was shaken out, exclaimed over and hung up, while Rowena sipped her chocolate and issued orders from where she reposed on a couch.

And all this has nothing to do with the wedding, Sylvia mused. Another orgy of shopping will take place before I'm finally led to the altar. It's so unreal. I don't feel as if I'm engaged to be married. I haven't clapped eyes on my bridegroom yet and there seem to be no immediate plans to introduce us.

She admitted to a surge of annoyance that many of the purchases had been made by Rowena, who seemed to be spending Sylvia's money regardless. Now, having shooed everyone out, with the exception of Mary and Cora, her aunt wanted her to take her clothes off.

'I don't wish to,' she announced, chin lifted proudly. 'I prefer

64

privacy when I disrobe.'

'What nonsense!' Rowena said, brushing aside her objections. 'Don't put on a show of prissy modesty for me, girl. We're all women here. Nothing to be shy about... unless you're hiding something. Are you, Sylvia? Have you a guilty secret?'

Despite her resolutions, Sylvia hung her head, her cheeks flaming and her lips trembling. She had hoped the weals would have faded before she had to expose herself to her aunt.

'No,' she whispered.

'Really?' Rowena said, her eyes glowing as she put down her cup and stood up. 'Are you quite, quite sure about that?'

'Yes,' Sylvia murmured, in great distress, though the pulse between her legs quickened.

Rowena's hand came to rest on her head, nails digging into her scalp as she forced her to meet her eyes. 'I think you are withholding the truth, Sylvia,' she pronounced. 'Do as I say. Remove your clothes.'

Sylvia did not stir, bewitched by her aunt's beauty, imagining that hand moving down over her breasts and belly to stroke and play with the fair down covering her mons. What delights could such a woman teach her? Things Sylvia had not yet even dreamed existed.

Mary and Cora had put their mistress's purchases away in the dressing room that linked the boudoir with the bedchamber beyond. Now they returned to their posts, heads down, hands folded, waiting instructions.

Shades of evening were drawing in and the candles already lit. The magnificent apartment glowed, an exotic paradise of sumptuous red and gold hangings, couches and carpets, ornaments and glass, a perfect setting for Rowena.

'I have invited friends to dine tonight,' she said, and her fingers trailed down Sylvia's cheek and throat, then touched the tip of her right breast. 'You will attend and I shall select your attire, but first, I want to look at you.'

She stood back and waited, her expression indicating that

Sylvia would be wise to obey.

Sylvia hesitated, torn between the desire to expose herself and unpleasant memories of the humiliation she had endured in the hands of Mrs Dawson.

'And if I refuse?' she challenged.

'Then I shall give you a lesson in discipline,' Rowena answered calmly. She removed her bonnet and coat in a gesture that signified she was readying herself for action.

Sylvia's eyes cut to the great Ming vase wherein rested the canes and rods. Would her aunt use these on her? Looking at that haughty, impassive face, Sylvia did not doubt it.

Mary came behind her and helped her out of her pelisse, then unfastened the tiny ball buttons at the back of her dress. Sylvia eased her arms from the tight, ruched sleeves. The gown was taken from her and given to Cora, the whole process carried out in an almost ritualistic manner. No one spoke. No sound broke the silence except the crackle of the fire and Sylvia's own hurried breathing.

Her chemise was flimsy and she could feel her aroused nipples rubbing against it, such stimulation communicating itself to her damp labia and the tiny tyrant that swelled from its hood. Mary's fingers worked on the buttons and ribbon and opened the chemise wide. Then that, too, was handed to Cora.

I can't hide my marks of degradation much longer, Sylvia thought. In a second Rowena will know. She could feel the blood suffusing her face, pounding through her body, filling and expanding her secret places, her hidden self ripening and blossoming.

Would Rowena understand if she confessed that she enjoyed touching her bud? And what would she say if she knew that she had longed to feel Henry's penis in her mouth, wanting to fasten her lips round his masculinity and suck it dry? Would Rowena punish her for her wickedness? She thrilled at the thought, sexually hungry and wantonly aroused.

Rowena nodded and Mary stripped off the chemise. Sylvia's long, wheat-gold hair had come tumbling down, hiding her face and resting in fat ringlets over her breasts. She was naked now except for the white stockings gartered above the knee, and her small flat pumps.

Rowena leaned forward and lifted the screening locks aside, running her eyes over those pearly mounds, crowned with rose-pink nipples.

'Ah, such beauty,' she sighed, and took them in her fingers. They crimped, rearing upwards in pursuit of that tingling touch. 'Theo may be the one to possess you, but I shall taste your treasures, too.'

Mary loosened the tapes that upheld Sylvia's petticoat and it dropped to the carpet, leaving her naked. Instinctively, Sylvia's hand shot down to cup her mound, and she stood there shyly, half excited, half shamed by her nudity.

Rowena eyed her up and down before walking round in back of her. The silence was absolute, then,

'My God! Who has been instructing you in pain!' Rowena shouted.

'Mrs Dawson,' Sylvia muttered, wishing the floor would open and swallow her up.

'And your crime?'

'I answered back,' Sylvia confessed.

'Did you so? This seems to be one of your failings, my dear. And was this your first intercourse with the cane?'

'No, madam. Stripes have been my bedfellows for many a year.' Sylvia was crying now, the hot tears streaming down her face to drip from her chin.

'Don't cry, pet,' Rowena said tenderly. 'In time you will be grateful for your early indoctrination, for it will make you soften more easily.'

'Soften? To whom?'

'To your lord and master… your husband.'

Sylvia flung her hands over her face, crying all the harder. 'No,' she sobbed. 'Keep a part of my money if you must, but let me go away to Monk's Park. I'll trouble you no more.'

'Don't be silly!' Rowena cracked out, her patience exhausted.

'You are committed. There is no turning back.'

She picked up a hand bell and rang it. At once Farid entered. His satin uniform was gone and he was naked to the waist, muscles rippling under that shining dark skin. He had removed his turban and his hair fell across his shoulders.

He wore a gold, spiked collar round his neck and wide damascened bracelets banded his wrists. Emerald green silk pantaloons covered his legs, gathered in at the ankles and girded by a jewelled belt at the waist. Below this the trousers were open, his prick jutting forth from the ebony thicket between his thighs. It was big, up-thrusting, the bare head a deep purple colour.

With one hand Sylvia vainly attempt to conceal her breasts. The other covered her mons, yet her womb spasmed with yearning as he advanced, his penis swaying from side to side. She ached to touch him, to feel that oiled skin and fondle the dusky nipples. He was a blackamoor, bought at auction by Rowena, becoming her page, lover and pampered plaything, yet he had the dignity of a prince from an Eastern fairytale.

He knelt in front of Rowena and kissed her feet, but not before throwing Sylvia a warm, affectionate glance from his melting, peat-dark eyes.

Rowena reached down and idly caressed his crisp curls. 'Get up,' she said, and when he had risen to top her by several inches, her hand closed over his phallus, arousing it even more with long, slow strokes. Her other hand cradled his balls, palpating the crinkled sac.

His lids drooped, and his eyes became unfocused. His teeth gleamed as his full red lips parted over them. He stood passive, apart from the slight undulation of his hips as he met that steady, up and down motion of Rowena's hand.

She smiled and subjected his inflamed organ to a series of short, hard slaps, and Farid groaned, almost reaching his pinnacle. Rowena pushed him away but when he grabbed at his tormented member to bring it to completion, she brought her hand down across his arse with punishing force.

'Leave it alone,' she snapped. 'Only I shall bring you relief, if and when it pleases me to do so. I have other work for you. There is an arrogant chit who needs to be schooled. Do it.'

Farid approached Sylvia calmly, seized her in his strong hands, seated himself on a chair and bent her naked body over his lap. She was aware of many things at once: his stiff manhood pressing against her belly; the cinnamon scent of his skin: the chill air on her bare buttocks and the vulnerability of her love lips, a secret no more, on view between her parted thighs.

She struggled, but Farid held her effortlessly with his left hand clamped round her wrists. Rowena was beside them, watching keenly.

'Make him release me,' Sylvia pleaded, turning her face to address her aunt, tears making a damp patch on the silk covering Farid's knee. 'I'm sorry I was defiant. I'll do better in future, I promise.'

'Hush, now. Accept your punishment,' Rowena said implacably, and she placed a hand on Sylvia's neck, massaging it, then reached under to where the full breasts hung down on the far side of the young man's lap.

Rowena pinched them, and stretched the nipples, one by one, letting them spring back, then tweaking them again. Sylvia flinched, breaking into fresh sobs as she tried to avoid that teasing touch.

'I'll do anything you ask, but don't let him hurt me,' she begged brokenly.

'You are very lovely when you cry,' Rowena murmured absently and nodded to Farid.

He brought his open palm down across Sylvia's rump, the impact shattering in its intensity. She yelled and struggled, but he did not waver, spanking her again and again, till the flesh turned beet-red, the already sore nether cheeks smarting and burning. In its own way it was as painful as the cane, coming as it did on recently inflicted wounds.

'There is something immeasurably thrilling about the sound

of a hand striking a bare arse,' Rowena enthused, fingers clasped round her pubis, stimulating the sensitive membranes of her delta through the light fabric. 'Flesh on flesh... it's music to my ears. Continue, Farid, give her no quarter.'

Though Sylvia instinctively sensed his liking for her, he was a slave and forced to obey and he laid the slaps on unrelentingly. His hand shaped itself to her contours, descending with all the considerable strength of his muscular arm. Sylvia cried and screamed, kicked out and writhed, but was unable to avoid those remorseless smacks.

'Enough,' Rowena said at last, and leaning over, touched Sylvia's anal fissure and her pursed sex. 'As I thought,' she added with satisfaction. 'You are wet and swollen with desire, and your nubbin is hard. You want Farid? Is that it? Stop crying and talk to me, girl.'

'I've nothing to say,' Sylvia replied, dashing the tears from her face with her hand as Farid released her and she staggered to her feet.

'Still rebellious?'

'I've said I was sorry. What more can I do?'

Rowena regarded her thoughtfully for a second, then said, 'It is time you were prepared for this evening. Is the bath filled, Mary?'

'Yes, mistress, all is ready,' Mary murmured, casting a glance at Sylvia's crimson bottom before lowering her eyes.

'Very well. Farid, bring Miss Sylvia.'

The bathroom was as decadently luxurious as every other part of the house. The walls were of Islamic tiles, the oblong bath sunk into the marble floor. Candles burned on glass shelves, their flames reflected in mirrors. Others stood in a circular brass ring suspended from the domed ceiling, sending dancing light across the blue, scented water. Perfume rose on the steam, the potent, heady scent of dried flowers and herbs.

Sylvia marvelled at this miracle. She had never seen the like, used to washbasins and water jugs and a slop pail. Drainage and sanitation were new to her, as was immersion of the entire body. She guessed that the servants had lugged up buckets of water to fill the bath. Indeed, several large pitchers containing more stood on the tiles.

Rowena started to undress, and the misery between Sylvia's legs increased as she watched the uncovering of that superb body. Her nipples hardened, her vagina pulsed as she watched each delicate garment discarded. Now the pale flesh came into view, and Sylvia nearly gave vent to a cry of surprise when she saw the little gold rings piercing her aunt's nipples and labia majora, and the bruises scoring her flanks.

Rowena gave an amused smile, twirling the rings and saying, 'You see, darling? My master has laid his brand on me.'

'But you have not softened and become submissive,' Sylvia gasped.

'Little do you know, my dear,' Rowena answered, and sadness lingered on her features. Then she gathered her thoughts and her voice echoed under the cupola. 'Farid, lay her on the couch and remove her maidenhair, then she must be oiled and massaged before joining me in the water.'

'Remove my bush? But why?' Sylvia cried, longing to shield that badge of womanhood she had been so proud to acquire.

Rowena stretched her arms over her head, exposing herself fully. Her shaved pubis stood out prominently, swollen with sexuality. The lack of hair and the little rings sharply defined the cleft, which rose high, offering itself to the gaze.

'In the harems of the East the lack of pubic hair is much admired. They say it enhances sensation,' Rowena began, running her fingers over the smooth, split mound that thrust itself forward invitingly. 'You too shall be denuded of that unsightly growth.'

It was as if the last defence was to be removed, her most intimate parts laid bare. But Sylvia could do nothing but lie on her back on the couch, though the pressure on her sore behind cost her dear. It was a high bench, padded and covered in a white sheet. Sylvia stared up at the rainbow hued stained glass of the dome, listening to the splashing sounds Rowena made in the bath, and the swish of razor on leather strop as Farid honed the blade.

He returned to her side, carrying a small ceramic bowl of water and a bar of soap. He smiled at her encouragingly, showing an expanse of even white teeth, then nudged her knees gently, indicating that she should splay them.

Sylvia trusted him, though she could not quite understand why. He was no more than a lad, yet fully developed. He, too, was a captive in this gilded cage. She spread her legs obediently, holding her thighs open with her hands. Her lower lips unfurled, revealing the dark pink crevice between and she felt a tingling in her clitoris as it began to swell.

Farid wetted the sensitive, hair fringed labia with warm water, then worked the soap over it till sweet scented foam joined the oceanic fragrance of Sylvia's own juices. She gasped, relaxed and opened wider under the slippery caress of the soap, wishing he would touch it to the tip of her nub which ached to be stroked, but Farid was careful to avoid that spot, concentrating on making sure that every inch of fluff was lathered.

'You'll feel so fresh when it's done,' Rowena said from where she relaxed in the bath. 'Lie still and don't object, or I'll order Farid to pluck out the hairs instead of shaving them, and I warn you this is a painful process.'

'Yes, Rowena,' Sylvia answered dreamily. She had not the smallest desire to move or object, giving herself over to Farid.

The cutthroat razor gleamed as he pushed her crack together with one hand, stretching the skin downwards as he began to shave her mound with sure sweeps. This brought pressure on her bud, the heel of his hand resting directly over it. Sylvia sighed, closing her eyes in ecstasy, as a cat will when stroked.

Why, she thought impatiently, doesn't he slip a finger between my slit? Work it over my kernel – softly, secretly, till I come. It would take hardly a second.

But though Farid's naked penis was fully erect, he did not do so, simply lifting the razor. Sylvia caught a glimpse of it, her fair floss mingling with the suds that coated the glittering blade. Then Farid rinsed it in the basin, bringing it out clean and shining. He moved to Sylvia's other side, repeating the movements, giving no ease to her thrumming clit.

The already depilated mound felt cold, stinging slightly, the sensations exacerbating her arousal. Her frustration increased when Farid slid his hand under her hips and eased her down so that her legs dangled over the bottom of the couch. He positioned himself between her wide open thighs, and this was even worse because now she must work with him, lifting her legs one at a time, to enable him to seek out the stray hairs that sprouted from her perineum and even around the tightly closed rosebud of her anus.

Her control slipping, she thought wildly of pulling Farid down on her and impaling herself on his engorged prick. He was more than ready, she could see, the glans glistening with the dew escaping from its eye. But even greater was her need for a finger against which to grind her clitoris until she exploded into orgasm.

'Have you nearly done?' Rowena asked, her voice cutting through Sylvia's fevered longings.

'Yes, mistress,' Farid replied in his dark, honeyed accents. 'You wish to see her?'

'Not yet. Massage her first and then bring her to me.'

His hands gentle as a woman's, Farid bathed Sylvia's naked mons and labia and dabbed it dry. She grew hotter, burning with want, longing to feel his mouth on hers, his tongue probing between her teeth, his thumbs circling her taut nipples, and then the blissful release as he caressed her nub with fingers and lips.

He did neither, saying, 'Roll over, Miss Sylvia, if you please.'

How can he be so calm? she thought as she did so, his solid shaft on a level with her eyes as she lay on her stomach. He's huge and ready, already stimulated by Rowena. If I opened my mouth and stuck out my tongue, I could lick the bulging helmet. Would he spurt over my face? Her womb contracted and fresh juice oozed from her vulva as she conjured up this scenario.

Farid poured a puddle of aromatic oil into his palm and she felt his touch on her shoulders, strong, knowledgeable fingers massaging the tender area at the nape of her neck, then progressing down her back, kneading away every ache. They moved towards her buttocks, and Sylvia felt the sores and welts springing into life, the oil burning slightly as he added more drops, working on her reddened flesh.

She winced, but pleasure underscored the pain. Over each cheek he worked, and then across the backs of her thighs. She could not resist parting them a little. His fingers went between them, caressed the moue of her arsehole, reached lower to touch the as yet sealed opening to her womanhood, and, joy of joys, probed the little nodule that crowned her nude cleft.

It was supremely sensitive from that angle, his finger hooking under it slightly, catching the base of the head, causing mayhem in her loins. She was so very nearly there, straining to reach the peak, then,

'You are not to satisfy her,' Rowena cried sharply. 'I forbid it.'

The touch was withdrawn and the hands continued their progress down her bruised thighs, the backs of her knees, her calves, ankles and finally, every muscle in her feet. Sylvia's desire subsided, replaced by a dull, tormenting pain, tears scalding her eyes. Was she not to be granted release from this agonising frustration?

Farid straightened up and, holding out a hand, helped her to stand. Her legs felt wobbly, as if every bone had turned to jelly under his loosening touch. He guided her to the rim of the bath. Within seconds she was in the water with Rowena.

'Pretty one,' her aunt murmured, a catch in her voice. 'Such a lovely, lovely girl. Isn't she lovely, Farid?'

'Very lovely, mistress,' he answered, standing straight and tall, arms at his sides, his penis ramrod stiff.

Rowena reached up an arm, the water trickling back over it, and fingered his erection. 'Perhaps I will allow you to pleasure me later,' she said. 'But now, wash me, Farid.'

He dropped to his haunches and took up a large sponge, then commenced to bathe his mistress, the water cascading over her shoulders and breasts. She rose, like some magnificent goddess leaving the sea, and stood before him, parting her legs so that he might attend to her intimate parts.

She let her head sink back, her long throat arched, her breasts jutting towards his mouth. Farid sucked them, drawing each teat in turn into his mouth. Then he sank lower and, as Rowena stood knee deep in water, ran his tongue over her navel, across her lower belly, and into her crotch.

He used his hands to open it, revealing the jewel within, lapping the clit-head where the membrane was almost transparent. Rowena's legs shook. She lifted her hands and pinched her nipples between her fingers as Farid brought her steadily to climax.

She gave a great cry, seized his dark head and held it to her mound as the spasms rolled through her.

Sylvia watched breathlessly, her fingers seeking the unusual smoothness of her mons and the little pink organ that poked between the lips. She rubbed it as Rowena climaxed, but was unable to join her in completion before she recovered, pushing Farid aside and saying,

'Now bathe Miss Sylvia. Bathe her, nothing more. She is to be kept on the edge. Understand?'

'Yes, mistress,' he said, licking his lips as if savouring her juices that clung to them.

He was suffering great discomfort, Sylvia could see. His penis was hugely swollen, the purple glans shiny with jism, the balls between his legs so distended that he walked with difficulty. Rowena watched him, and smiled her cruel, musing little smile.

When Sylvia had been thoroughly washed, her hair too, then skewered on top of her head, Mary wrapped her in a big fluffy towel and she was taken into Rowena's bedchamber.

Mary began dusting her mistress all over with fragrant powder, and brushing out those luxuriant russet tresses. Cora's task was to arrange madam's evening attire, spreading it out on a chair for inspection. The room matched the boudoir for opulence, dominated by a massive bed with plaster ostrich plumes on every corner of the draped canopy. Still naked, Rowena strolled over to it and patted the gold embroidered coverlet.

'Join me, Sylvia,' she said. 'Time to relax while your new clothes are brought from your room. I thought it would be amusing if we dressed together tonight. You will need a personal maid of your own, and a suitable girl must be selected. Till then, Cora and Mary shall look to your wants.'

Sylvia sat down carefully. The quilt's gold thread and beadwork chafed her tender buttocks, digging into each red mark, but she kept silent. Looking up, she saw the astonishing sight of her own nakedness in the large mirror angled against the tester where it could reflect every aspect of the bed's occupants and their activities.

A hot blush spread up her neck and over her face. What scenes must that glass have mirrored? Rowena and her lovers, and she was sure by now that they were numerous. The lady had no shame, it seemed, as comfortable naked as when clothed, even more so, perhaps. Sylvia burned as she recalled Farid's tongue working between those silken pubic folds. In her secret fantasies she had imagined a man placing his mouth to her own lower lips, but had not thought it really possible.

Now she had seen it – knew it was a reality – yearned for someone to do it to her.

Rowena edged closer and her hands alighted on Sylvia's breasts. 'Such delectable little nipples,' she whispered and, lowering her head, breathed gently on each one.

Sylvia's hands clenched on the rich material beneath her. Strange and wonderful sensations lapped her, communicating with her bud, forming a trinity of sexual stimulation.

Rowena's tongue advanced to lick one ardent peak, then sucked it into her mouth. Sylvia shut her eyes, pitched into darkness while passion bloomed between her thighs.

Rowena pushed her back until she lay among the silken cushions. Sylvia kept her eyes tight shut. Whatever happened, and there was no doubt Rowena had some intention in mind, she felt better able to cope with it if she did not see.

It was impossible to resist peeping, however, as the bed creaked and they were joined by Mary and Cora.

'Let us see how experienced our little novice is,' Rowena said quietly. 'I want to see her bud, test it's reactions, find out whether or no it has been well exercised.'

Sylvia felt her arms seized and held apart, then fingers were at her breasts, Cora's and Mary's, rolling and roiling the eager tips.

Farid brought over a seven-branched candelabrum, placing it so that it illuminated her pubis. Sylvia squirmed. This was too much. Were they about to invade her most private place?

'Be still,' Rowena commanded, and pinched her thigh hard.

Sylvia whimpered and allowed her limbs to grow slack.

The delight lavished on her nipples was echoed in her needy kernel. She no longer cared what they did to her as long as that craving was satisfied. Vivid pictures flashed across her mind: Mary and Henry Lanston: the barmaid being whipped by Rawley: Mary's bare backside jerking under Rowena's rod and, finally, Farid licking his mistress to orgasm. Naked pricks. Naked cunts. She wanted it all – even the pain.

Rowena leaned forward, her ripe breasts swinging. She parted Sylvia's legs and moved her hand upwards along her thigh, then trailed a finger across the lips of her sex. Sylvia shivered and her legs fell apart. Now Farid's two fingers held back her labial wings, opening her fully and his mistress's middle digit wandered up the wet pink cleft towards the quivering clitoris.

'Oh, Rowena,' Sylvia moaned. 'I'm aching with want.'

'You know the sensation and it's cure,' Rowena whispered. 'You've played with yourself, haven't you? Done it often. Permitted your girl friends at school the liberty, and pleasured them in return. Isn't this so?'

'Yes… oh, yes… I admit it.'

'You love the wonderful feeling… the build up of tension… the little death of orgasm.'

'Yes, I do.'

'She is experienced,' Rowena said to her servants. 'It is evident by her eagerness. See how the lower lips part, thickened and red with desire, and note the copious liquid flowing from her vulva. And her nub… rarely have I seen a finer example. So large and eager.'

Sylvia began to moan and whimper, pleading for release. Mary and Cora continued to excite her nipples, and Rowena sank a fingertip into her entrance and spread her juices up the throbbing avenue to her clitoris. She massaged it with slow strokes, easing her finger back and forth over the tingling head.

'What are you feeling, darling?' she asked.

'So much pleasure,' Sylvia panted, her heart pounding wildly. 'Oh, please don't stop… go on stroking it. There… that's right… touch me there!'

She wanted nothing to interrupt her gradual ascent to heaven as Rowena and her servants brought her closer and closer to her goal. She was almost there – up and up, with waves gathering, ready to bear her aloft and carry her to the acme of sensation.

Then, with brutal abruptness, all touch ceased.

Sylvia's eyes snapped open. They were standing by the bed, looking down at her, while her blood throbbed and the pre-orgasmic waves began to retreat.

'Why have you stopped?' she demanded, her eyes flashing angrily.

'You are not to reach fulfilment yet. There is a long night ahead and I have guests who require entertainment,' Rowena answered coldly, though her nipples were erect and there was a sheen of moisture between her smooth crack.

'You can't do this to me,' Sylvia stormed, beside herself with rage and frustration. She sat up smartly, opened her legs and ran her finger over her pulsating bud. 'If you won't pleasure me, then I'll do it myself.'

Rowena's blue eyes were icy. 'No, you won't. I forbid you to touch yourself.' She raised her arm high and brought her hand down across Sylvia's with a stinging slap.

Sylvia jumped, her breasts bouncing. 'How are you going to stop me?' she snarled.

Rowena smiled and turned away. 'You'll be with one of us every moment,' she said evenly. 'And when you finally go to bed, I shall fix clamps on your lower lips so that you can't toy with yourself.'

'How can you be so cruel?' Sylvia whispered, every good feeling she had had shrivelling and dying.

Rowena looked back over one bare, shapely shoulder, saying, 'I have been taught by experts, my dear.'

Chapter Five

Sylvia stood nervously outside the door of the great reception room. She wanted to run away, but Mary guarded her on one side and Cora on the other. Both women were most immodestly clad, their outfits bringing blushes to Sylvia's cheeks.

Mary's huge breasts were barely contained by the tight stays that restricted her waist and forced those luscious globes above the lacy cups. Her skirt was transparent, her voluptuous belly and sturdy thighs easily seen, her glossy black pubic hair showing through the white muslin. Behind, the skirt was tucked up high, displaying her generous bottom and the red marks imprinted on it.

Cora, too, was semi-nude, while Sylvia felt worse than naked in a high-waisted, diaphanous chiffon robe with a revealing neckline and girlish puffed sleeves. Her hair was dressed in the popular Grecian style, drawn up at the crown with loose ringlets falling about her jewelled ears. It was a simple robe reminiscent of paintings depicting pastoral scenes in ancient times, when goddesses and nymphs frolicked with fauns, goat-legged men and lusty young shepherds.

The fact that she was about to face Rowena's guests in such an outrageous state of undress did nothing to lessen her discomfort. There were sounds from within: laughter, the rise and fall of conversation, the pop of champagne corks and the tinkling strains of a gavotte. The door was thrown open and a footman announced her name in ringing tones, 'The Honourable Miss Sylvia Parnell!'

Mary gave her a little jab in the ribs and, stiffening her spine and holding her head erect, she stepped over the threshold into a dazzle of light. A sea of faces turned towards her.

She heard 'Oohs' and 'Aahs' of admiration and Rowena

calling, 'Over here, darling one. Let me introduce you.'

The room was huge and extremely ornate, its many vases filled with hothouse flowers that exuded a heavy fragrance. There were some three dozen ladies and gentlemen gathered around Rowena who was holding court in a throne-like chair set on a dais attained by a shallow step. A multitude of candles flickered, bathing the scene in a radiant glow.

As Sylvia advanced towards her aunt, her train whispering over the parquetry, she watched her progress in one of the several full-length Venetian mirrors. She was embarrassed by the way her breasts were defined, the rosy studs of her nipples poking through the silk. As she moved the material undulated, sometimes clinging, sometimes drifting away from her limbs, and her eyes were drawn repeatedly to the triangle of her mons, so vulnerable without it coating of fluff.

She was so acutely self-conscious that it took a moment for her to register Rowena's companions. Then the blur cleared and she realised they were obviously from the nobility, the men in military uniforms or faultless evening suits, the women like gorgeous blossoms in an array of pastel silks. The light scintillated on tiaras and necklaces, medals, decorations and sword hilts. She reached Rowena's chair and dipped into a low curtsey. The voices murmured appreciatively again.

'She is quite charming,' lisped one agreeable beau, taking Sylvia's hand to raise her.

'Theo Aubrey is a deuced lucky dog, damn me if he ain't,' remarked another, lifting a languid wrist and applying one nostril to the little dune of snuff balanced at the base of his thumb.

'Has he seen her yet?' asked a vivacious, dark-haired lady, flirting her fan at the gentlemen.

And, as in the dress shop when Monsieur Andre mentioned him, Sylvia was aware of an underlying thread of excitement, as if the very mention of his name roused lustful passions.

'No. I am reserving that pleasure for later,' Rowena replied, and rising gracefully, she slipped an arm round Sylvia's waist and led her to the long dining table at the far end of the room.

Everyone took their places, ladies alternating with gentlemen, and the conversation was light and frothy. The rosewood table glittered with silver plate, Sevres china and Waterford crystal. Flowers spilled from a magnificent central epergne decorated with a female figurine, naked and with a man lying between her thighs, his phallus upward pointing.

The food was sumptuous in the extreme: salmon, turbot and trout, each with an accompanying sauce, quail and roast chicken, with vegetables swimming in butter, ice-cream and puddings and fruit. Yet nothing was heavy, the dishes designed to titillate the taste buds rather than satisfy the appetite.

A different wine was served with each course and the voices became louder, less controlled.

Sylvia was puzzled. She had expected something other than this rather decorous gathering. True, the ladies were as scantily clad as herself but this, she supposed, was high fashion. As the wine flowed more freely, so they began to discuss subjects other than politics, the latest theatrical productions and horse racing. Now they amused themselves with risqué anecdotes concerning the love lives of certain actresses and gossip about the Prince Regent's mistresses, but even this brought hardly a blush to Sylvia's face.

Perhaps I have been mistaken regarding Rowena, she thought. I know nothing of how court circles conduct themselves. How could I, a simple girl from the provinces?

The orchestra played softly, the talk hummed and she noticed that the dashing hussar seated by Rowena had his hand in her lap, caressing her mound through the silk, while she, serene as a nun, carried on a conversation with the man on her other side.

Sylvia shifted uneasily in her chair, moving her hips away from the dandy next to her who was engaging her in small talk. What should she do if he tried the same thing? she wondered.

Her clitoris tingled. She had not been allowed to play with

it, her senses stimulated even further by the attentions lavished on her body as Mary and Cora robed her. She was very afraid her wayward flesh would respond if the dandy touched her. On fire inside, she longed for him to do so, yet was ashamed of her wantonness.

She was not put to the test, for Rowena led her guests from the table into a further room whose doors were opened by two footmen, then closed firmly after they had passed through.

This was a very different apartment, no less luxurious but darker, draped in scarlet, and containing curious instruments – a wooden crosspiece – a bench like a vaulting horse – hooks suspended on chains from the lofty ceiling.

Sylvia stared, apprehension knotting in her gut.

There were other things, too – a selection of rods and canes, whips and flails, chains, handcuffs, blindfolds and gags, hanging neatly against the panelled walls. The servants were different from those who had waited at table, the women dressed like Mary and Cora. The men wore leather straps across their chests and bellies, from which stretched chains linked to manacles at their wrists and ankles. The straps passed tightly round their genitals, lifting their cocks and balls high.

Some went on all fours, their buttocks raised. Others crawled, their arms forced behind their backs and fastened there. Farid was in charge of them, pacing along their ranks, flourishing a many thonged whip with knotted ends, which he applied rigorously at the slightest provocation. He was naked, save for his collar and linking chains, his cock erect, held firm by a metal band round the base.

A remarkable change came over Rowena's guests. They openly inspected her servants, probing into fundaments and vaginas, pinching male and female nipples. Some took up paddles and made them whistle through the air before bringing them down across posteriors, breasts and thighs. The sounds of slaps were punctuated by gasps, squeals and sobs.

'To me,' Rowena commanded Farid, who shuffled across to her on his knees. 'Do you want him, Major?' she said to the handsome hussar. 'He is one of my favourites, a model of good behaviour. He'll do anything you command.'

'Anything, madam?' the soldier said, stroking his moustache thoughtfully.

She nodded and held out a small jar of oil. The major opened his breeches, drew out his engorged organ, anointed it with the lubricant, kicked Farid's legs apart and mounted him, driving that huge, greasy weapon into his nether orifice. Farid grunted, but took the whole, hard length of it.

'You see, Sylvia?' Rowena asked, blue eyes fixing her. 'This is true submission... an art you will acquire with my careful tutorage.'

'Never!' Sylvia burst out, as Farid gave vent to a moan under the major's rough, swift thrusts. 'No one shall use me thus!'

The major came with a shuddering groan, his hands gripping Farid's hips as he stood there letting the final convulsions of ejaculation judder through him. When he withdrew, his prick was coated with creamy fluid.

As Sylvia stared, disgusted yet aware of a dark coil of desire, Rowena smiled and said,

'Stand on that table over there.'

'I won't,' Sylvia declared.

At a nod from Rowena, Farid rose, picked Sylvia up and deposited her on the inlaid surface of a buhl table placed before a huge mirror in a carved and gilded frame.

'Gather round, my friends,' Rowena cried, that fiery haired votary of Venus, her gown flowing open, showing her pierced nipples, smooth belly and denuded cleft, the lips connected by a fragile gold chain passed through the rings. 'Here, for your delectation and delight, is my niece, Sylvia Parnell... Lord Theo's bride-to-be.' Sylvia kept her chin raised, looking above and beyond the heads that now clustered below her, ignoring the smiling, lecherous faces, the lustful, animalistic eyes. But she could not escape their hands.

Fingers crept over her curves and into her hollows, tweaking her nipples, which rose in response, sliding over the slight curve of her stomach, feeling her plump, hairless mound, dipping into her furrow.

In vain, she fought to control the tremors that shook her as one finger in particular found and played with her clitoris. She hated herself for the waves of pleasure that swept through her, but could not control them. The torment was worse than ever. Fingers on her nipples and in her cleft. One even circled her anal opening. Male or female, she did not care, just as long as she was not left strung on the rack of unfulfilled passion.

Rowena clapped her hands, shouting, 'Enough. There are other pleasures for you to sample. She is obdurate and needs training,' and she seized Sylvia and spun her round.

Sylvia could see herself in the mirror, her eyes wide and wild, her lips parted, and breasts rising from the low cut bodice with the force of her agitated breathing.

Farid passed Rowena a flexible paddle, and then gave her his hand that she might climb up beside Sylvia. The audience shouted their approval.

The paddle twanged as Rowena pressed in down with her thumb and then let go. Sylvia looked at it, aghast. It was white, smooth and pliable. Surely it won't hurt as much as the rod, she thought frantically, or even Farid's hard hand, yet her bottom was very sore and she knew it would sting at the lightest blow.

'Hold up your dress,' Rowena said, and when Sylvia hesitated, did so herself, hooking the long train up across Sylvia's shoulder leaving her backside and thighs bare.

'You can't do this to me,' Sylvia blurted out, tears of indignation wetting her face, the image of herself and the room behind her reflected in the looking glass.

'No one says "can't" to me,' Rowena answered and the paddle came down with a loud swish, landing on Sylvia's weals with terrible accuracy.

She leapt to one side but could not escape, the tabletop small and ringed with spectators only too ready to hurl her back to her tormentor. The paddle struck her repeatedly and Sylvia's sobs turned into shrieks as it spanked her rump.

'Stand still, girl,' Rowena said contemptuously. 'You *will* submit, so do it gracefully. Lord, but you've a great deal to learn!'

She passed the paddle to Farid who handed her a broad leather strap.

'That's it, Rowena! Show her what's what!' cried the major. 'By God, a flogging is the only thing to cure rebellion. It never fails to curb mutiny in my regiment.'

The belt struck Sylvia with a resounding crack. Her knees buckled as the pain scalded through her. Rowena pulled her up by the hair, forcing her head back till she thought her neck would snap. She had no option but to spread her legs to keep her balance.

The strap landed again and again. Sylvia howled in agony as the pain built up in her buttocks. She felt she might faint – longed to fall down in a swoon, avoiding further torture, but this was not to be.

In the mirror she could see the guests transported by lust at the sight of her flesh splotched with red welts, the ladder of stripes running up her thighs, the crimson blush spreading across the underside of her lower cheeks. They were fornicating even as they watched her – men with women, men with men, women with women. Wherever she looked there were naked limbs, bare cocks, cunts slippery with juices. Some, inspired by Rowena's treatment of her, were whipping the servants, chasing them across the floor and lashing them repeatedly. Others, even more perverse, presented their own buttocks to the whip. This impression lasted for a flash, no more, before the next blow fell on Sylvia's cringing body, and the next, till it seemed she was swimming in a sea of pain – a salty sea whose waves thrashed her mercilessly.

Rowena used the strap with skill, and at last made it lick at the pouting purse protruding from between Sylvia's thighs as she bent over.

'Oh… oh…' Sylvia sobbed loudly, her pubis flooded with

fiery pain. She could not tell which was worse, the agony of her bruised labia or the humiliation of her position.

'You are nothing… nothing,' Rowena hissed, the sweat of exertion trickling between her breasts.

Sylvia opened her eyes and stared at herself in the mirror, at her tear-streaked countenance, her disordered hair and clothing, her flushed breasts, and she thought, I *am* someone, a living, breathing woman, not a thing of no importance. She can't break my spirit. I refuse to admit defeat, even were she to flay every inch of skin from my body.

Rowena flung the strap aside and slid her hands under Sylvia's armpits, reaching round to fondle the bunched nipples, and a hot well of wanting opened in Sylvia's womb.

She could not help leaning back against her tormentor, all the strength draining from her, riven with pain and desire.

The secret room was dim, contrasting vividly with the light drenching the scene portrayed in the trick mirror which, from this side, was a window giving an uninterrupted view of all that took place. Theo stared as Rowena held Sylvia before him. His cock was swollen in his breeches, coming erect while he had witnessed her flogging. Now he impatiently opened the buttons and took it in his hand.

So this was Sylvia, his betrothed.

He smiled sombrely, well pleased. Not only did she own a substantial fortune that would pay off his gambling debts and keep him in the manner to which he was accustomed, but she was a beauty into the bargain. Wilful, too, judging by her defiance under the paddle and strap, refusing to back down. He admired her spirit. It was so much more rewarding to break a lively filly than have her meek and compliant at the start.

It was as if Rowena was looking directly into his face from behind the girl's shoulder, smiling in her catlike way, knowing he was watching. Rowena – his partner in debauchery, almost as wicked, very nearly as dissolute – but not quite.

She's doing it for me, he thought. And why not? I answer

that deep, dark hunger in her as no one else can.

Theo stroked his burgeoning member, caressing the heavy testicles, tracing the line between them before going back up to his shaft. The helm was moist and his fingers worked that warm wetness over it, pushing down the foreskin so the ridge stood out tensely.

He watched Sylvia as he did so, seeing how she leaned against Rowena as if half fainting with pleasure as his paramour teased her dusky rose nipples. Then, moving slowly to tantalise the watcher, Rowena reached down to lift Sylvia's skirt, gradually raising it till he was afforded the bewitching sight of the girl's shaven pudenda.

He stared at it as Rowena's fingers advanced, but carefully, never obscuring his view. Go on, Theo urged in his mind, his hand moving ever faster over his tumescent member. Open that lubricious furrow. Open it for me.

As if reading his mind, Rowena paused over the line marking the division, then, placing a finger on either side, unfurled the wet sex lips. Sylvia's features lost their sadness. Her green eyes looking blindly at Theo were now heavy, her lips fuller and more lustrous, slightly parted over her perfect teeth. He could see the tip of her little, slippery tongue peeping between them.

Theo pulled at his penis, sliding the foreskin over the head, and then rolling it back again. His cods ached for release, but he held off, prolonging the moment of sublime pleasure.

Rowena's hands worked on Sylvia, whose legs were now spread, her pubis lifted towards that seductive finger which flicked at and massaged the crest of the clitoris poking out boldly from the labial folds.

Theo could almost smell her essences, taste the slightly salty, sea-washed juices, and feel the extreme smoothness of her silky delta. His fingertips tingled as he rubbed his own centre of sensation, his cock. It needed sucking, and he wanted Sylvia to do it, relishing in advance the joy of teaching her fellatio.

He dreamed of what he would do to her after the wedding

ceremony.

First, he would whip her with his riding crop, bringing her to her knees, that proud, defiant girl. Then he would lay her back on the great seigniorial bed and open her with his hands, using an antique ivory lingam to rupture her hymen. This being done, his tongue and fingers would bring her to orgasm, whether she was willing or no.

Finally she would thresh and scream with pleasure, beg and implore him to possess her, and he would scissor her legs over his shoulders and plunge his organ into her virgin body, pumping and thrusting until he spent himself.

After that, another beating perhaps, and then he would make her take him in her mouth and, later, turn his attention to that other untrodden path – her arsehole.

Theo smothered a groan, the burning heat of lust making his cock-head ever more slippery. His fingers curled round the shaft and rubbed the glans, repeating the motion in a frenzied manner, sensation pouring through him as he brought himself closer to crisis.

He saw Sylvia arch, her face intense and beautiful as she abandoned herself to orgasm. The fierce heat of Theo's release thundered through his loins, ejecting a stream of milky semen with such force that it spattered the trick window.

'He's taking tea with us this afternoon,' Rowena said, idly combing the tan and white fur of the miniature spaniel on her lap. 'Sit still, Fleur!' she scolded sharply as she fixed a blue ribbon to its topknot.

'Who is coming to tea?' Sylvia asked, showing little interest, worn out by last night's excesses.

'Your fiancé, Lord Theo, is visiting you,' Rowena answered, staring at her over the little dog's head.

'Oh, no! I'm in no fit state…!' Sylvia began, starting up, her hands flying to her face.

Rowena laughed and turned Fleur over to Farid, saying, 'Take her for a walk, and no idling in the park with lecherous soldiers. Return here smartly.'

'Yes, madam,' he murmured, liveried once more, no longer the enslaved denizen of Rowena's secret playground for courtesans and rakes, peers and great ladies.

'I thought you would be anxious to meet the man whom you are to marry,' Rowena continued.

'Will he take me away from all this?' Sylvia asked anxiously, spreading wide arms to include the boudoir where Rowena insisted she spend much of her time.

She had a room of her own, a lovely room furnished in walnut with dainty flower sprigged curtains and hand painted wallpaper, but Rowena wished to have her constantly under her eye. They had shopped again, then had luncheon, and now it was afternoon and she had made her alarming announcement.

'I assume you'll live in his house... Burbank Abbey, which lies beside the river at Richmond,' Rowena went on, shifting her legs beneath her coffee-coloured silk skirt, a demure garment with long ballooning sleeves and a short bodice with a frill bordering the deep valley between her breasts.

'No doubt he'll take up residence at Monk's Park, when the fancy takes him... or you might even go abroad. He has a villa on one of the Greek islands, I believe.'

'What is he like?' Sylvia asked eagerly, hugging her knees as she sat on the stool at her aunt's feet gazing up into that lovely, aristocratic face. 'Is he kind? Will he treat me well? Is he good looking?'

Rowena ran a finger round the edge of Sylvia's bodice, dipping inside and tracing over one nipple. 'So many questions,' she chided with a chuckle. 'Theo? Well, my dear... he's just Theo. A law unto himself. He's intelligent and educated, went to public school and then Oxford University. He's dabbled in poetry and astrology, rubbed shoulders with Lord Byron and other notable rakes... has travelled a great deal. An expert horseman, a crack shot, a brilliant and deadly duellist. You want to know what he looks like? He's tall and straight, and beautiful as a fallen angel. As for kindness? You will have to decide for yourself.'

None of this was reassuring, but Sylvia felt a prickle of excitement running along her nerves. Lord Theo was calling on her. Soon she would meet her destiny.

'How well do you know him?' she asked, puzzled by something in her aunt's eyes.

Rowena did not reply for a moment, a cloud passing over her face, then she said, 'As well as anyone possibly can. He is something of an enigma.'

The hours dragged slowly, yet seemed also to fly by. Sylvia was in a high-strung state, one moment longing to see Theo, the next plunged into fearful trepidation. Her bottom stung from her beating, and she was near to weeping every time she moved, but she could not forget the extreme pleasure Rowena had given her, almost as a reward.

Later, she sat with her aunt in the drawing room, a splendid apartment where the predominating colour was yellow. The ceiling was tented in saffron silk, the windows draped in topaz damask. They were open, giving on to a balcony overlooking the green lawns and trees of Hyde Park. The afternoon sunshine streamed in and Sylvia felt herself bathed in gold. It heated her, roused her desires, dread and longing making her damp between the thighs.

A footman brought in the tea tray with its chased silver pot and eggshell china cups. These were blue, with gilt edgings. A small silver kettle steamed on an ornamental stand, heated by a little charcoal burner.

'He's late,' Sylvia said, hardly able to speak for the constriction in her throat.

'Theo is always late,' Rowena remarked, from her place on a dainty walnut daybed. 'It is a demonstration of his ability to manipulate people. They are in his power while he keeps them waiting.'

Sylvia felt as if she was sitting on thorns instead of a comfortably padded chair. Her buttocks had never been so sore, even after being whacked by Mrs Dawson. She hoped she would be able to keep facing Theo, for her dress was thin and she had been forbidden to wear a petticoat. Her mirror had shown that her posterior shone bright pink through the white muslin. The thought that he might see it was torture to her. She would never survive such shame.

She trembled, her face flushing then turning pale as the butler opened the door, announcing: 'Lord Aubrey, milady.'

Sylvia stared, and then caught her breath, dumbstruck by the individual standing at the entrance.

Later, all she remembered of this first impression was height and inexorable power, an angular face with high cheekbones, an aquiline nose and sensual lips, framed in curling, raven black hair.

Older than Sylvia had expected, or maybe it was just his cynical expression, he was a picture of sartorial male elegance in his plum velvet cutaway tailcoat. Gold fobs shone from his watch chain. His long narrow trousers fastened under his polished shoes. They clung like paste around his lean flanks, and outlined his phallus clearly.

His linen was spotless; a high stock fastened beneath his firm jaw; lace showed at his cuffs; a diamond pin glittered amidst the frills of his shirtfront. He was a fine figure of a gentleman, yet cold fingers ran down Sylvia's spine.

'Rowena,' he said, and his deep voice seemed to penetrate Sylvia as surely as if he had already taken physical possession of her.

'Theo,' Rowena answered, her smile deepening as he came across and raised her hand to his lips.

He straightened and looked directly at Sylvia, and a spark crackled between them. She could feel it tingling down to her clitoris and erupting in an exquisite pain. Yet over all and above all, she still felt chilling terror.

She heard Rowena saying, 'This is Sylvia,' but was helpless to do other than stare at him, mesmerised by his amber eyes, his crooked smile, that aura of sinister sensuality that surrounded him.

'I'm enchanted,' he said, very low.

She felt his cool, strong fingers on hers and her nipples crimped. Then came the brush of his lips on the back of her hand. His hold tightened and she felt his thumb-pad in her palm, tickling it. Her skin burned. Her weals pulsed. Her mouth was dry, her sex wet. All reason and commonsense slumped into abeyance.

Rowena's eyes glittered as she watched them, then, 'Sit down, Theo,' she said, and made room for him on the couch.

She poured the tea and handed round the fragile little cups. Sylvia sat across from them, but did not dare look at him again, lost and bewildered. The magnificent room, its equally impressive owner, faded into insignificance in this man's presence. He was arrogant, self-assured, the sort of person who would undertake anything with force and precision. There would be no half measures with him.

I can't possibly marry him, Sylvia thought. He will destroy me.

'I've taken the liberty of inviting Mr Middleton to attend us,' Rowena said, passing the cake stand to Theo, who declined.

Sylvia's ears pricked up. The lawyer. They were losing no time then, concerned about settling the deal. I feel like a heifer in the market place, she reflected angrily. Am I to have no say in the matter?

She spoke before she could stop herself, the words coming tumbling out. 'Why the hurry? Surely it would be better if Lord Theo and myself became acquainted before we involve Mr Middleton?'

Their eyes switched to her, and she felt herself wilting.

'My dear young lady, I already feel that I know you,' Theo began, a predatory smile playing round his lips. 'Lady Rowena has told me so much about you and, now that we've met, I confess myself to be bewitched. Certainly, we shall go out and about together, once the settlement is signed, and the wedding will take place within a short while.'

Trembling at her own boldness, Sylvia looked at him, though this was almost her undoing. Rowena had warned her that he was irresistible, and she felt herself drowning in those fierce, tigerish eyes. She dragged her gaze away.

'It is too soon, my lord,' she whispered.

Theo leaned back, one arm resting behind Rowena along the couch. 'I think not,' he vouchsafed. 'Your coming into your inheritance hinges on you marrying. You'll not be permitted to manage it alone.'

'That is monstrous,' Sylvia exclaimed. 'I don't want to marry anyone... particularly you.'

He smiled sardonically, drawling, 'How unflattering. Can it be that my person offends you?'

She blushed hotly, and he reached across to place his hand on hers. A spasm of voluptuous pleasure shot through her, wrenching at her womb and making her wet inside.

'No sir, but I repeat, it is too soon,' she stammered.

'Where is that fellow, Middleton?' Rowena said suddenly, rising to her feet with a rustle of silk. 'I shall go and find him. I said four o'clock. How dare he keep us waiting?'

'I'll go, Rowena,' Sylvia offered, leaping up.

'No, my dear, you stay and talk with his lordship.'

'But...'

'Do as I say,' Rowena commanded, the steel in her voice making Sylvia's welts throb.

She hung her head miserably and sat down again. The door closed with a click and she was alone with Theo.

He patted the space beside him vacated by Rowena. 'Come over here,' he said.

'I'm perfectly comfortable where I am, sir,' she answered icily, though her cheeks were almost as red as her bottom.

'Come here,' he repeated, scowling at her.

'No!' She lifted her head and met his gaze square on.

She found herself rising and going to him. He watched her with his mocking smile, and then pulled her down beside him.

'You were slow in answering my command,' he said in those

fluid accents. 'You will have to be quicker once we are man and wife.'

'I'll never marry you, Lord Aubrey,' she cried, but was terribly aware of the personal odour of his body and hair – a sensual, woody smell with the aromatic undertones of perfumed pomade. 'You can't force me. I have rights. I'll appeal to the Courts of Justice.'

'Do that, if you so desire,' he replied suavely. 'No doubt they'll listen, then throw your case out of court. You are a young woman adrift in a wicked world and no one will give you permission to inherit such an important estate as Monk's Park without a husband at your side. Rowena is responsible for you, and as your only relative has the authority to commit you to an asylum if you prove too troublesome.'

'She wouldn't do that!' Sylvia stormed.

'Would she not? Indeed people would think you mad to refuse a man like myself,' he said, and gripping her by the shoulders, pushed her back amongst the soft sofa cushions.

He leaned across her and laid open her bodice. Her nipples hardened as his fingers stroked over them. She moaned under his expert touch, feeling herself melting away. Her hair had come unpinned, falling like a scented curtain over her shoulders. Theo buried his face in it, then seized a handful and gave it a sharp tug.

She cried out and struggled, but he reached down and lifted her skirt. Now her torso was exposed to his gaze – her waist, belly and thighs, and the cleft dividing her bare mound.

She tried to fight him, but felt him rubbing, gently circling and fondling her navel. He was nowhere near her clitoris yet it was affected, swelling from its delicate, wet folds. She pressed her legs tightly together, but he thrust a knee between them and opened her, then found her bud with practised ease and began to finger-stroke it.

To her bitter shame, Sylvia felt herself responding as he fondled the nubbin as delicately as if he touched silk. It was a deeply seductive touch and she gave a little melodious groan as she neared the acme of her bliss.

Theo laughed quietly as he stared into her passion drugged eyes and whispered, 'Not yet, my flower. You have only just begun to discover the meaning of pleasure.'

In a trice, he had her across his knee, skirts flying up around her buttocks. 'What are you doing?' she screamed, jolted out of the sensual dream into which the friction of his finger had plunged her.

'Examining your backside, darling,' he said harshly, running his hands over the welts and stripes. 'What a naughty little wanton, eh? A young lady who thinks she can be independent and survive without a husband. Rubbish, my love. You need a man to fuck you every day and beat you regularly. Like this!'

Sylvia jerked as his hand hit her flesh. She bit her lip to prevent herself from crying out, and he hit her again. This time she could not restrain a sob. Theo paused, and she felt his fingers exploring the amber furrow of her arse, dipping lower and finding the hot mouth of her vulva. He wetted his finger, lifted it to his nose and inhaled her strong fragrance, then dabbled in her dew once more, spreading it upwards to her thrumming clit.

He massaged and teased it, till she was almost screaming for release. He chuckled again and flattened out his right hand, delivering a series of hard, stinging slaps on her crimsoned buttocks.

Sylvia bucked and threshed but there was no escape. She could feel the solid bough of his cock rising under her as she sprawled over his lap, and, maddened with baulked passion, tried to rub against it.

'You can't have it… not yet,' he whispered into her ear. 'You'll be wearing a wedding ring before I let you even see it.'

Sylvia was sobbing now, her rump on fire, her clitoris a swollen berry needing instant relief. 'Please…' she cried, grinding her pubis against his thigh. 'Please, help me.'

At that moment Rowena came in at the door, accompanied by a gentleman. He was tall, spare and angular, his black suit and thin legs making him look like a stork, as did his high-domed, balding head.

Rowena took in the situation at a glance, but ignored Sylvia's flushed, dishevelled appearance and Theo's very obvious erection. She swept across the floor with her usual confidence, saying, 'I've found Mr Middleton. He's brought all the necessary documents with him. All we need is for Sylvia and Theo to add their signatures.'

'Miss Sylvia... how do you do?' Middleton remarked in a nasal, whining voice, bowing from the waist. 'I knew your father... a most noble gentleman. His death... such a loss to the Government. Ah, well... and now you will carry on the line... with a little help from his lordship here.'

He means none of it, the hypocrite, Sylvia thought savagely. They have me trapped between them. What can I do? I've no intention of signing the wretched papers. Give my property to Theo and become his slave? Over my dead body!

Yet she had to get away from him before her weak flesh succumbed to his blandishments. He was just too expert a libertine for her to resist for long. Even now, she yearned to be in his arms again, with those elegant fingers stroking her bud to fulfilment.

Sudden inspiration flashed across her mind. She must play for time, dissemble for a moment, beat them at their own deceitful game. That way she might be able to make her escape. Surely there was someone who would help her? Maybe the Prince Regent would champion her if she went to Carlton House and threw herself on his mercy.

She simpered at Mr Middleton and settled herself close to Theo on the couch, looking up at him adoringly, acting the part of the coy fiancée. Rowena gave her a sharp stare and raised an eyebrow at Theo, who merely smiled in response, thinking he had won the day.

'I'm so glad to meet you, Mr Middleton,' Sylvia gushed. 'London is wonderful and Lady Rowena the soul of kindness. As for my betrothed? He is all I could have hoped for, and more. The answer to a maiden's prayer.'

'I'm so pleased to hear that, Miss Sylvia,' Middleton said, and took a bundle of papers from beneath his arm, bending his lean frame to spread them out on the table. 'Let us delay no further. Have you a quill and ink, Lady Rowena?'

'I have indeed,' she cried gaily, and went to her desk, taking out the required tools and bringing them over to the table.

'Oh, one moment, if you please,' Sylvia cried, jumping up and turning towards the door. 'The excitement, you know… it has quite upset me. I beg to be excused for an instant, if I may.'

Rowena frowned, then smiled, 'Very well, my dear. Don't be long. We await your return to complete this important matter.'

Sylvia dipped a curtsey to her aunt and Theo and then ran from the room. She fled to her bedchamber, seized her coat and bonnet, paused outside the door to make sure the coast was clear and then bounded down the backstairs that led to the servants' quarters, and the garden. Luck was with her, and very shortly she let herself out of the kitchen gate, leaving Laurel House behind her and escaping into the anonymity of the London streets.

Her spirits lifted and she almost danced along the pavement. She was free.

Chapter Six

It was fun at first, a jaunt across the park where gentlefolk strolled, enjoying the spring sunshine, but as Sylvia put distance between herself and Laurel House, so doubts began to creep in.

Running away was all very well, a brave act of defiance, but where was she to go?

There were five guineas and some copper coins in her handbag, a silver comb, a pair of pearl eardrops and a matching necklace, but nothing more. She had not thought to pack a change of clothing. Hot-headed and rash, she chided herself, you should have stopped to think it through. But there had been no time. She had panicked, concerned with nothing but getting away from her aunt and Theo.

Now she was alone in the vast, noisy city.

She did not dare linger. A hue and cry would be raised as soon as she was missed. She sped on, considering and discarding several plans of action. There was the Prince Regent, but would she ever gain audience with him? And where was Carlton House located? Perhaps she should try to find a posting inn and take a coach to Hampshire and Monk's Park. But even if she was successful in this enterprise, would it not be one of the first places Rowena would look for her?

By far the wisest course would be to slip into that part of the town far removed from the gentry, there rent a room in a tavern, eat and rest and reconsider her plight.

She trudged on, leaving Mayfair behind her and entering the squalid, twisting streets well beyond the mansions of the rich. She found herself jostled on all sides by dirty, shabby people who eyed her fine clothes suspiciously. She hid her fear, walking along the side of the unpaved road as if this was her route every day of the week.

The cobbles were slippery with muck and rubbish, while the three-storey, gabled houses leaned drunkenly across the streets, shutting out the daylight. The smell was almost overpowering. Open sewers ran down the centre of the roads, a repository for garbage, kitchen waste and the contents of chamber pots. The acrid smoke belching from chimneys added to this nauseous stink.

At last, hungry and tired, Sylvia stopped outside a dilapidated tavern that bore a creaking, weather-beaten sign on which was inscribed: *The Blue Boar*.

Screwing up her courage, she stepped through the open doorway, finding herself in the taproom. It was thick with the fumes of ale and tobacco, filled with workmen, travellers, layabouts and flinty-eyed factory girls who all turned their heads to look her over.

Sylvia stuck out like a diamond on a dung-heap, well dressed, beautiful, and unaccompanied.

Ignoring them, she picked her way over to the bar, intending to ask for lodgings. One of the men, winking at his companions, reached up an arm as she passed. He was a big, unshaven ruffian. He swung her round to him, dragging her across his knee, his face pressed close to hers, grinning into her wide, startled eyes.

'Care for a drink, deary? Old Danny will look after you, never fear, as long as you let him fuck you,' he growled, blowing his sour breath into her face.

One of his dirty hands slid up under her skirt and invaded the privacy of her sex, a finger wriggling into her cleft. He gave a harsh burst of laughter as she wrenched herself free, the angry colour flaming in her cheeks, her green eyes shooting sparks. He merely grinned the wider, and sniffed his finger with relish, shouting,

'Ah, lovely! There's nothing like the smell of juicy pussy, and this one's smooth as silk, boys.'

He was suddenly knocked from his stool by a gentleman

who materialised from the crowd. The labourer rose, shaking his fist and mouthing threats, but his mates restrained him, roaring with laughter, full of ale and bonhomie.

'Let that be a lesson to you, fellow!' Sylvia's rescuer barked, dusting his hands together, then turning to her and bowing as he added politely, 'Madam, we've not been introduced, but I beg that you will sit at my table and partake of a little refreshment.'

There was nothing exceptional about him. A young man of wiry build with sallow, acne scarred skin, sandy hair and watery blue eyes. His clothes had a kind of spurious elegance, yet the material was of inferior quality. However, Sylvia was badly shaken by her encounter and he was offering protection. She had no choice but to accept.

She threw him a tremulous smile, and placed her gloved hand on the arm extended to her, allowing him to lead her to a table in the corner.

'Thank you, sir,' she said, as they sat down. 'A lady travelling alone is prey to such unmannerly louts.'

'Indeed, yes. You're alone, you say?'

'I was on my way to board a carriage journeying to my village in the country, but I'm lost. I don't know the name of the inn from which it was due to leave, and have wandered far from my destination, I fear,' she said, having decided it was prudent to lie.

'Dear me, I must see if I can help you,' he soothed, pouring her a glass of wine. 'Robert Kelly, at your service, a student from Kent residing at the Inns of Court where I'm studying law.'

Law? Could he be useful in pleading her case? Sylvia wondered, and relaxed a little, opening her pelisse, the creamy skin of her throat and the upper curves of her breasts gleaming between the folds.

'And I,' she said, with an appealing lift of her dark lashes, 'am Miss Anne Rankin, a vicar's daughter, about to return home from the city. I have been staying with my grandmother.'

'You are journeying by yourself, Miss Rankin? Is it not risky for so charming a young lady to go about without a chaperon?'

Sylvia noticed that he was sitting with his legs open, knees pointing towards her. His breeches were tight, and she could see the firm curves of phallus and testicles between his thighs. He leaned a little closer and the bulge enlarged. She realised she must use her assets to aid herself.

Sighing helplessly, she adopted the affectations she had seen Rowena and Mary employ, giving him a flirtatious glance and saying, 'You are right, sir, of course. Under normal circumstances my dear Papa would not permit such an indiscretion, but poor grandma is unwell, and he can't leave his parish. They could not manage without him, even for a single day. Mama has been dead these many months, and there was no one else to go with me at such short notice.'

'You are quite alone, then?'

She nodded, and his arm brushed hers as he eased nearer, while she kept her eyes down shyly as she said, 'I am, sir, and don't know what to do.'

'If you will allow me to advise you,' he breathed, seeming quite captivated, daring to take her hand in his. 'It is too late to find a coach tonight. I suggest that you hire a room. Don't worry. I'll arrange everything with the host, if I may.'

'Couldn't I pass the night under your roof?' she asked. 'No doubt you have lodgings hereabout.'

Something flashed in his eyes and she wanted to pull her hand away, but remained passive. She was becoming desperate. What had seemed an exciting adventure was turning into a nightmare. She cursed Rowena and Theo for forcing her into such a position. They should have been more honourable, guarding her zealously, instead of subjecting her to exploitation.

'As a student of modest means, I'm forced to share my apartment with some rather rowdy companions,' he replied, with an apologetic shrug. 'They are lewd-tongued and might offend you. However, another thought has occurred to me. I'll take a room here, next to yours, so that I may be on hand if you need me, and tomorrow will make sure you are safely settled on the right coach for home.'

'You are too kind,' she murmured, and her clitoris pulsed as she wondered if he intended to try and share her bed.

He could not be described as handsome, but the heaviness at his crotch promised that delight she had not yet experienced, the forbidden joy of full intercourse. The stimulation given her by Theo had left her craving satisfaction, coming as it had directly after the stresses and excitements of Rowena's party and the awakening of that eroticism rooted in her innermost core.

Sylvia's curiosity had been aroused to fever pitch, and here was a virile man eager to show her more. She forgot the dangers this might entail, putting her trust in him and, after she had drunk two more glasses of wine, he seemed quite attractive, assuming the role of knight-errant.

He left her for a moment, and she saw him across the smoky room, deep in conversation with a burly individual wearing a hessian apron and that air of command that proclaimed him to be the owner of the hostelry.

Robert returned, all smiles. 'Everything is arranged, Miss Rankin,' he announced. 'There are two rooms available and I've ordered dinner. You will be my guest, naturally.'

The food was well prepared, and they ate in a partitioned cubicle. Robert seemed ravenous and, with hardly a pause, he tucked into soup, roast mutton and potatoes, followed by apple-pie and cream, biscuits, cheese, and a great deal of wine.

Sylvia, too, had found her appetite, her spirits reviving. She congratulated herself on having come out of this ordeal unscathed. It seemed that fate had already decided on her course of action. Not the Prince Regent then, but Monk's Park. She would find Nanny Talbot, gather faithful retainers around her and defend herself against Theo Aubrey. Robert should be her ally.

'Tell me, Robert,' she said; they had been on Christian name terms for some time. 'You study law, you say?'

'That's true, Anne,' he answered, helping himself to another wedge of Stilton cheese.

'I have a friend… a young women of means, who is being forced into marriage.'

'Indeed,' he said, staring at her owlishly. He slid a hand on to her knee under the table, squeezing and fondling, moving up her leg towards the dampness of her mound as he murmured, 'May I hear more?'

Sylvia closed her knees firmly and moved away from that tantalising exploration as she answered, 'This lady has a considerable fortune, but has been told that she can't claim it unless she marries the man her guardian has selected. Could you take on her case, and help her free herself from this odious match?'

'For you… and your friend… I would do anything,' he vowed. 'We'll talk of it further tomorrow. I'll give you my address and you can forward it to her.'

Does he guess I speak of my own situation? she wondered, but was feeling too dizzy with wine to bother. Robert had an arm about her, and a hand inside her coat, cupping and caressing the under swell of her breast, his touch one that she found agreeable. The little beast within her cleft stirred wantonly, raising its head, longing to be stroked. Sylvia's control was slipping, Robert becoming more and more palatable and to her liking.

'You are a lovely woman, Anne,' he crooned into her ear, his breath tickling it pleasantly. 'I swear that I'm falling madly in love with you.'

Sylvia was torn, one part of her wanting to kick over the traces and yield to him, the other suggesting that this would be folly. But she had no one else to lean on, nowhere to go, and could not venture out into the dangerous night streets alone.

'You mustn't say such things, Robert,' she protested half-heartedly. 'I hardly know you.'

'That can be quickly remedied. Let us retire,' he whispered. 'I'll see you to your chamber. Don't worry. You have nothing to fear from me.'

She walked up the stairs on billowing clouds of alcohol, with Robert lurching after her. Somehow, she reached her room and collapsed on the bed. Everything whirled, and she plunged into an intoxicated sleep.

She was rudely awakened by someone slapping her hard about the breasts and thighs. Struggling out of oblivion, she found that her skirts were up around her waist and her bodice open. Robert was kneeling on the bed, shaking and smacking her, as he shouted,

'Wake up, Anne! You can't sleep. I didn't bargain for that. I want some action from you!'

He pushed her down amongst the pillows and groped at her breasts, pinching and twisting the nipples. His slack, wet lips captured hers, his big, fleshy tongue delving and probing into the cavity of her mouth. His breath was tainted with wine.

Still enmeshed in dreams, Sylvia's vagina clenched at the sensual feel of this invasion, her nipples stinging under his harsh handling, honeydew wetting her labial petals. She felt him fondling her thighs, and forcing his hand between them, his excited panting grating on her raw nerves.

She flinched as he crudely parted her delicate folds, homing on her clit, rubbing hard as if he was trying to remove a stain from a carpet. So harsh a handling brought her no pleasure, her bud retracting into its hood to escape such brutality. She raised her knee, trying to jab him in the groin and free herself, but he gave a her resounding, backhanded blow across the face, half stunning her.

He tore open his breeches, releasing a short, thick cock. His adoring manner had vanished, and now he was insolent, coarse and overbearing. His vulgarity shocked and disgusted her as he shouted,

'You're no lady, Anne Rankin… or whatever the hell your name is. You're a whore… a filthy, shameless little whore under that dainty pose. I know your type. You thought you could gull me, but you met the wrong man here. I'm nobody's fool. Now you're going to get what you asked for.'

He knelt astride her and, grabbing a handful of her hair, pulled her head between his thighs. He thrust his hard, pale-skinned prick towards her lips, nudging them open with the shiny red helm.

She could not escape that agonising grip and the pressure of his thick tool driving into her mouth. She gagged, could feel herself choking, but he ignored her, pushing in harder till her nose was buried in the musky smelling, reddish fur of his lower belly. He put his hands each side of her head, fingers still buried in her hair, and rocked her back and forth on his cock.

Her jaw was aching, the taste of him rancid and strong, nausea rising in her stomach. Oh, yes, her curiosity was being satisfied without doubt, but not the yearnings of her sex, even though he was savagely ravishing her virginal mouth.

He was careless, concerned only with his own pleasure, his chest heaving uncontrollably as he moved faster and faster, thrusting against the back of Sylvia's throat. With a shuddering cry, he exploded in rapid-fire action, a great spurt of hot juice choking her and running from the sides of her mouth and down her chin.

Coughing and spluttering, she succeeded in pushing him off, revolted by the taste of his secretions. She struggled to the edge of the bed, leaned over and vomited on to the floor, hanging there half conscious.

She revived enough to be aware of Robert hitting her violently with his hands and then attacking her with his belt. She quivered under the brutal beating, the vile taste of vomit mingling with his semen on her lips. Robert had betrayed her. They had all betrayed her. The sacred temple of her mouth had been violated, her trust, dreams and expectations ground into the dust.

She wept, allowing the tears to swamp her.

'Stop that blubbering! D'you hear?' Robert shouted, emphasising each words with a blow. He rolled her on to her back and tipped the remainder of the wine bottle over her, a steady stream pouring into her mouth.

'Dirty whore!' she heard him muttering, and his voice sounded distant now. 'Whore... all women are whores...'

Sylvia could fight no more. Sobbing and very drunk, she plunged into a sleep of utter despair.

She woke to the sounds of street cries and the rumble of traffic. Somewhere, high above, came the pealing of bells. The sweet, clear ringing mingled with the other noises; the clamouring music of London.

The greyish light of a rainy morning penetrated the bed curtains, and it took a few seconds to gather her wits. Her head pounded relentlessly and her eyes hurt. When she moved, every inch of her seemed to have its own particular ache, her buttocks a burning sea of pain.

Memory started to return and, with a cry of horror, she reached down and felt between her legs. She was moist there, but not unusually so. Robert had not attempted to penetrate her vagina. Though her mouth tasted foul and she remembered his invasion of it with a shudder, her maidenhead was still intact.

She felt fouled by his touch. She got up swiftly, afraid that he would return and demand a repeat performance of last night's pillage. Swinging her legs to the floor, she tried to rearrange her torn dress and crumpled coat. Gazing into the fly-spotted mirror as she bathed her face at the washstand, she thought,

Lord, what a sight I am, with my ashen cheeks and red eyes with those dark smudges beneath them. A far cry from the ladylike Miss Sylvia Parnell of yesterday.

Never mind. Robert had promised to help her. She could forgive him his rough usage if he would work diligently to free her from her obligation to Theo.

But where was he?

She peered into the next room but the bed stood undisturbed. It had not been slept in. She returned to her own chamber and waited, tapping her foot impatiently and reviling him for an oaf who had gone down to breakfast without her. The novel sounds of the waking tavern caught her attention. There were footfalls and laughter as the servants went about their chores.

It all sounded reassuringly normal, but where was Robert? Suddenly a horrible suspicion flashed across her mind. She remembered stuffing her purse under the pillow when she arrived in the room last night. She whipped back both pillow and bolster, even the mattress, finally stripping the bed in her frantic search before accepting the bald truth.

Her money and jewels had gone. And so had Robert Kelly.

Dark clouds hung like a pall over London, rain sluicing down from a lead coloured sky. Though not yet eight o'clock, the streets were filling and the shops opening, tousle headed apprentices banging back the shutters.

Sylvia had been walking for some time, not knowing which direction to take, her one thought to escape from the tavern.

For a while after discovering that Robert had absconded with her money, she had been stupefied with shock. Then, rising anger against his dastardly behaviour and her own gullibility had galvanised her into action.

What a fool he must have thought her to be so easily duped!

Lawyer be damned! He was nothing but a thief and trickster!

With quick, enraged movements, she had fastened her coat and put on her bonnet, knowing she must disappear before the landlord demanded settlement of the considerable bill. She had not the faintest hope that Robert had paid it before his cowardly flight.

It was too risky to use the main staircase, so she had opened the door leading to the gallery and slipped down the wooden steps to the courtyard, attempting to appear casual and unconcerned lest anyone see her and become suspicious. This was impossible to do and, in the end, she had rushed out beneath the arch, reaching the street, taking a turn to the right and dashing headlong down it.

At last she paused for breath, a stitch clawing at her side, trying to formulate a plan of action. She would not return to Laurel House. The idea was untenable. Could she find someone who would give her a lift to Monk's Park? But what could she do without money?

She left the doorway where she had been huddled and set off again, trying not to show her confusion, while inside her heart was sinking and fear stalked beside her. She traversed the alleys, appalled by the abject poverty on all sides, glad that her bonnet drooped, rain dripping from the brim and her coat was muddied to the knees. That way she was a little less conspicuous. She tramped for hours, wandering deeper into the warren of fetid streets, hungry, wet through and lost.

She had no idea where she was to spend the night and, wearily, turned into yet another dingy side-street. In doing so, she had to pass two women dressed in gaudy, tattered finery. Their faces were heavily painted, and their shawls flung back to display naked breasts with rouged nipples. They lounged against the wall, haggard and disease ridden, on the alert for customers. Even Sylvia, green as she was, recognised them as harlots of the lowest order.

God help me, she whispered to herself as she shrank from their fierce stares. Will I have to become like them in order to survive?

'What's all this?' one of them demanded in a ripe Cockney accent, regarding her with open hostility. 'Who are you? Some rich man's doxy who's been turned out for stealing? You can't work here, you know. This is our pitch.'

'I don't understand,' Sylvia said, outfacing them with a boldness she was far from feeling. 'I'm not looking for work.'

'Oh, hoity-toity! D'you mean to say you're not on the game?' the woman mocked, looping an arm round her friend's shoulders, one hand coming across to idly play with the puckered, carmined nipples.

'Game? What game is that?' Sylvia asked, wondering if she might dodge round them and pelt off down the alley.

'The game of tits and bums, sweetheart. The game of sheath

109

the pork sword,' the whore answered, hands on her hips now, legs astride, her skirt open to show the dark, matted triangle of hair at the apex of her thighs. 'Gord love us! Comes to something when a posh tart muscles in on our turf.'

'I'm not doing anything of the kind,' Sylvia insisted, alarmed by the crowd gathering from the shadows, staring at her with prurient interest.

A gaggle of snotty nosed urchins lurked on the periphery. One of them picked up a stone and threw it. It landed in a swampy puddle near Sylvia's feet, splashing her coat.

'Oh, yes, pull the other leg, it's got bells on it,' the whore taunted. 'Why else would a ladybird like you be wandering in this neck of the woods? Different if you was a gent. They comes to shoot the spunk from their balls. This is the place for it… a sixpenny fuck up against the wall.'

Sylvia tried again, though terrified of the hands that were touching her hair, her bonnet and her person. 'I'm not here to deprive you,' she insisted. 'Can you direct me to a coaching inn? That's all I seek.'

'Reckon I might,' the whore replied. 'Let's trade. What you got to give me in exchange?'

'She has nothing for the likes of you, Nelly Grimes,' came a crisp voice from across the lane. 'Just you let her be. I'll look after the young lady.'

The crowd parted like a muddy tide to let the speaker through. She was big bosomed, wide hipped and dressed entirely in rusty black. No longer young, she yet possessed a magnetic presence. Her clothing and confident bearing suggested that she did not live in squalid misery, as they did. They lowered their eyes, and dared not show resentment. She seemed to have a stranglehold over them and was backed by a hulking, broken nosed man swinging a cudgel.

'I meant no harm,' Nelly muttered. 'And you, above all people, would want to know what she was doing, wouldn't you?'

'That's as may be,' the woman snapped. 'Now get about

your business. The night is young, and plenty of punters out there hot for a lively wench. Scarper, before I lose my temper.'

She was close to Sylvia now, and her face, though gaunt, with thick black brows and broad cheekbones, wore a friendly smile.

'Thank you, madam,' Sylvia ventured. 'I appreciate your assistance.'

'Think nothing of it, my dear,' she replied, and placed a hand on her arm. 'I can't bear to see young ladies being threatened, and by the likes of Nelly Grimes. Now, how can I help you?'

Having learned a salutary lesson with Robert, Sylvia was not prepared to be frank, sympathetic though the woman appeared to be. 'I've lost my way,' she said, hoping that she looked less bedraggled than she felt. 'I should be on a stagecoach heading for the country but I fear I've missed my connection.'

'I see,' the woman said thoughtfully, and Sylvia was uncomfortably aware of her close scrutiny, those opaque eyes like lumps of coal in the pasty face. 'Well, I'm not concerned with your reasons for being here. I never ask people's business. I'm known as Mother Challis.'

'And I am Miss Anne Rankin,' Sylvia brought out, though having the awful feeling that Mother Challis would know she lied.

'Fine. That will do. I take it you're seeking shelter?'

'Yes.'

'Look no further. Come with me.'

With a hand clamped firmly round Sylvia's arm she set off down yet another alley, the only light from smoky flares set in the walls, here and there. Her bully loped behind like a trained mastiff. They passed shabby taverns from which shouts and raucous laughter burst, and small shops trading in gin. Though the night was foul, figures lurked in doorways, accosting passers-by with their whining, hard luck stories, though usually dismissed with a blow or kick.

'Beggars!' Mother Challis commented disdainfully. 'Scum of the earth. Don't you have no dealings with them, my dear. There's no need for it. Work can be found if one applies oneself.'

They came to a slightly more salubrious area, and stopped outside one of a row of houses, though even these were rundown and sadly in need of a coat of paint. Mother Challis produced a key and opened the door. A smell wafted out; a stale combination of boiled cabbage, kippers, cats urine and dirt.

'Come in, come in. Welcome to my home,' Mother Challis said. 'It may not be a palace but at least it's dry.'

Sylvia crept in behind the bulky figure, becoming more depressed by the minute. The hall was dingy and poorly lit, the walls panelled in dark wood, with a flight of narrow stairs corkscrewing up into deeper darkness.

'That will be all for the moment, Fergus,' Mother Challis said, dismissing the bodyguard who sloped off into the dimness out back, then, 'Flo!' she shouted. 'Where are you, you idle slut? We've a visitor.'

A shuffling of footsteps answered this summons and a blowzy women appeared from somewhere at the end of the gloomy passage. Her hair straggled down from the bun atop her head, and she was frumpishly clad in a faded dress, with half-moon sweat stains at the armpits.

'What's up, missus?' she asked in a guttural voice.

'The young lady's hungry, and so am I. Bring us supper in the parlour, and tell Miss Emily and Mr John to join us,' Mother Challis ordered and led Sylvia through a door on the right.

The chill of the room was barely alleviated by the few knobs of coal smouldering fitfully in the cast-iron grate. It was a dark, over-furnished apartment with a musky smell. Not only did it contain chairs, a sofa and a table, but there were other items stacked against the walls; pictures in wooden frames, ornaments, clocks, statues, items of clothing, giving the impression that this was a repository for pawned or stolen goods.

Mother Challis weaved her way through the clutter to the

fire, and gestured to Sylvia. 'Take off you coat and bonnet, Miss Rankin,' she said, and her attitude suggested she was not to be gainsaid.

'But I'm cold,' Sylvia protested.

'You'll soon warm up,' Mother Challis replied, brushing her protests aside. 'It's been a long time since I've clapped eyes on a girl with such a pretty face. I want to see the rest of you.'

Sylvia untied the ribbons of her hat and removed her pelisse with the greatest reluctance. She shivered in her thin cotton gown, feeling near naked.

Mother Challis looked her over, her lips pursed, her eyes narrowed. She reached out and grabbed one of Sylvia's breasts, her calloused fingers jagging over the nipples, making them rise through the tight bodice.

'Good, good,' she murmured. 'Nice tits, deary, and a sweet little cunt, I'll warrant.' Her hand darted lower, pressing between Sylvia's thighs, finding her lower lips and squeezing them, then caressing the swell of her clitoris. 'Are you a virgin, by any chance?'

'Yes, and I'll thank you to unhand me,' Sylvia said, her voice rising an indignant octave.

Mother Challis laughed, and something malevolent sparkled in her eyes. 'No need to be coy with me,' she commented, and continued in her exploration of Sylvia's sexual parts, running a finger up the furrow between her buttocks. 'But I'll need to be sure your hymen is intact. I can't open my house to wantons. Lay on the couch.'

She swept aside a pile of newspapers and books heaped on the sagging seat and pushed Sylvia down on it. She was a strong woman and Sylvia's struggles were in vain. Mother Challis slapped and pinched her till she subsided and lay supine, too terrified to move.

She bent over Sylvia, her rank odour stifling. Sylvia gave a cry as her skirt was raised and Mother Challis's big, raw-boned hands opened her thighs wide. 'Ah, as delicious a little pussy as ever I've seen,' she muttered, a flush spreading up her face and a hot, eager look in her eyes. 'Who's been shaving you, sweetheart?'

'I don't wish to discuss it,' Sylvia murmured, flushing to the roots of her hair.

'Someone with unusual tastes, I'll be bound. There's more to you than meets the eye,' Mother Challis went on, her fingers even more invasive. 'Let me open the lips and see your kernel. An eager bud, I've no doubt.'

Sylvia closed her eyes, horribly humiliated, yet unable to restrain the thrill that warmed her labial lips as they were parted and examined, fondled and teased. 'Please leave me alone,' she begged. 'You have no need to do this. I am a virgin. I swear it.'

Mother Challis's finger circled Sylvia's clitoris and she was unable to help grinding her hips under that seductive touch. The woman smiled darkly, saying, 'You need it rubbed? Is that it? Rub it yourself, do you? I'd like to watch that sometime. Now, for your maidenhead,' and she eased a fingertip into Sylvia's vulva, giving a grunt of satisfaction as she met the obstructive membrane. 'Ah, yes… so you're telling the truth. A virgin, eh? A chaste, unsullied maid. You are sitting on a fortune, deary, or didn't you realise this?'

'Leave me be!' Sylvia snarled, breaking free and covering herself. 'I came here because you promised me lodgings, and for no other reason. I'm not like Nelly Grimes.'

Mother Challis plonked herself down on a chair, facing Sylvia, not in the least abashed. 'Not yet, perhaps. But she was a virgin once, though it's hard to believe. Right. Lodgings it is, but it will cost you.'

Sylvia shrank into a corner of the couch, her legs tucked under her, arms clasped tightly around them. 'That is a problem,' she confessed, then blurted out, 'I was robbed last night. I have no money, but if you'll trust me, I promise to pay you as soon as I reach my home. I will sign an IOU.'

'No money?' Mother Challis repeated slowly.

'I'm sorry,' Sylvia stuttered. 'I was going to tell you.'

'Lying bitch!' Mother Challis shouted, and jabbed a finger at her. 'No one cheats me and lives to tell the tale. I'm not known for charity.'

'I'll go,' Sylvia said, getting to her feet. 'I'm sorry to have troubled you.'

'Go?' Mother Challis thundered, looming over her. 'Oh, no you don't, my fine lady. You've wasted my time and I don't like it.'

'It was a mistake. I didn't mean any harm,' Sylvia protested.

Flo appeared at the door, carrying a tray. Mother Challis spun round on her, shouting, 'Take that back to the kitchen. This trollop tried to cheat me.'

Flo backed out, her broad face quivering with fear.

Sylvia made a lunge for her coat, but Mother Challis was too quick, snatching it up. 'Give it to me,' Sylvia cried.

'Oh, no… it'll be worth something… and your fancy hat, too. Take off your dress. I'll sell that as well.'

'I can't. Let me go,' Sylvia shouted, running for the door, but Mother Challis was there first.

She grabbed Sylvia roughly. 'Take it off,' she repeated, a grim smile lifting her lips. 'Do it carefully. I don't want it damaged.'

'I'll scream,' Sylvia threatened. 'I'll run for the constables.'

'Ha! Foolish girl,' Mother Challis said scornfully. 'No one will come. And the constables are all in my pay. You're here, Anne, and here you'll stay, till I decide who shall buy you.'

'You can't sell me. I'm not an animal,' Sylvia yelled.

'Aren't you? What difference is there between you and a prime piece of meat? And I shall find the right buyer. The dress! Get it off!'

She thumped Sylvia so hard that the breath was knocked out of her. Too frightened to do other than obey, she unbuttoned her gown and dropped it to the floor.

Another blow followed. 'Pick it up,' Mother Challis roared, her face a vicious mask. 'And I want the chemise, the petticoat, your stockings and shoes... everything.'

When finally completely nude, Sylvia pressed her thighs together, one arm hiding her breasts, the other hand nestled protectively over her pubis. She was shivering uncontrollably with cold and fright.

'You won't get away with this,' she whimpered through chattering teeth.

For answer, Mother Challis picked up a cane and tapped her palm with it, her eyes feeding on the half-healed stripes scoring Sylvia's buttocks. 'You claim to be innocent, yet you wear the marks of punishment,' she said in a slow, considering way. 'A woman of mystery, eh? Yet one who has known a master's hand.'

The cane whistled and slashed across Sylvia's rump, making her dance, the pain erupting along her muscles and nerves. She could not restrain a cry, and this seemed to inspire Mother Challis, the rod rising and falling with dreadful regularity.

Sylvia collapsed to her knees, and the woman seized her by the hair and thrust her face against her evil smelling black shirts, pushing her in hard so that she felt the pubic bone beneath the layer of clothes.

'You've a new mistress now,' Mother Challis panted hoarsely, and then gave her a shove so that she sprawled on her back. 'Get up! The kitchen is the place for you.'

So saying, she drove the cringing, sobbing Sylvia into the passage and down rough stone steps at the back. Forced to bend double, Sylvia cried out as the end of the cane poked between her nether cheeks, the tip teasing the tightly closed mouth of her anus. There was no escaping it, though Sylvia's naked feet pattered fast over the cold, bare floor.

She found herself catapulted through a door and into a stifling, airless kitchen. Eyes swivelled towards her and she was agonisingly conscious of her naked state, trying to hide herself until her arms were beaten down by the cane.

'A new playmate, children!' Mother Challis proclaimed, and thrust her into the centre of the room.

A lank-haired slattern wearing a sack tied round the waist with a length of rope, looked up from where she was scouring greasy pots in the stone sink. Her hazel eyes held Sylvia's briefly, and there was a spark of sympathy in their depths. The other occupants of the filthy room were Fergus, slouched by the fire, Flo, engaged in serving a mess of stew, and a youth and a girl, better dressed than the others, who occupied a bench on one side of the table.

'What have you brought us, ma?' the girl asked.

'A dainty lady, Emily. She says her name's Anne... Anne Rankin, but I expect she's lying. She's haughty, and that wicked pride needs beating out of her. She'll learn obedience, service, and how to be a slave,' Mother Challis replied, aiming a kick at Fergus. 'Out the way! Give me that chair!'

Sylvia was left standing, her head down, long hair streaming over her breasts, her arms limp at her sides. Emily rose and circled her slowly. She was comely, with dark curls and eyes, but there was something deliberately insulting in the manner in which she wrinkled up her nose as she looked at Sylvia, as if aware of a bad smell.

'You're right, ma,' she said, pausing in her perusal. 'She looks a mighty high-flown jilt to me.'

The florid-faced young man drained his tankard and came over to put an arm round his sister, gazing insolently at Sylvia's body. A lecherous smile settled on his plump, heavy features. His slightly protuberant eyes went to her denuded mound and he lowered a hand to stroke over the pink flesh. 'I think you've made an excellent choice, Ma,' he said, and pressed a finger between her legs. 'We'll have sport taming her.'

His trousers were tight around the crotch, and Sylvia, who dared look no higher than that area, was appalled to see the way his cock strained against the material.

Their mother smiled fondly at them, saying, 'I'm glad you're pleased, John. I rely on you and Emily to instruct her. We'll have a skivvy and toy in one. What d'you say, Phoebe? Thank me nicely for finding someone to share your duties, in every

117

way.'

The girl at the sink nodded, and muttered, 'Thank you, ma'am.'

Though there remained a trace of desperate defiance in her attitude towards Mother Challis, she was pale and starved looking. The enormous tabby cat taking its ease on the hearthrug was far better fed than her. A fearsomely ugly beast, it squinted balefully at Sylvia with its one eye, while Mother Challis bent to rub it under the chin, crooning to it lovingly.

John's clammy hands were all over Sylvia's body, rubbing between her thighs, pinching her welted rump, bouncing and squeezing her breasts. His erection enlarged as he thumbed her nipples, fascinated as they rose, succulent as strawberries.

'I'll wager you know all about cock,' he said crudely. 'You've lost count of how many you've had, haven't you? Long ones, thick fat ones... tell me about them. Speak!'

He thrust his pelvis against her, rocking his hips backwards and forwards, his prick hot and damp through the fabric. This was too much. Sylvia pushed him in the chest with both hands.

'Let me go, you vile wretch!' she cried.

'What's all this? Still rebellious?' Mother Challis growled, leaving her cat and towering over Sylvia.

'Tell him to stop. I can't endure it,' Sylvia shouted, head back, shoulders straight, her hauteur almost halting her tormentors.

'Stop? But we've only just begun,' Mother Challis hissed menacingly. 'I've been too lenient with you. That will change forthwith.'

'Can I have her, ma?' John bellowed, rubbing the bulge inside his breeches.

'She's a virgin, and thus she'll remain till I find a generous purchaser,' his mother snapped. 'You can use her other orifices, but not her cunt-hole. Understand? I don't want her belly swelling up.'

'Yes, ma,' he said sullenly.

'I suppose you'll use her like you do me,' his sister cried, jealously. 'You're a dirty rotten rat, John, after anything that breathes. I don't know why you look elsewhere. Lord knows, we get pleasure enough from one another.'

'Be silent, Emily,' Mother Challis growled.

'But, ma… you always favour him. It's not fair,' Emily said, lips dropping sulkily.

'Shut up moaning. You can have her, too,' her mother replied, but indulgently. 'You are good children, the pride of my life. You both sprang from my loins and I've reared you without the help of those two despicable, useless wretches who pumped their seed into my womb. I soon got rid of them, I can tell you.'

Brother and sister, though sired by different fathers. Incest, Sylvia thought desperately. Was nothing sacred in this horrendous place?

'Take her outside, John,' his mother commanded. 'She's to spend the night in the yard. Tie her securely or it will be your arse that smarts under my rod.'

John grabbed Sylvia's waist and marched her through the backdoor. It was dark in the small, cluttered area without, lit only by the fitful glow of the candles in the kitchen feebly penetrating the sooted windowpanes. The rain had slowed to a fine drizzle. It fell on Sylvia's head and bare shoulders, bedewing her breasts and trickling slowly over her belly and thighs.

John bound her wrists behind her back with a length of twine. Her breasts jutted forward and he stared at them, licking his lips hungrily. Then, moving dextrously, he attached the rope to the iron handle of the pump, binding her securely.

'On your knees,' he muttered, his hand forcing her obedience.

There was just enough play on the rope for her to sink down, her legs contacting the hard, wet paving stones, the harsh hempen bracelets cutting into her wrists.

John was busy with the fastening of his breeches and, in the yellowish uncertainty of diffused light, she saw his erection poking from the opening.

'No,' she whispered, despairingly.

'But yes,' he answered. 'You're going to satisfy me or I'll beat you black and blue.'

His cock was erect, red and engorged. He spread his thighs, lowering himself slightly, and touched Sylvia's mouth with the end of it, then her ears, her neck, and finally rested it between her breasts. Taking the firm globes in both hands, he pressed them together forming a channel for his ardent weapon.

Sylvia shook, the lower half of her body disregarded by John. In spite of the degradation of her position, kneeling in front of this uncouth young man, her nipples hardened, honey flowing from her sex.

She needed to be touched there, would have welcomed even his fingertips on her clitoris.

Heaving, grunting with pleasure, he moved faster, the deep avenue slippery with his juices now, performing the service of a vagina. He swayed, his cock giving a final, convulsive jerk as he sprayed up into her face. He looked down, watching his semen spurt, smiling stupidly as it drenched her cheeks and lips and spattered her hair.

'That'll do to be going on with,' he muttered, and returned his limp cock to his breeches.

'You can't leave me out here all night,' she grated hoarsely. 'I'll catch my death of cold.'

'You'll be all right. It isn't winter,' he answered offhandedly, and turned for the door, leaving her to sink down in misery and endure the hours of darkness alone.

She sobbed quietly, feeling the sodden stones beneath her buttocks, the cold metal of the pump against her back. Her sex throbbed, but there was no release for her.

The cat stalked out, hissing when she spoke to him. He leapt to the wall and made off about his nightly patrol. The light in the kitchen was extinguished and the house fell into darkness and sleep.

Chapter Seven

Sylvia dozed, exhaustion taking over from bodily discomfort and agony of mind. It may have been an hour, or possibly more, when she was roused by someone touching her gently and a voice saying,

'I've brought you some stew. You must be starving hungry.'

Sylvia opened her eyes and could just make out Phoebe's pale face in the gloom. She was holding a bowl, the smell of warm food rising on the steam.

'Oh, thank you. That's so kind, but won't you get into terrible trouble?' Sylvia whispered, moving awkwardly in her bonds, her body smarting with pain, the rain chilling her to the marrow.

Phoebe smiled and lifted her thin shoulders in a shrug, saying philosophically, 'What's another beating? I get into trouble when I've done nothing, so might as well be hung for a sheep as a lamb. Open your mouth – I'll feed you.'

The ladle was brought close to Sylvia's lips and she opened them, accepting Phoebe's help like a baby. 'Are they asleep?' she asked, as the girl gently wiped away a dribble of gravy with her fingertip.

'Yes, snoring like the pigs they are,' she answered acidly.

'I must get away from here.' Sylvia exclaimed, frantic to escape.

'That makes two of us,' Phoebe grated. 'But it's easier said than done. Mother Challis owns the neighbourhood. She's a fence, a bawd and a moneylender. No one will dare help us. They're all scared shitless.'

'How did you fall into her clutches?' Sylvia asked, the bowl empty now; plain though it was, the food had been good.

'I was a maidservant, but lost my job when the son of the

house said I'd seduced him. Course, it was the other way round really,' Phoebe answered, with a dry chuckle. 'He was dirty bugger, and no mistake. I was lucky he didn't get me with child. Anyway, I was flung out with no money, only the clothes I stood up in, and no reference.'

'Haven't you parents and a home?' Sylvia asked.

Phoebe shook her head, hair twisting lankly each side of her face. 'No... a workhouse brat who was sent to a factory when I was ten. I lived rough with a couple of the other girls, then got out of that death-trap. Terrible they are, those factories, it eventually kills you. I worked in pubs, gathered dog turds for the tannery at a penny a bucketful, shovelled horse muck from the roads, did anything to scrape a living, then got this job as maid to an alderman's wife. She thought she was posh, but her son was at me from the word go. Wouldn't leave me alone. He took my virginity. Lord, he had the biggest cock I've ever seen... like a bloody donkey's prick. Brought tears to my eyes, I can tell you.'

'How dreadful. Wasn't there anyone to help you?' Sylvia exclaimed, remembering the relatively soft existence she had led at the academy, the canings and humiliations as nothing compared with the sufferings of this streetwise girl.

'Who's going to help the likes of me?' Phoebe asked bitterly. 'I'm the lowest of the low... a bastard... workhouse born. I just had to make the best of it, put up with him getting at me night and day, and then, when she found out, start all over again. That's how I fell in with Mother Challis. She found me, wanted to make me a whore, but I refused. That's something I've never done, not even when I was starving. So she brought me here to do her dirty work, and it is dirty, too, emptying their slop pots, slaving, putting up with John and Emily fingering me whenever they fancy... and her as well. She's not above taking her pleasure.'

'But why can't you run away? Steal some of her money if you have to, but get out of here,' Sylvia whispered, comforted by the feel of Phoebe's small, calloused hands smoothing her hair.

A shudder run through the girl. 'I can't,' she answered. 'She'd have the constables after me. They'd catch me, fling me into Newgate Gaol and then send me to the gallows as a thief. She twists everything and uses everyone. There's no escaping Mother Challis.'

'I shall escape her!' Sylvia declared, the food in her belly putting new life into her. 'She'll not hold me for long.'

'Be careful. She's a monster,' Phoebe warned, glancing fearfully over her shoulder as if she could see her storming from the house. 'I must go. Take my advice and do as you're told. That way, you have a faint hope of surviving. I'll do what I can to ease your lot.'

Phoebe kissed Sylvia's cheek and slipped off the way she had come.

Sylvia sank back against the pump, the future spreading out like a murky cloud before her. Spend the rest of her life under Mother Challis's domination? Not me! she promised herself.

But as the weary hours passed, so her courage faded. It continued to rain and the stew gave her gripes. Her bowels churned and she could do nothing but void them, then try to move out of the way of her excrement. She was cold, miserable, smeared with her own filth, almost regretting leaving Laurel House.

Mother Challis found her thus as a fresh, pink dawn pearled the sky, the rain clouds moving off.

'What's all this?' she cried, entering the yard and staring at Sylvia. 'No fine lady now, eh? A drab... an animal paddling in its own manure. Phoebe!' she yelled over her shoulder. 'Bring a bucket. This dirty bitch needs sluicing down.'

Phoebe answered her call, a wooden pail in her hand. Mother Challis seized it and Phoebe worked the pump handle, the bucket thumping against it. When it was full Mother Challis swung it with all the strength of her brawny arm and the contents hit Sylvia with full force.

She gasped with shock and cold, the water pouring over her

in an icy torrent. Her tormentor repeated the action, then set the pail down and tweaked Sylvia's crimped nipples.

'Lovely dugs,' she muttered, and lowering her head, fastened her teeth on the tender nubs, gnawing at them. Sylvia cried out in pain, and Mother Challis looked up with a cold smile, adding, 'I'll take my fill of these later.'

She yanked off the ropes that had tightened in the rain, and Sylvia fell to the ground, chafing her wrists where the flesh was red and swollen. She expelled a grunt as Mother Challis's foot caught the underside of her rump, almost lifting her from the ground.

'Indoors, slut, there's work to be done,' she shouted.

Emily was still in bed, but John was there, yawning, scratching and breaking wind, while Flo filled his tankard with ale and prepared him a breakfast of fried gammon and eggs. He leered at Sylvia and pinched her buttocks, then caressed her mound. The skin was stippled with goose bumps, but he withdrew his finger, looked at his mother and said,

'Her cunt's prickly, ma. She needs another shave. Can I do it?'

'No. I want some work out of her. Go and play with your sister,' Mother Challis answered crisply. She turned back to Sylvia, saying, 'You'll work through the day and entertain me tonight. D'you hear?'

'If I must,' Sylvia returned haughtily.

Mother Challis goggled at her. 'What did you say?' she rasped.

'I said, I'll work if I must.'

'Oh, you must. There's no doubt about that. Flo!' Mother Challis bawled, and the slattern looked up from where she stoked the fire.

'Yes, ma'am.'

'Bring her something to wear.'

'Yes, ma'am,' said Flo and lifted the lid of an oak chest, taking from inside a skirt made of sacking and a blouse of the same harsh material.

'But first, she needs punishing for her insolence,' Mother Challis went on, picking up a length of plaited leather and flexing it in her hands.

Sylvia was seized by Flo and flung, face down, over the seat of a chair. Her naked breasts swung loosely, her hair falling forward, her belly and mons pressed into the cane rushing. Flo held her by the wrists which throbbed painfully in response.

Sylvia saw the shadow of Mother Challis's arm as it rose, then felt scorching flame searing her buttocks as the leather strap slashed across them. She clenched her teeth and forced down a cry.

Mother Challis lashed her again, but on the backs of her thighs this time, shifting position for a more accurate aim. The next blow caught her across the shoulders, then curled round to hit the side of her breast. The woman took an almost professional pride in her skill, ensuring that each lash landed on an unmarked portion of Sylvia's flesh, then cut across the existing weals, causing untold anguish.

Sylvia howled, throwing back her head, her mouth a rictus of agony. 'How many lashes did your master give you?' she heard Mother Challis ask, a strange, gloating note in her voice.

'I have no master,' Sylvia yelped as another punishing cut connected with a particularly tender bruise.

'I'm not suggesting he was your master in the accepted sense of the word,' Mother Challis went on, pausing for breath. 'But I feel sure you've subjected yourself to a man… probably some titled rake who delights in meting out punishment. Isn't this so?'

'There's no such person,' Sylvia said through gritted teeth.

'No?'

'No.'

The leather swished as it flew through the air, and Sylvia bucked in Flo's grip. She stared into the servant's ugly face, and remembered – ah, so much. The lovely Rowena – the handsome Theo. Why, oh why, had she run away?

Now there was only ugliness and squalor.

With a final blow that seemed harder than all the rest put together, Mother Challis nodded to Flo to release Sylvia. She flopped across the chair, limp as a rag doll. By now she had stopped sobbing. Her blazing posterior was numb.

She felt Mother Challis open her from behind, and slide her fingers into the amber cleft between her bottom cheeks, opening them more fully. The fingers went lower, stroking the lips of her pudenda, moistening them in her vulva and using that wetness to anoint her clitoris. Sylvia could not restrain the quiver that ran through her as her bud swelled from its little cowl.

'Tonight, you'll play with it for my amusement,' Mother Challis breathed in her ear. 'Till then, I forbid you to touch it. D'you understand?'

'Yes…' Sylvia said, choking back a sob.

'Yes, mistress!' Mother Challis snapped, plunging her hand into Sylvia's hair and jerking her head up.

'Yes, mistress…'

After this she was allowed to put on the skirt and blouse, the dun-coloured material of coarse weave that chafed her weals and rubbed the delicate skin of her underarms. It made her itch as if it harboured an army of fleas. Wearing this garment that was the equivalent of a hair shirt, she was set to perform the hardest, most degrading and menial tasks.

To her fell the distasteful job of emptying night-soil from the family chamber pots, collecting up and washing John's sweaty underclothes and hose, and enduring Emily's jibes as she threw a heap of stained shifts and stockings at her. Mother Challis insisted that Sylvia haul up coal from the cellar, scrub floors, scour the filthiest of cooking pans, and clear up the cat's faeces which it had deposited in a corner.

A great vat of vegetables had to be peeled; a hand of pork prepared; a chicken drawn. Sylvia had performed none of these chores before, but Flo stood over her, wielding a large wooden spoon and bringing it down with a crack on hands, head and back if Sylvia did not do the work properly, or was too slow.

Tears were near at all times, but Sylvia stubbornly refused to shed them. Even through her misery she kept her wits alert, listening if Mother Challis had callers, trying to find out something with which she might compromise the women and, more important of all, to discover where she hid her money.

Escape was the one thing on her mind.

At nightfall she was allowed a crust of stale bread and a mug of water, huddled by the backdoor while Mother Challis and her children dined on a mountain of food.

'Let me see,' the woman said, leaning back in her chair and thoughtfully picking her teeth with her fingernail. 'Where shall the new slave sleep tonight? In the yard again? Or shall it be the coal-hole?'

'Aw, ma…' whined John, rubbing a hand over his gross belly and farting loudly. 'Can't she stay in my room? You said I could have her. You promised!'

His mother shot him a glare that had him cringing. 'Stow it!' she grunted. 'I'm in charge here and don't you be forgetting it. No, I've other plans for her ladyship.' She fixed her cold black eyes on Sylvia and said, 'You, girl. I'm going upstairs now, and you'll join me in a while. Phoebe, carry the bottles.'

Sylvia, who had been considering the possibilities of grabbing a few scraps when she cleared the dishes, stared balefully at the bulky woman who now retreated towards the door.

'Old bitch!' John snarled, and then grabbed hold of Emily. 'I suppose I'll have to make do with you.'

His ungracious remark seemed to please her, and she looked up at him with a doting expression, dropped a hand into his lap and cupped his stiffening bulge. 'That's right, John. You know I can pleasure you, don't you?'

'I wanted a change,' he grumbled, his stubby fingers diving into the neck of her bodice and rubbing her nipples. 'Tired of the same pussy… needed something new, and fresh, and juicy…'

Sylvia shuddered. Whatever Mother Challis had in store for

her, it could hardly be worse than having to submit to that loathsome youth.

Phoebe came to fetch her a little later.

Stumbling in darkness relieved only by a single rush the girl carried, Sylvia followed her up the stairs. She knew the layout by now, and was not surprised when they entered Mother Challis's bedchamber. The sight that greeted her, however, was totally unexpected.

Mother Challis lay on the big bed. She looked different with her hair unpinned, younger... with a trace of the good looks that might once have been hers. She wore a silk dressing robe, the material fine and costly. This was open, displaying a body coarsened by age, with a pair of large, sagging breasts and a corpulent belly. Her thighs were thick, the mottled skin showing above the tops of black woollen stockings. Between her fork sprouted a dense thicket of dark pubic hair.

She held a tankard in one hand, and her slanting eyes smiled, but not her lips as she said, 'Ah, my little Anne. Come closer, pretty darling. Don't be afraid. Remove your clothing.'

With the greatest reluctance, Sylvia did as she was bidden, then forced her dragging feet cross the floor till she stood by the bed. It resembled a curtained catafalque, gloomy and sinister, the bloated white flesh within contrasting with the shadows, as if it was a web containing some ghastly female spider.

Mother Challis extended a hand and massaged Sylvia's breasts, prodding them, testing them for firmness and resilience. She handled Sylvia's thighs, too, and then made her sit on the bed. Sylvia tried to close her legs, but Mother Challis pushed her knees so far apart her pelvis rose. She almost squatted, her lower lips protruding, split like a ripe peach.

Mother Challis slid a hand beneath her, palming the whole of Sylvia's pudenda, feeling the roundness of the lips and the wetness that seeped from her vulva.

'Ah, so you want it, do you, little kitten?' she muttered, her breath larded with gin. 'Like a cat in heat, you'll rub yourself

128

against almost anything. Isn't that so?' And she squeezed Sylvia's labia together, bringing pressure to bear on her clitoris.

Sylvia hung her head, flooded with shame, admitting to herself that need boiled within her. She tingled everywhere as Mother Challis fondled her nipples with one hand and tweaked her love-bud with the other. She trembled violently as, against her will, she felt herself commanded by this masterful woman who was making her passion bloom and burn.

She did not want to yield to this witch woman, this ogress who was amusing herself at her expense, but she gave an open-mouthed moan as her sex pulsed against the knowing finger that flicked and caressed it. Her pubis jerked as the pleasure between her thighs washed over her. She started to gasp, but just as she was about to peak, Mother Challis suddenly pushed her away and withdrew her hand, smiling.

'Do it yourself,' she said silkily, and lay back among the pillows, arms folded beneath her head.

'I can't,' Sylvia protested, her face flaming with embarrassment and desire.

'It's the only way you'll be satisfied tonight,' the woman continued. 'Frig yourself, or remain frustrated.'

'Oh, no... don't make me,' Sylvia pleaded.

'I'm not forcing you to do it. Don't you want to? Aren't you dying to toy with that slippery cleft and work your button till it explodes with joy?' Mrs Challis said, then motioned Phoebe to come closer, adding, 'Bring the candle. I want light to watch Anne masturbating.'

Her words were inflammatory, bringing back a rush of memories. Sylvia recalled the numerous occasions when she had brought herself to orgasm, seeking private places in which to indulge her lust. She grew hot as she thought of the wonderful fusion between her finger and her bud... the terrible, beautiful little death when she lost touch with the world, transported by bliss.

Hardly realising what she was doing she splayed her legs and, after lightly rolling her nipples with her thumbs, reached down, walked her fingers over her mound and parted the damp petals of her labia. She was wet there, producing that fragrant honeydew which she now spread over her vibrant clitoris that eagerly responded to the stimulation.

She was no longer aware of Mother Challis or Phoebe, caught up in the spell evoked by her touch on her nub, working it gently at first, then faster. She let her finger slide over it, back and forth. The pleasure was extreme, and she panted as the ecstasy mounted, straining to reach completion, terrified lest someone snatch it away.

As she reached that point of no return when the crest of orgasm was about to break over her, she opened her eyes and stared into Mother Challis's, meeting an approval that spurred her on. She cried out and came, every muscle tense as the spasms poured through her.

'Good girl,' whispered her mentor and, lying prone, legs slack and relaxed, Sylvia felt a hand joining hers across her throbbing nubbin and heard her say, 'Now, I want you to touch me just there.'

She looked up and saw Mother Challis reclining against the pillows, her legs wide apart, the great dark gash of her delta fully exposed. Phoebe leaned over her, playing with and sucking the huge, brown nipples that jutted from those heavy white breasts.

Sylvia rose to her knees and crawled up the bed till she rested between Mother Challis's legs. She was repelled yet fascinated, her hands stroking over the fat thighs, approaching ever closer to the inky forest at their apex, smelling the piscine odour of the woman's sexual arousal.

Saliva dribbled from Mother Challis's slack lips, echoing the moisture running from her channel and glistening like silver on her labia. She moaned as Phoebe attended to her teats, which grew ever harder and infused with blood. 'Do it… do it…' she babbled, and grabbed Sylvia by the hair, dragging her face down to her crotch.

Sylvia hung over her, then placed her thumbs each side of

the brownish slit that lay between the hairy lips. She pressed lightly and they parted, swelling visibly, with a plump clitoris standing proud at the crown, as red and engorged as a penis.

Unable to control her fascination with these obtrusive female genitals, Sylvia dipped a finger into the odoriferous fountain of Mother Challis's vulva, and stroked the thick, turgid lips and the fissure between.

'My clit!' Mother Challis gasped. 'Rub it, girl! Now!'

Heat laved Sylvia's own throbbing organ, and she ached inside. Her desire made her lean closer, all else forgotten as she ran a finger over the bulging clit-head straining towards her. The powerful aroma filled her nostrils and made her mouth water. She stretched the lips down so the nub stood out even more, and worked fluid over its tip. Mother Challis's hips heaved and she groaned loudly.

Greatly daring, testing her own feelings and instincts, Sylvia bent lower and placed her mouth over that swelling nodule. The upheaval below her increased, with her victim screaming her pleasure.

Sylvia smiled a dark, secretive smile and advanced her tongue, allowing it to play over the hard pistil flowering in Mother Challis's overblown garden. Then, gradually, increasing the torture bit by bit, she closed her lips round it and sucked it into her mouth.

She felt it pulse, felt Mother Challis buck and plunge and heard her yells of ecstasy. The juices flooded from her, smearing Sylvia's mouth. It was strong, salty but far from unpleasant. When the great body collapsed on the mattress, she remained there for a moment, caressing the convulsing organ with her tongue.

Within a short while snores erupted from Mother Challis's mouth as she sprawled there, satiated and deeply asleep.

Sylvia looked down at her, disgust crawling in her stomach. Now that it was over, she could hardly bear to think of what she had just done. How could she have placed her lips on the woman's most intimate parts? Yet there was satisfaction to be had in knowing that the dominating mistress had been her slave, if only for a few moments. She had been helpless under Sylvia's tongue, prey to her own lust.

And, in the deepest, darkest recesses of Sylvia's psyche, glowed a fiery ember, desire flaring up as she thought of other women who had demanded her submission.

It had begun with Nanny Talbot, long ago in the nursery. Then there had been Mrs Clara Dawson at the academy, followed by Lady Rowena. Each in turn had fulfilled a deep-seated need in her. Fight it though she might, there was this longing to be destroyed and remade by someone who would recognise the depths of her submission and love her for it.

The thought threw her into a panic.

'You did well,' Phoebe said, and curled up beside her at the foot of the bed. 'At least we'll be warm and comfortable tonight. She'll be dead to the world till morning. We're safe for a while.'

Sylvia opened her arms and Phoebe crept into them and they lay there, breast to breast, their thighs wound round one another. Inevitably, they began to kiss and caress, seeking solace, then relief. Sylvia, her passions unleashed, needed one orgasm after another, and Phoebe knew how to please her, while she, in gratitude, was more than willing to perform the same service for her friend.

Nelly Grimes stepped into the parlour where Mother Challis sat at a leather-topped desk, working on her accounts. A great ledger was opened in front of her and she was entering columns of figures with a quill pen.

She looked up, saying irritably, 'What d'you want? If it's more time to pay your rent, forget it. You'll be out on your ear by the end of the week.'

''Tisn't the rent, though you're a fucking bloodsucker,' Nelly stated, flinging back the mangy fur tippet that part covered her pockmarked breasts. 'I've made a lot of coin for you. Why can't you give me more time? Christ knows, I've earned it.'

Mother Challis laid down her pen, snapped the ledger shut

and fixed the whore with frosty eyes. 'And why shouldn't you?' she barked. 'You're good for nothing but lying on your back with your legs open. What's the matter, Nell? Getting past it, are you? Finding it harder to find punters?'

'I ain't been well,' Nelly grumbled, her cheekbones flushed with fever. Then she edged nearer, a desperate woman with little to lose. 'Any road, d'you want to hear what I've got to tell?'

'Maybe,' Mother Challis conceded dubiously.

'It'll likely do you a bit of good,' Nelly continued, and eyed the decanter on the desk. 'Any chance of a drop of gin?'

Mother Challis pushed it towards her and the whore tipped it to her lips and took a deep swallow.

'That's enough,' Mother Challis said sharply, grabbing it off her. 'Don't waste my time. Out with it.'

Nelly smirked slyly, saying, 'How about if I was to tell you something about that girl you brought here lately? Something to your advantage?'

A coal dropped into the ash pan, and a gust of smoke billowed across the room. The smell added to all the other odours, including the whore's cheap and pungent perfume. Mother Challis drummed impatient fingers on the desk, considering her in a slit-eyed, suspicious way.

'Spit it out,' she ordered.

'What do I get in return?' Nelly asked, sharp as a razor. 'Will you wave the back rent?'

'I may… that depends.'

'Well then… here goes,' said Nelly and, without being asked, dropped into a chair and crossed one leg over the other. 'You know old Jamie Wheeler, who used to be a lawyer?'

'Aye, till the drink got the better of him. So, what's he to do with this?' Mother Challis asked, and gestured to a quantity of books stacked against one wall. 'I've got most of his library here. He needed the money for booze.'

'I know all that. He's a kind old bloke, the only one that treats me like a lady,' Nelly said with a sniff. 'I've slipped him a farthing or two, when I've been flush.'

'You're too soft, Nell.'

'I know, and that's something you can never be accused of. "Skinflint" will be carved on your tombstone,' Nelly replied pithily, throwing her a look of pure venom. 'He came to see me last night, said he'd seen a notice pinned on the wall in a tavern. He'd managed to steal it, and asked me if I'd buy it from him. He was that desperate for a drink... had the shakes, he did, so I gave him a penny and got him to read it to me.'

Mother Challis sighed heavily and glanced at an ornate chiming clock set in the centre of the mantelpiece. 'Get on with it,' she complained. 'Talk about long-winded.'

Nelly preened herself a little, enjoying having the upper hand for once, keeping her waiting. Then she said, 'Seems like it offered a reward for any information leading to the whereabouts of a certain young lady what had disappeared. Name of Miss Sylvia Parnell. Fair-haired and green-eyed, so it said. She went missing a week ago.'

Mother Challis sat up abruptly, grinding out, 'A reward? How much?'

Nelly sat back and examined her nails, then pursed her lips and remarked, 'What do I get for telling you? I've even got the notice with me, if you wants it.'

'All right, I'll let you off the rent, though some would say I'm going weak in the head. Hand it over,' Mother Challis snapped ungraciously.

Nelly stuck a hand down the front of her stained bodice and produced a folded paper. She tossed it on to the desk. Mother Challis leapt on it, smoothed it out and leaned over to read, then said,

'You're right, Nell. It's all here just as you said, and I'll wager that Anne Rankin and Sylvia Parnell are one and the same. But who's this Lord Theo Aubrey who wants to find her? Let's see... ah, yes... he's her fiancé. He gives his address and all. Burbank Abbey, Richmond. Interesting. Very. And he's offering twenty-five guineas for information. Why didn't you go for it? You could have shopped me. You knew she was here.'

Nelly flung her a sceptical look, a wry smile twisting her crimson mouth as she replied, 'It would've been more than my life was worth. I know you, Mother Challis, and what you do to anyone who betrays you. I don't want to have my face slashed... or worse... or end up in the Thames. No, I'm content to be let off the rent. The rest is up to you.'

For days Theo had been in the blackest, dirtiest, most evil temper that his household had ever witnessed. His fury at losing Sylvia knew no bounds. It was awe-inspiring.

Money was at the back of it, of course, though her beauty and innocence had stirred his loins. In fact, he had been walking around with an erection ever since viewing her for the first time, a swelling of the flesh that could not be fully relieved by visits to Rowena or several whores of his acquaintance. Rowena, in fact, had received the backlash of his rage, and he had whipped her almost raw, his anger no way appeased because she so obviously enjoyed the experience.

He had retired to Burbank Abbey and there put a plan into operation. Like many men of his ilk, his influence was widespread, and not only in select circles. His interests took him to areas inhabited by the lowest echelons of London. He went to prizefights, wrestling bouts, cock fights, gaming rooms, and brothels.

Always accompanied by ex-pugilist bodyguards, he rubbed shoulders with the criminal element and had several villains on his payroll. He set enquiries in motion through the underworld grapevine, besides having broadsheets displayed in public places and it was not long before he had a result.

Seated brooding at the refectory table of the magnificently furnished great hall, he twirled a cut glass goblet of red wine between his long, strong fingers, hardly able to contain his frustration. *Sylvia had to be his*. There was no question about it. He wanted her, and what Theo wanted he always got.

Scrope, one of his henchmen, tapped on the mighty oak door before sticking his battered face round it, and announcing, 'There's a person to see you, my lord.'

'Who?' Theo growled, turning to look at him, his lips set grimly, the flickering light of a candle filled girandole giving a demonic slant to his face.

'A woman, my lord. Says her name is Mother Challis,' Scrope replied, rubbing a hand over his shaven pate. 'Says she's got news she thinks you'll want to hear.'

Theo's heart leapt and his cock stirred within his buckskin breeches. News of Sylvia? It had to be!

'Show her in,' he commanded, his voice ringing through the vastness of the room, its stone walls of unremitting grey, its ceiling rising thirty feet to black timber arches.

Scrope vanished, to return almost at once accompanied by a dark clad figure. Theo was not impressed. As the women moved closer to him he caught a whiff of musty clothing covering a dirty body. She was tall and unlovely, wearing an absurd, tasteless hat. Theo took one look at her and shuddered fastidiously.

'You wished to see me?' he said, his voice as cold as a wind blowing over Arctic wastes.

'I did, your honour... begging your pardon. Mother Challis, at your service. I understood you were looking for a certain young lady,' she began, shuffling her large, booted feet, her eyes roaming the room as if making an inventory of its contents.

'You know where she is?' Theo thundered, pushing back his carved chair with a sudden grating noise, and rising to his full, impressive height.

'I do, sir... least ways, I think I do.'

His lip curled disdainfully and the wine reflected in the facets of his glass shone like blood red rubies. He looked her up and down, and his sneer deepened.

'Well, do you or do you not know where Miss Sylvia Parnell is at this precise moment?' he asked with an arrogance that reduced her to jelly.

'I do, your lordship,' she ventured, then gathered her wits and clung to the vision of financial gain that floated in her brain. 'I've seen the notice you distributed, and understand there's a reward.'

'The reward. Ah, yes. You're attitude confirms my view that all men are venal, women too,' he pronounced cynically. 'Are you a business woman, Mother Challis?'

'Oh, yes, my lord,' she replied, almost genuflecting in his presence. 'I make a living of a sort. Not the kind of income you're used to, I expect, but enough to keep body and soul together.'

She stared at him as he stalked towards her, the steel tips of his riding boots striking sharply on the flagstones. He carried his glass, and she licked her lips, but he did not offer her a drink. The thought of having this grotesque hag seated at his table and supping his rare vintage was anathema to him.

'Then you will appreciate that my time is money,' he said brusquely. 'Tell what you know, and, if it proves to lead me to Miss Sylvia, then you shall be paid, never fear. You have my word on't.'

'Oh, yes sir. Of course, sir. That's good enough for me, sir,' she blustered, sweat beading her upper lip. 'There's this girl, see. I found her starving in the gutter and took her in, out of the goodness of my heart, you understand.'

Theo's amber eyes bored into hers as if he could read every shady secret of her mean soul. He smiled thinly, and said, 'You did not expect gain?'

'Bless you, no, sir,' she protested, twisting her hands together in their faded mittens. 'Ask anyone in my street and they'll all tell you that Mother Challis is there for them… night or day… whenever they need help.'

'Yes, yes. A saint, no doubt. Where is this girl?' Theo snapped, taking to a restless pacing.

'In my house, sir. I've kept her close like, so as she didn't take no harm. Young girls are delicate blooms, aren't they, sir. They have to be looked after,' Mother Challis stammered, mesmerised by that tall, distinguished figure, probably the most handsome man she had ever seen.

He stopped short in front of her, demanding, 'What's her name?'

'She calls herself Anne Rankin, but her clothing was of the best. She weren't no ordinary waif, your honour, and I thought at the time that she wasn't being truthful. Told me she'd been robbed on her way to the stagecoach. Said she was heading for the country.'

'What makes you think she is Miss Parnell?' Theo asked calmly, but people who knew him well would have trembled had they seen him. When Theo Aubrey was being calm and reasonable, he was at his most deadly.

'It was worth a shot, sir,' Mother Challis answered boldly, that native cunning which she owned aplenty recognising his hidden agitation. 'Seems too strong a coincidence, if you take my meaning. Your betrothed scarpering, and this girl turning up on my doorstep.'

'When can I see her?' Theo said evenly, putting a curb on the excitement tingling through his body.

'Whenever it suits your lordship. D'you want me to bring her here?' Mother Challis asked, hands clenching into hard knuckled fists as if she could already feel the gold filling them.

'No... I've a better plan,' Theo answered, his mind working at full stretch. 'The young lady is reluctant to become my bride. She has some silly, romantic notion that marriage has to do with love.'

'And it hasn't, of course,' Mother Challis agreed.

'Not necessarily,' he concluded, replacing his glass on the table and folding his arms across his chest. 'Happily, this blessed state may follow, but whatever the outcome, she must do her duty. Her aunt is Lady Rowena Bancroft and, as her legal guardian, she concurs with me on this issue.'

'I'll do whatever you require, sir,' Mother Challis said with an oily smile. 'Just tell me your wishes.'

Theo ran a hand over his smooth-shaven jaw, and his eyes

took on an even more dangerous slant. 'She must have no inkling that I'm on to her,' he said, thinking aloud. 'If it is her, of course. Tell me what she looks like.'

'She has brownish hair, with golden lights, and her eyes are green. Her body is slim, but her breasts are rounded, and she speaks like a lady, carries herself like a lady… I'm sure she *is* a lady,' Mother Challis enthused, determined not to lose her chance of the glittering prize.

'Is she well? You've not harmed her, I hope?'

'Goodness gracious no, sir!' Mother Challis averred indignantly. 'She's still a virgin. I made sure of that, your honour. Couldn't take no flighty doxy into my house… I've got children to consider.'

Theo's eyes narrowed and he was as controlled as a hunting panther. 'You've not damaged her maidenhead? I want her intact. Breaking her hymen is my task,' he said, his sternness chilly and uncompromising.

'She's intact, I promise you,' Mother Challis quavered. 'Though I had to use the rod on her… just a little… to make her behave. Very defiant, she is, sir.'

'I know,' Theo answered heavily, and his phallus jumped as he visualised Sylvia's buttocks marked with fresh stripes. There was no doubt in his mind that Mother Challis was understating the severity of her treatment.

A dark skein of pleasure rippled right through him. The girl needed discipline and he felt no pity for her. There was a lump in his throat, a thudding in his heart and pressure in his groin that needed immediate relief. He would toss himself off as soon as this greedy piece of filth had removed herself.

'But she'll learn, my lord, once she's in your hands?' Mother Challis murmured with a crafty smile as she considered the cruel slant of his mouth, the fire and force of him, and that air of hubris that humbled her.

'She will indeed,' he replied sardonically, then moved with a swiftness that made her jump. 'Here's what we'll do,' he continued.

'You'll tell me where you live and, tomorrow morning, will take her out, as if you are going to market or some such. I shall be waiting in my carriage. I'll recognise her instantly and make my presence known, but gently, as if I'm rescuing her. I take it that she isn't happy with you?'

'No sir, very ungrateful,' Mother Challis answered, beady eyes fixed on his face.

'Capital,' Theo said flatly. 'Make sure you ill-treat her between now and then, that way she'll be more than willing to come with me.' He permitted himself a grim smile, adding, 'She may even end up looking on me as her hero.'

Mother Challis clapped her hands together, exclaiming admiringly, 'A capital plan, your honour! It shall be done as you say, to the letter, sir, I can assure you.'

'Good. Then tomorrow it is, Mother Challis,' Theo said, and snapped his fingers at Scrope who leaned with his back against the wall, arms folded over his barrel chest. 'Show the woman out.'

Mother Challis hesitated, her eyes darkening and her mouth setting like a rat-trap. 'The money, sir,' she reminded.

Theo spun round on his heel and the look on his face was terrifying. 'Money, woman? You shall have it after I've assured myself that it is really Miss Parnell you are selling. Don't even consider the possibility of crossing me, not if you wish to live, that is. Good evening to you.'

With that he turned his back on her, and she could do no other than follow Scrope out of the door.

Chapter Eight

It was a grey day, just another in the long line of grey days that constituted Sylvia's existence.

Her only comfort was Phoebe, and she dreaded to think what she would do if she was not there. The workload was crippling. If she had thought for a moment that Mother Challis would be easier on her after the episode in the bedchamber she was very much mistaken. Nothing changed.

Though she had slept in the mistress's bed, she was kicked awake at daybreak, lashed thoroughly and set to work without breaking her fast. Mother Challis mocked and tormented her for days to follow, giving her no peace, but on returning home on the previous evening her mood had been one of gloating triumph as she announced,

'You girls are to come to the market with me tomorrow. You'll get up extra early to get the chores done before we leave. Are you listening, Anne, you stubborn trollop?'

'Yes, mistress,' Sylvia muttered, though her heart lightened at the prospect of an outing, be it never so humdrum. She had not set foot beyond the house since her captivity, apart from nights spent chained in the yard.

'You say it with bad grace, girl,' Mother Challis declared and reached for her plaited leather thong.

Sylvia's flesh cringed, but she withstood the assault, almost accepting that she merited this punishment, unworthy of anything better. But when she was pushed into the blackness of the coalhole, a fearsome place inhabited by rats and spiders, she broke down, crouching at the bottom of the steps and burying her face in her hands.

Now it was morning and Phoebe unbolted the heavy door and let her out. 'She's so cruel,' she whispered, and held Sylvia

141

in her arms momentarily. 'I'd like to see her dead. Dance on her grave, I would.'

'You mustn't say such wicked things,' Sylvia remonstrated, though echoing these sentiments in her heart.

She was starving, smeared with coal-dust, her feet lacerated, her back throbbing with pain, her hair falling in greasy snarls around her face. I can't stand this much longer, she thought desperately. Oh, God, help me to escape!

By eight o'clock their tasks were completed, but Mother Challis kept them waiting while she ate a substantial meal. They were denied even the usual bread and water.

'Hunger is good for you,' she declaimed piously, chewing her way through yet another pork chop. 'Keeps you on your toes.'

'Can I come with you, Ma?' Emily asked, dragging down to the kitchen, a wrapper clasped about her. Bleary-eyed and yawning, she scratched at her tangled hair.

'No, but I'll be back for you later, my love,' her mother answered, and she seemed to be in an unusually amiable frame of mind. Emily brightened. 'Can we take a trip to the second-hand clothes dealer?' she asked eagerly.

'No, we can't,' said her mother teasingly then, smiling into Emily's crestfallen face, she continued, 'You deserve a treat, but no cast-offs for you this time. We'll get something new.'

'But it isn't my birthday,' Emily reminded, puzzled by this sudden burst of generosity on her mother's part.

'That don't matter. Nothing's too good for my precious,' Mother Challis cried, beaming widely. 'Don't you worry, pet. All being well, your clever old ma is about to strike a deal.'

Sylvia stared at her in astonishment. It was the first time she had seen her so jocular, and this was even more alarming than when she stormed and raged. What was going on? Had there been a burglary? Were stolen goods about to be delivered? Something momentous must have happened.

'Don't stand there gawking, Anne!' Mother Challis shouted and gave her a hard cuff. 'Fetch the basket. I'm almost ready.'

She shrugged a cloak over her shoulders and tied the black bonnet strings under her chin. Sylvia and Phoebe followed in her wake as she sailed through the front door. They wore nothing but their hessian garments, their naked feet squelching through the mud.

Even so, Sylvia lifted her face to the sullen skies and took a deep breath. The air was hardly pure, but it felt like heaven to her after the confinement of the house. The street was busy. Whores lingered in doorways, painted young ones, toothless old ones. There was a conglomeration of vagabonds and beggars, toil-worn women and wizened-faced children. Their misery settled round Sylvia like a familiar pain. They muttered greetings as Mother Challis passed. Servile and afraid, the majority of them were in her debt.

The shops had been open for some time, dingy establishments unlike the ones Sylvia had visited with Rowena. Drunks reeled down the middle of the road, shouting abuse at passing carts. There was a reek of gin, bad drainage, and the stench of the nearby tannery. Her attention became focused on a commotion at the bottom of the alley, the clatter of iron-shod hooves and the rumble of wheels. People were moving aside to avoid being crushed by the coach that suddenly appeared under the arch. It came on at a brisk trot.

Sylvia pressed back against the wall lest it mow her down. A pair of equine heads hung above her. She saw fiercely rolling eyes and great mouths flecked with foam, flowing manes and glittering harness. The coachman bellowed and hauled on the reins and, with rattle, the vehicle stopped abruptly. The door opened wide. A dark figure was framed there, and she found herself staring up into Theo's face.

'Sylvia!' he exclaimed and, before she could move or protest, reached down, gripped her under the armpits and dragged her inside.

She was too stunned to struggle, but Mother Challis was right behind her, leaning in at the door, tugging at her skirt and shouting, 'What's going on? You can't take her. She's my servant.'

'This is no servant, woman! She is my betrothed, and I've been seeking her all over London,' Theo cried, holding Sylvia close in an iron grip.

She was crushed against the softness of velvet and fine linen, inhaling the fresh, clean smell of him, feeling the long, strong finger of his phallus rising to meet her hip. Her emotions were on a seesaw – one moment appalled, the next relieved.

Theo had saved her. How, she could not guess. Suffice to say, he had snatched her from the clutches of the devilish Mother Challis. She forgot that she had once run from him, blanking her mind to the reason.

All she was aware of was smooth fabric under her hands, sweet smells in her nostrils, warmth and luxury and the promise of a bath and clean clothing. His maleness overwhelmed her, the muscular strength, the air of authority.

'I need her,' Mother Challis roared, her eyes linked with Theo's. 'It'll cost me to replace her.'

'Take this, and bother me no more,' he snarled and plunged a hand into the pocket of his triple-caped coat, drew out a purse that clinked invitingly and threw it at her.

'Thank you, sir,' she said, catching it promptly. A shutter came down over Theo's features, transforming them into a cold mask. 'Now get away from here, and I never want to see your ugly face again,' he growled menacingly.

'No, wait!' Sylvia said, recovering her wits and struggling into a sitting position. 'I won't go without my friend.' She pulled away from him and leaned out of the door, shouting, 'Phoebe! Come here!'

'Leave her, Sylvia,' he said impatiently, clamping an arm about her waist, but she fought him off.

'She must come. I want her as my maid,' she insisted, a savage-eyed termagant, her raised knee threatening to catch him in the balls.

'Sweeting, I can get you a dozen maids…' he began.

Her eyes sparked and her chin set in that mulish way which

always spelled trouble. 'No,' she declared. 'I want Phoebe.'

Theo shrugged his wide shoulders and retreated, saying, 'Very well. Have it your way. Get the wench inside, and hurry.'

Needing no second bidding, Phoebe jumped in beside Sylvia, falling with her into the plush depths of the seat. Mother Challis opened her mouth to argue but Theo slammed the door shut, rapped on the roof with his cane and the carriage lurched off over the cobbles, quickly leaving the slums behind.

'So, Sylvia, you thought to give me the slip,' Theo said slowly. He was seated opposite her, and she could not help recalling Mr Henry Lanston on the stagecoach from Bath.

She was lost for words, dry-mouthed, aware of a head spinning intoxication, the inability to respond, the throbbing ache between her legs that made her want to writhe on the padded upholstery, hotter than a bitch in season.

These gentlemen, so fine and personable, were insidiously seductive. Henry with his large cock and Mary so eager to accommodate it. Now there was Theo sitting there with his curling black hair, a low-crowned beaver hat, a long, full-skirted overcoat and shiny top boots. How far removed he was from the disordered inelegance and crudity of John Challis.

Theo's every movement was one of studied negligence and grace. She could not but admire the way in which he flicked back the lace at his wrist, took out his gold snuffbox and applied a pinch to each nostril, then dabbed his nose delicately with a spotless white kerchief.

'Well?' he continued in a cool drawl. 'Have you nothing to say to me? Cat got your tongue? If I recall, you aired your views clearly enough on the last occasion we met.'

'I'm sorry. I was obviously mistaken about you. Is my aunt very angry with me,' she stammered, and all the time her eyes were locked with his steady, compelling gaze.

'She wasn't over pleased,' he said, touching the head of his cane to his lips pensively. 'But all is forgiven now, my dear. The arrangements can go ahead. The marriage will take place on the morrow.'

'What?' Sylvia cried, frozen to her seat.

'The wedding, my sweet. Everything is ready. Rowena has prepared your trousseau, the flowers are ordered, the feast prepared. Now that the bride has been restored to us, there need be no further delay.'

'But how has this been done? You couldn't have known where to find me. I planned that you should not. It was pure chance that you happened upon me today, wasn't it?' Sylvia asked, bewildered by the swiftness of events.

He raised an arched eyebrow, saying, 'It was inevitable, considering that I had been searching for you night and day, sparing no expense. Aren't you impressed by my devotion? At my express orders, the wedding had merely been held in abeyance. A word from me and it will happen… at noon tomorrow.'

'Wait!' she implored, though her spine tingled and her secret lips were wet with love-juice. 'Please, my lord. You've been patient so far… have overlooked my transgression. I beg you, give me more time before we're wed.'

Theo sighed and shook his head, murmuring, 'Child… child… don't you know that any delay to a bridegroom is extremely irksome?'

Ignoring Phoebe who was watching him with wide eyes and her mouth an O of astonishment, he leaned across the gap between the seats and hooked a finger at the opening of Sylvia's sacking blouse. It fell apart, exposing her breasts and, as the breeze played over her nipples, they rose into peaks.

Gripping her knees between his so that she could not move, he bent and showered kisses on her throat and breasts. The expert caressing of his lips made her breath shorten and her body quiver.

'You like me more than you did, surely?' he said, the beautiful articulation of his voice making the down rise on Sylvia's limbs. 'Haven't I just saved you from a terrible fate? That woman! Faugh! What a horror! My poor darling, how you must have suffered. But that's all over now. You are safe

146

with me.'

Safe was the very last thing she felt, but hypnotised by his eyes, desire overcame trepidation, lust of the flesh drugging her so that she ignored the tocsin in her brain that warned of dangerous shoals ahead.

Theo curtly signalled Phoebe to move and settled himself at Sylvia's side, his arm holding her comfortingly. She relaxed, for he did not seem about to take liberties, and she was grateful for that, yet regretted it, too.

'I may have misjudged you, sir,' she said, resting her head against his shoulder. 'Perhaps we can start over again.'

His lips touched her hair where the white parting showed at the centre, though his nostrils flared at the stench of the slums that clung to her.

She shifted position so that she might look up at him, but his eyes were unfathomable as he murmured, 'Of course, dearest. Anything you say. Tomorrow we shall be united, and I'll show you pleasures far beyond your wildest dreams.'

No expense had been spared in the wedding preparations. Sylvia, swept up in the flurry of it all, was yet aware that it was her money they were spending. But she was so engrossed in her new, bewildering emotions concerning Theo that this was of little consequence.

She felt like Sleeping Beauty who has been awakened by a prince's kiss after years of incarceration. I must have been blind, she scolded herself as Rowena embraced her warmly when they arrived at Laurel House and all was bustle and excitement. Why didn't I want to marry him? Why did I run away? Her actions now seemed incomprehensible.

Only Phoebe dared voice the tiny doubt lingering in the back of her mind. Phoebe who said, after they were installed in Sylvia's bedroom,

'This is a rum go, ain't it, miss? You sure you're doing the right thing?'

Sylvia, who was lying in a tub of warm, deliciously scented

147

water, squinted up at her and said stiffly, 'Of course I'm sure. What's the matter with you, Phoebe? And why are you calling me "miss" all of a sudden?'

Phoebe took up a big sponge and trickled water over her mistress's breasts. She now looked the part of lady's maid, scrubbed clean by Mary Standish and equipped with a striped cotton dress, a snowy mobcap and frilled apron.

'I can't call you Anne no more,' she said, respectfully. 'You're Miss Sylvia till tomorrow, then you'll be Lady Aubrey. Things have altered, and you've changed… all starry-eyed and cock-struck.'

'I'm not!' Sylvia snapped crossly, then suddenly grasped Phoebe's hand and held it tightly in her slippery wet fingers. 'You mustn't ever leave me. I need you.'

'Don't you fret. I'm yours for keeps. You've saved me and I'll always bless you for it,' Phoebe said, her hazel eyes shining with sincerity. 'It's only that I fear for you. That man you're promised to… he's an odd one. I find him scary.'

'You're wrong. Theo is wonderful,' Sylvia enthused, her nipples rising at the remembrance of his touch, her love-tunnel aching to have him fill it, consummating their marriage.

'You didn't always think so, else why did you leg it?' Phoebe asked, ever practical.

'I must have been crazy,' Sylvia cried, and smiled widely, raising her arms above her head, her breasts rising from the soap bubbles.

Phoebe shrugged, her generous mouth pulled down at the corners, and helped Sylvia from the tub, swathing her in a big soft towel.

Sylvia chose a gown from the vast selection awaiting her, all ordered by Rowena. Theo awaited her downstairs, along with Mr Middleton and her aunt. The lawyer had the betrothal papers with him, and it was necessary for her to add her signature.

Later, standing with them in the drawing room, a chill finger touched Sylvia's spine as Mr Middleton pushed the parchment towards her and, through a blur, she saw the copperplate writing and impressive red seals which would bind her to Theo as his wife. "Chattel" was the unpleasant word that sprang in mind.

'Sign, my love,' he murmured seductively into her ear, his lips setting the diamond pendant swinging.

He was close behind her and she could feel the swell of his erection against the division of her buttocks. She could imagine that formidable weapon naked to her touch. The thought made her languorous with need, and sent her nipples peaking under the fragile silk of her simple, tube-like dress.

Without giving herself time to hesitate, she took up the quill, dipped it in the brass inkwell, and added her name to Theo's almost indecipherable scrawl. Then she reached for the pepper pot shaped container and shook sand over the wet ink.

The die was cast. She now belonged to Theo. And he to her? Somehow, she could not visualise him belonging to anyone.

Despite the congratulations, the lifting of champagne flutes and the toasts drunk to the happy couple, she was aware of a chill creeping through her body, an insidious cold that seemed to freeze the blood throbbing in her veins.

The music soared, the sweet voices of the choir rising to the arched roof of the church. Sylvia stood at Theo's side, her gown of heavy slipper satin encrusted with silver embroidery and seed pearls. White kid gloves reached her elbows, though she had slipped her hand out of the left one to bare her finger for his ring.

Her wheat-gold hair flowed down her back beneath a veil held in place with a circlet of orange-blossom. The scent of the flowers was powerful, almost narcotic, making her head swim. Rowena stood behind her as matron of honour, wearing poppy-red bombazine and a magnificent tulle turban. An elderly colonel in full dress uniform had led Sylvia up the aisle. He was one of Rowena's cronies who had been pressed into giving the bride away.

Why do I feel like a victim about to be sacrificed? Sylvia fretted as the priest mouthed the solemn words of the marriage ceremony.

The shining brass vessels were misty through the veil – the censers, the flowers, the statues of saints – the elaborately robed priest. She felt Theo take her hand in his, firm, cool fingers slipping on the heavy gold band. She thought of the bondage she had witnessed at Rowena's orgy, the slaves in manacles, the chains linking their body piercing. The fading bruises on her buttocks tingled. Her nipples hardened. Her clitoris pulsed.

I don't want to go through with this, she suddenly panicked.

It was too late. The priest pronounced them man and wife.

She wanted to run, screaming, from the church.

Theo lifted her veil and kissed her full on the mouth, holding her hands close to the ruffles on his chest. She felt the secret probe of his tongue, just the tip pressing between her lips. He lifted his head and her heart skipped a beat, reading nameless perversions in their amber depths. A pang of lust shot through her, so sharp it made her catch her breath.

He knew her, this husband of hers, better than she knew herself, was aware of the longings, hungers and strange fantasies that she dared not admit to, even to herself.

She had the dizzy feeling of falling into space, and his hand became a lifeline to which she clung. Once more in command of herself, she held her head high and walked down the aisle with her fingers resting on the velvet sleeve of his jacket. Even as she pasted a smile on her face and glanced at the packed pews filled with his and Rowena's friends, so she felt the muscles under his sleeve, and the movement of his lithe body, and could smell his musky odour with the spicy undercurrent. Soon it would be her wedding night, and the final mystery revealed.

Outside the uncertain English weather decided to be clement. Theo and Sylvia hurried to the beribboned coach, dodging showers of rice and rose petals. She crouched in a corner of

150

the swaying chaise, as far away from him as possible, busying herself with settling her train. He merely smiled and looked out of the window, ignoring her. This was disconcerting. He was moody and temperamental. Sylvia could never be sure what he would do next. It made her jumpy and on edge.

Laurel House glowed, polished and flower decked. Musicians played while flunkies moved among the guests. It was a most decorous gathering, everyone behaving with the greatest propriety. This, too, unsettled Sylvia, who had half expected the wedding breakfast to dissolve into a saturnalia, like the party she had attended before.

Could it be that Theo was more circumspect?

She did as she was told; moving here, standing there, introduced to this person and that. She had no hope of remembering their names. Everyone wished her well and called her 'Lady Aubrey'. She hated it.

She was aware of eyes on her at all times, assessing, considering, even envying, particularly the women. And she had to admit that Theo was looking remarkably handsome in his black velvet breeches and tailcoat. Black silk hose and shoes with cut-steel buckles completed his finery, and his ruffles were black, too, shot through with silver thread. He wore a court-sword at his left hip, sparks scintillating from its beautifully worked hilt.

He smiled ironically every time he caught her looking at him, and sat with her at the head of the long table with forty guests on either side. She could not eat, nerves cramping her stomach, laved in heat and longing for the feast to be over, yet dreading the moment, too.

What next? she wondered.

'The coach is waiting to convey you to Burbank Abbey,' Theo said, placing a bejewelled finger under her chin and raising her face to his. 'Your maid will accompany you.'

'And yourself?' she asked, while her heart raced.

'I shall join you later.'

'But... I thought... imagined...' she stuttered, amazed by

his abandonment at a moment when he should have been eager to be alone with her.

'That I would take you home, throw you on your back and assert my rights as your husband?' he said, stifling a yawn behind his hand. Then he bent closer, and his breath carried a sweetish odour, mingled with that of claret. She had noticed it before, and wondered as to its origin. 'I'm engaged to play cards at my club,' he continued, and his lips curled in a sombre smile as he added, 'Your eagerness is flattering, but we have all our lives before us in which to enjoy the rutting heat of the marriage bed.'

His hand dived beneath the white damask cloth and landed in her satin lap. She started, but his eyes smiled into hers as he slid a finger into the hollow between her legs, the frisson between his digit and the silk causing mayhem in her loins. Her pubis was smooth again, shaved that morning by Farid, ultra sensitive to Theo's expert massage. She gave a little moan and,

'Hush, my dear wife,' he whispered, nodding across the table to where a red-faced, bedizened duchess was talking to the colonel. 'They mustn't know what I am doing. Ah, I can feel your naughty bud swelling... that's beautiful...'

'Oh, Theo... you can't leave me like this,' she murmured.

'I can and I will. Waiting will sharpen your appetite,' he said, and removed his finger, wiping it on the sparkling napery.

Tears sprang into Sylvia's eyes. He played with her like a cat with a mouse. It was humiliating and worst of all was the fact that he could see she was dismayed, confused and disappointed.

'Do as he says, my dear,' Rowena advised, from her other side. 'Theo has commitments, you know. Don't worry, he plans a surprise for you tonight.'

He stood up, bowed and excused himself, leaving with half a dozen male companions, all joking, making sly comments behind their hands and laughing. Theo joined in and his laughter cut Sylvia to the quick. No one seemed surprised at his cavalier action, those remaining at table carrying on eating and drinking. She hid her pain, cool and dignified, nodding in agreement when a little later Rowena suggested she might like to leave.

The afternoon was well advanced and the guests stirred themselves to give her a warm send-off, clustering round the chaise which was gaily decorated with white ribbons and silver bells, the horses bearing ostrich plumes on their heads. Sylvia smiled stiffly, longing to be alone, the strain of keeping up appearances making her head ache.

'I'm proud of you, my dear,' Rowena said, balanced on the step in order to reach in and peck her cheek. 'I shall see you anon.'

Sylvia did not answer and, when the horses broke into a trot, sank back against the beige upholstery, tears welling up and spilling over.

'There, there, don't you take on so,' Phoebe comforted, taking out her kerchief and handing it to her mistress. 'You're a lovely bride, and he's a damn' fool! What sort of a game is he playing?'

'I don't know,' Sylvia sighed, dabbing her eyes, veil and wreath askew.

'I hate to say "I told you so", but I did,' Phoebe pronounced sagely, then she grinned, a far cry from the skivvy Sylvia had first met, pert and pretty in her sprigged dress, the perfect lady's maid.

'Cheer up. Maybe when he comes in, he'll be too drunk to fuck you.'

'That's what I'm afraid of,' Sylvia confessed, and they both laughed.

Their laughter died, however, when they reached Richmond, where they had their first glimpse of Burbank Abbey. The coach left the highway, turning in between wrought iron gates guarded by a pair of stone griffons and set in a high wall topped with iron spikes.

'Look, my lady!' Phoebe gasped, and they both stared

through the window at the fantastic silhouette looming against the fiery sunset sky. It looked like a fortress, with curious pinnacles and towers and twisted, ornamental chimney pots.

'Burbank Abbey,' Sylvia whispered.

'Your husband's house and your home from now on.'

'Be quiet, Phoebe. I don't wish to be reminded,' Sylvia said. The coach stopped at the foot of granite steps leading up to an imposing arched door. The house beetled over them, and Sylvia felt a shiver run through her. Despite the lights blazing in many of the mullioned windows, the impression was one of overwhelming gloom.

She jumped as a peculiar scream rent the air.

'It's only a peacock, Lady Sylvia,' said a suave voice, and the dark-clad figure of a woman appeared and walked down the steps towards her. 'Allow me to welcome you. I'm Nairi... Lord Theo's housekeeper.'

She was thin and classically beautiful, her skin sallow, her eyes slanting. Not English, Sylvia concluded, but some exotic creature Theo had acquired during his travels.

Sylvia was nonplussed, then managed to say, 'He did not tell me about you.'

Nairi smiled and said, with a deprecating gesture, 'There was no reason why he should, milady. I have orders to conduct you to the master bedchamber and prepare you for his coming.'

Sylvia could do nothing but follow the woman inside, with Phoebe behind her, holding up her train. The great hall lay before her, where, under the light cast from huge flambeaux, more than two dozen servants waited in line to greet her.

It was solemn, almost awesome, and in complete silence she walked between the ranks of liveried men in tobacco brown and women in plain, dark dresses, relieved by splashes of white.

The housekeeper led her up a large intricately carved staircase, along a corridor of such grandeur that Sylvia was spellbound and then paused before a door of inlaid marquetry, saying, 'This is the master bedchamber.'

She opened it and stood back so that Sylvia might precede

her. The curtains were pulled across the windows, and the fire in the enormous hearth leapt in the sudden draught and the candle flames slanted.

Sylvia paused on the threshold, reluctant to enter, but felt Nairi's slender hands on hers, encouraging her in. 'Come, milady,' she said. 'There is much to do and we must not keep the master waiting.'

'It's so big,' Sylvia quavered, wanting to add 'and so strange', but not quite daring. No doubt the woman was one of Theo's spies. Everything she said and did would be reported to him.

Nairi looked around it with a hint of pride, saying, 'Milord has garnered many treasures from his frequent travels. He is a lover of art, madame, a connoisseur.'

The room was panelled in oak and sumptuously furnished in Gothic style. The air was sickly sweet with perfume rising from incense smouldering in ornamental dishes. Added to this were idols and artefacts from as far afield as India and China, rugs from Persia, drapes from Turkey and Hindustan, and statues from Ancient Greece and Rome. Sylvia was flabbergasted. She had no idea that Theo was knowledgeable, finding it hard to correlate this with his hedonistic lifestyle.

'Is he a pagan?' she asked, alarmed by the full-sized statue of a strange goddess with bare breasts and several pairs of arms.

'He studies many religions and worships at different shrines, including this one. Isn't she beautiful?' Nairi murmured and rearranged the white lilies with thick, fleshy leaves and flamboyant orange stamens that stood in a vase before the deity.

'She's hideous!' Sylvia cried, staring at the fierce expression, the outstretched tongue, the third eye in the centre of the forehead, the girdle of severed heads.

'Not when you understand and revere her,' Nairi whispered, hand touching her brow and breast as she made obeisance. 'She is Durga, the demon slayer. She blesses you, the new bride, and welcomes you to your lord's house.'

'Nasty heathen nonsense,' Phoebe muttered in Sylvia's ear. 'Don't you have nothing to do with it, my lady.'

But Sylvia had little say in what happened to her, Nairi taking control. First, the housekeeper clapped her hands and a manservant appeared promptly.

He was young and very handsome, almost femininely pretty. His skin was oiled and his body nude, apart from a wide, jewelled collar and a tiny apron that dangled from his waist in the front. It shifted when he moved, displaying his penis and the taut globes of his balls. His nipples lay like two pennies on his well-defined pectorals, thin onyx rings passing through them. As Sylvia stared, unable to keep her eyes away, she glimpsed another shiny black hoop that passed through his fraenum.

He dropped to his knees in front of her, bent and kissed her foot, while Nairi said, 'Hot water for her ladyship's bath, Caton, and bring us wine. I have prepared a special vintage for her… one of Lord Aubrey's own.'

She seized a switch that lay on the table and brought it down in a vicious swipe, catching his bare shoulders and chest. He made no sound and retreated, crawling backwards to the door, never raising his eyes above floor level.

Sylvia was appalled that such a beautiful young man should abase himself in such a way, her nerves still vibrating to the sound the bound twigs had made when they scored his flesh.

Nairi glanced at her, a little smile on her red lips. It was as if she knew Sylvia's own skin was smarting in sympathy.

Caton returned with a silver tray on which stood a decanter and a crystal goblet. Nairi poured the wine carefully and handed the glass to Sylvia.

She sipped cautiously. It had a sweet, fruity flavour, seeming to carry in its heart the warmth and languor of Italian vineyards where grapes ripened beneath a hot sun. There was a slightly bitter aftertaste, but she wanted more, her thirst increasing. She drank a second glass.

'Your bath is ready, Lady Sylvia,' Nairi said softly, but when

Phoebe stepped forward to accompany them, she was dismissed with a brusque, 'Not you, girl. Go and supervise the unpacking of her ladyship's belongings. They have arrived from Laurel House.'

Feeling as if she was cloud borne, Sylvia drifted into the adjoining room. It glittered, marble tiled and ornate, even more luxurious than the one Rowena used for her ablutions. Here, the perfume was more pronounced, and this, combined with the wine, added to Sylvia's feeling of disorientation.

'Allow me to disrobe you,' Nairi said. Just for an instant Sylvia tried to protest, but she felt weak and helpless, robbed of strength and coherent thought. Caton was as obedient as Farid, though fair as an angel compared to the African. He kept his eyes averted as he tested the temperature of the water and assisted Sylvia to immerse herself.

When she was thoroughly cleansed, hair as well as body, she was taken from the tub, encouraged to spread herself on a couch and massaged from head to toe. Another glass of the aromatic wine was brought to her and she could feel herself slipping away. Then consciousness returned sharply.

Nairi's hands worked fragrant oil into every inch of Sylvia's back, soothing the abrasions left by Mother Challis's rod. Her shoulders received particular attention, and she could not restrain a little moan of need as the fingers connected with that sensitive zone where her neck joined her spine. Her sex ached, and visions of Theo floated in her brain. It should have been he, not his servant, who aroused her to passion on this, their nuptial night.

'Please roll over, my lady,' said Nairi, in her soft, modulated voice.

Sylvia stretched on her back, completely vulnerable but unable to cover her nudity. She felt boneless. It was not worth the effort to move these relaxed muscles. She looked into Nairi's face as she bent to her task. Her features were impassive.

'Are you Theo's mistress?' Sylvia asked, amazed at her courage, the words coming without conscious thought.

Nairi smiled and answered, 'Are you jealous, my lady? If so, you're going to torment yourself unnecessarily. You'll be jealous of everyone, from myself to the meanest groom in the stables. Isn't that so, Caton?'

He nodded, his eyes lowered as he stood by the couch holding a jar of oil. 'Yes,' he said quietly.

This was an utterly new concept and one with which Sylvia would have wrestled, had she not felt so tired. Young men, too? Surely not?

Somehow, it didn't matter. All she was concerned with was the feel of those palms bringing her blissful feelings as they crawled over her body, seeking the most responsive spots.

Sylvia's sex swelled unbearably, her clitoris aching for the caress of the oiled, skilful fingers. Nairi circled her breasts, skimmed over the tender nipples, the touch just firm enough to be exciting. Then she kneaded the soft belly, dipping into the navel and out again to hover over Sylvia's mound.

She could not help writhing her hips, moaning quietly. Nairi signalled to Caton who gripped Sylvia's ankles and opened her legs wide, then slipped a silken scarf round each, tethering her to the couch.

Nairi rubbed each side of the labial lips, and examined her vulva, working a finger round its mouth. Sylvia rolled her head from side to side, burning for that touch on her clitoris, so ready it would have reacted instantly, sweeping her to orgasm.

But Nairi avoided the spot, nodding to Caton who released Sylvia's ankles. 'You may rise now, milady,' Nairi said. 'Your bridegroom and his guests are waiting.'

Sylvia was almost weeping with frustration, her loins on fire. In a daze she allowed herself to be led back to the bedchamber where, spread across the monumental four poster, was a white, gossamer thin gown.

Nairi picked it up and held it out. The light shone through it as if it were made of cobweb.

'I can't appear in that. It's indecent!' Sylvia cried.

'Lord Aubrey has ordered that you do so. He gave me *carte blanche* to beat you if you refuse,' Nairi replied, unemotionally.

'I thought he would come to me here… alone…'

'No, milady. I have my instructions.'

'Then where…?'

'The vaults, madame. Might I suggest that you sip your wine while I dress you?'

Why not? Sylvia thought bleakly, the language of the slums coming back to her. I may as well be drunk as a fiddler's bitch for all the good tonight will do me. His guests, indeed! What is this to be? A public performance of my defloration?

She stood like a lifeless statue as Nairi rouged her nipples and denuded sex lips and then slipped the flowing robe over her head and adjusted it. It was of so fine a weave as to suggest a mist rather than material, floating round Sylvia's limbs.

She stared at her image in the cheval glass. A golden cord banded her breasts and tied around her slender waist, throwing her carmined nipples into prominence. The darker shadow of her crotch was only part hidden by the fragile folds, serving to make her more alluring than if entirely naked.

Nairi brushed out her long hair till it coiled around her shoulders, and down across her back, held away from her face by a fresh wreath of flowers. She resembled a corn-goddess, a symbol of fertility – the earth mother herself, embodying all the dreams men have of golden-haired women.

Surely, they had added something extra to the wine, she thought, staring at herself and liking what she saw. Her nipples tingled and her vagina ached. She was filled with carnal heat. Her head span and as she accompanied Nairi through the door it seemed she was not touching the floor, but floating somewhere above it.

The house was huge and Nairi took her hand, rushing her through halls and along passages, passed paintings in great gilded frames, and suits of armour with sightless helmets. Crossed swords were hung on the panelling, and lances, too – tattered banners in muted colours, relics of long-ago battles.

Down they went, descending by a winding staircase, down and down into the bowels of the abbey. The air was damp and chilly, the darkness illumined by smoky flares set in iron rings. On and on they went, the floor rough under Sylvia's bare feet, the walls shiny wet and moss encrusted.

Now she could hear sounds in the distance. A drumbeat. Chanting. And, looming ahead was a large iron-studded door. The walls around it bore weird paintings of demons and devils fornicating with their screaming, tortured victims, lit by the lurid flames of hell.

Nairi tapped on the door. It opened and, her heart pounding violently, Sylvia stepped into the room beyond.

It was ablaze with candles that did not penetrate the gloom of the vaulted ceiling. Black and crimson drapes hung on the grey stone walls. Incense spiced the atmosphere. It was crowded with people wearing extraordinary costumes, bird masks and feathers, animal skins and leather, all sexually explicit and provocative.

Sylvia stood at the top of a staircase with shallow, carpeted treads. There was nowhere to hide, every head turned towards her, but she was hardly aware of anyone except Theo who lounged in a carved throne on a dais.

He fixed her with his tiger's eyes and rose to his feet, his deep purple cloak swirling around him. Sylvia advanced down the stairs like steel drawn to the magnet. Her dress displayed her body rather than concealed it. She had nowhere to run, nowhere to hide, prey to the eyes feeding on her from all sides.

She reached the bottom of the steps and Theo loomed over her. His robe parted with the sibilant whisper of silk and he pulled her into its darkness. He was naked, his phallus already hard, pressing into her belly.

He looked down at her and smiled grimly, 'Welcome to the Brimstone Club… welcome to the holy place where your virgin knot will be untied.'

Chapter Nine

'Not here!' Sylvia hissed fiercely. 'You can't mean to possess me in front of all these people!'

Theo chuckled wickedly, his arm holding her even closer to his aroused body, the other hand palming her breast. 'That is precisely what I intend to do,' he answered, not bothering to lower his voice. 'And you will obey, madam.'

Horrified, Sylvia made an attempt to struggle, but the wine fuddled her. Something was added to it, she thought, while it was possible to string coherent thought together. I've never felt like this before, filled with such a powerful, driving lust. Is it him, or some love potion I've drunk unbeknown?

Theo's cloak hung from his shoulders, fastened by a ruby clasp at his throat. His body gleamed through the opening, magnificently honed and muscular, the swarthy, darkly furred flesh bearing the livid scars left by opponents' rapiers. Sylvia stared at the phallus rising from its sable nest. His organ matched the rest of him in flamboyance, so huge that she trembled. Would her delicate channel be able to house such a daunting object?

The drugged wine coursed like fire through her blood and she was consumed with a wild longing to pit herself against his weapon. But not like this, reduced to a slave who must perform for the entertainment of decadent voyeurs.

'I refuse, sir,' she cried, all too aware of his thigh pressed between hers. She could not help gyrating her pubis against its steely strength.

Theo laughed, throwing back his head, the light dancing over his sinewy throat and raven locks. Her reluctance seemed to delight him and his fingers feathered over her nipples, sending spasms of desire shooting through her. She rubbed her clit against him harder, the diaphanous robe dampening as it was drawn tightly between the swollen lips of her cleft.

He sobered, and the eyes that now pierced hers held an age-old depravity. 'No one refuses me,' he growled, swivelling his hips, letting her feel the virile heat of his tumescent penis. 'Least of all my wife. It seems you've not learned obedience, despite your treatment by Mother Challis.'

'She needs a good thrashing, old boy,' advised the stout, ruddy-cheeked person whom she recognised as Sir Balty Stebbings.

He had acted as Theo's best man, a pushy individual, all too keen to "kiss the bride", and making free with sweaty hands as he did so. Throughout the ceremony and reception she had been acutely aware of him undressing her with his eyes.

Theo strode across the floor, dragging Sylvia with him. The room opened out into a small amphitheatre with tiered seats facing a circular stage. Flambeaux were placed round the edge, illuminating whatever performance, thespian or otherwise, was about to take place.

A collection of lovely women was chained at regular intervals on the topmost tier. They took up languishing poses, arms above their heads, eyes lowered, stripped bare except for black stockings upheld by frilly red garters and high-heeled shoes with rhinestone buckles. Blonde, redheaded or brunette, they were peerless examples of womanhood selected to suit every taste.

They formed an artistic frieze, some with flowing hair, others with short, springy curls. Some were statuesque, some slender as boys. Their forks varied, too, shaven or flaunting glossy plumage, plump pink wings folded modestly, or dark slits wantonly parted. But there was one thing common to all – the manacles banding wrists and ankles, with lengths of chain fastened to rings bolted into the wall behind them.

These symbols of bondage shone against their alabaster skin and, as Sylvia drew closer, she saw marks that made her own flesh burn – the familiar, flaming stripes on thighs and buttocks and breasts where they had been severely chastised.

In her intoxicated, high-flown state she almost envied them.

To be a slave seemed an enviable position. No responsibility, one's life governed by someone else. All that was required was total subservience. And there was extreme pleasure to be gained, expressed by the way in which the girls writhed their hips in supplication, their teats bunched with desire, honeydew bathing their inner thighs and glistening on their sexual parts.

Theo's carefully chosen audience lounged on the benches or fingered the tethered women or one another. Naked youths with pronounced erections moved around on silent feet, serving wine and delicacies, faces impassive as their genitals were examined and the hoops in their nipples and cock-heads tweaked.

Rowena smiled knowingly at Sylvia from where she reclined on a couch near the stage. Bizarre and beautiful, she was dressed in a red leather basque, her stone-hard nipples poking over the cups, as arrestingly rouged as Sylvia's own. She was bare from the waist down, her depilated pudenda stretched open, her legs hitched over the arms of the chair, calves and slender feet encased in tightly laced scarlet boots with spiked heels.

The dark promise of her furrow was dominated by her large, swollen clitoris, her female essences shining like the jewels in her unfurled labial wings. Even as she watched Sylvia approach, she did not stop caressing the two fine specimens of manhood who stood either side of her.

They wore nothing but chains, and she fondled the short, turgid prick of one, and licked the bulging glans of the other, taking his juice on her tongue. As she did so, she ran her whip between Farid's legs, teasing his jerking cock, and tantalising the area dividing his scrotum and arsehole. Mother-naked, he crouched before her chair, a studded collar round his neck from which a lead dangled.

'Suck me,' Rowena demanded, the whip coming down heavily across his backside, augmenting the welts that embroidered his lean flanks.

Farid took the force of the blow with a stifled grunt, then buried his face in her cunt and licked her clitoris, reaching up blindly to pluck at her nipples.

Excitement rippled through the crowd as Theo propelled Sylvia towards one of the stage props: a wooden triangle with an iron ring set at its apex and others at the lower corners.

Apprehension stirred in her gut as she stared at this contraption, ripening into terror as her glance encompassed a divan centre stage, heaped with tapestry cushions and black silk drapes.

'Our bridal bed,' Theo said, his smile savage, his eyes fever-bright.

'Oh, no… please, no…' she breathed, her cheeks burning with a fire that originated in her loins.

She was consumed with the rampant need to have Theo plunge his supremely erect cock into her virgin channel, lust like lava boiling inside her. Her eyes refused to function properly and the walls were shrinking and expanding, the ceiling shooting upwards, dissolving in space. All that remained was the craving that clawed at her vitals.

Theo gestured to Farid and Caton, who crawled over to him on hands and knees, their buttocks raised high.

'Up,' he commanded, and they rose, took Sylvia from him and directed her to stand before the triangle.

She whimpered in distress, looking imploringly at her husband, but he merely watched, his hand on his phallus, fingers stroking its length. The assembly murmured, attention riveted on the stage.

Farid took Sylvia's wrists and bound them with woven silk as strong as hemp, then secured them to the ring above her head. This made her stretch up, supporting her weight on the tips of her toes for a moment. Then Caton gripped her ankles, pulling them wide apart and binding them to the lower rings.

Now she was ready, taut as a bowstring, exposed to public gaze and her husband's whip.

The heat and arousal of the viewers was palpable. Lust seemed to shimmer in the air. Her own passion was at breaking point. She yearned for Theo's touch, his selected instrument of pain – and his cock. She embraced the wooden struts, fingers spread against the wood, welcoming its support, relishing the drag on her tethered arms and thighs. Her sex was displayed, buttocks wide, legs held firmly by the ankle bonds.

She hung there like a beautiful ornament, hearing comments from the crowd:

'By God, she's a beauty, Theo.'

'Will you whip her breasts and lay open her cleft?'

'Don't be too soft with her. If she were mine, I'd not be satisfied till she was shrieking for mercy.'

'Then I'd stick my todger in her quim and fuck her blind.'

Sylvia could not see Theo, but knew instinctively when he moved into place behind her. Just for a moment, she felt his phallus nudging the avenue between her lower cheeks. It felt heavy, its head pulsing, and she lifted her rump as far as she was able, pressing back against it.

'Do you want me to take you like this?' he whispered, and he reached round, brushed away the fragile silk and sunk his fingers into her cleft.

After dipping into her copious juices, he found her clitoris and drew back the hood. Pleasure rocketed through her as his thumb rotated on the sensitive tip. She gasped, but it was not the ultimate bliss, and her cry changed to one of frustration as he teasingly withdrew.

In an instant, he gripped the back of her gown and the material ripped as he tore it away from her body. A sob caught in Sylvia's throat and tears ran down her cheeks. But the aphrodisiac blazed through her, stoking her fires, and she could have climaxed at the slightest touch on her clit, her own or anyone else's. Most of all, she wanted her husband to bring her off.

Caton handed Theo a long, slender whip. A hush fell over the vault as he ran it through his hands, testing its flexibility.

Then he drew back his arm and sent the wicked looking strip of black leather zinging through the air to land across Sylvia's bottom with a sharp crack.

She registered a moment of blank shock, followed by a slice of raging agony. She yelped, body bucking as she strained at her bonds. Strung out on the triangle, she waited with baited breath for the next blow. Instead she felt him slide a hand between her legs from behind and cradle her vulva, his middle digit bent so that it worked her clitoris from below.

'Oh, Theo… for God's sake…' she whimpered as her tormented little organ trembled beneath his fingertip.

'Be patient,' he said, and stood back, raising the whip again.

This time it rent her with appalling agony, the dark lash descending almost too fast to see, cutting into the white flesh, burning, bruising. Sylvia's fingers scrabbled at the wood like a drowning man seeking dry land, but there was no rescue.

Theo laid six more lashes across her, and by the last one she had quietened, hanging limp in her restraints. He ordered her release, catching her in his arms and lifting her, his lithe strength supporting her as if she weighed no more than a feather.

She could hear laughter rumbling in his chest as he carried her over to the divan. By now she had reached the eye of the storm, sunk into a strange peace. The fire of the whipping seared her flesh, but contained a curious coolness, too.

Theo had shamed her, proving his mastery, but the drug she had consumed dulled the pain and fanned the flame of her desires. She loathed the idea of her exposure to the invited gentry, but could not bear it if he kept her waiting much longer.

Smiling into her eyes, he laid her down amidst the cushions, his saturnine face blotting out the light as he leaned over her. His lips fastened on hers, his breath tasting of wine, and his tongue delved into and explored the cave of her mouth, wringing such sweet sensations from her that she twisted in his arms, pressing her breasts against the crisp hair coating his chest.

He released her, shrugged off his robe and returned to her body, a hand sweeping her nipples, across her belly and parting her labia, making her sex-pulse flutter. Tossing her head wildly, she arched her back, the fresh weals adding to the sensation. He strummed on her bud, and she was rising on waves of pure delight, straining upwards to reach the precious peak, attaining it in all its glory and falling back down to earth.

Then Theo reared above her, parting her thighs with his knee. He poised there, looking down into her eyes while she murmured incoherent love words, unaware that she was doing so.

She lifted her legs and locked them round his waist. Taking his heavily swollen penis in one hand and supporting his weight on the other, he guided the throbbing helm to her vulva. She flinched, but he ignored her, thrusting with his hips, forcing it all the way in.

Sylvia screamed as her hymen ruptured. He filled her to capacity, stretching the ridged walls and butting against her cervix. She was slippery wet and pain receded as he dragged his phallus in and out, his movements quickening.

She heard the spectators murmur as they watched them copulating, but this was of no consequence. Let them watch. She cared for nothing but the feel of her husband possessing her. Pleasure flowed from his sap-filled bough to her female sheath, and she moved to meet his strokes.

A madness seized her and she ground herself against his pubic bone as it contacted her clitoris, impaling herself on his shaft, matching his rhythm. Her arms clasped him close, her nails raked his glistening back as she pumped harder, harder, wanting him to penetrate deeper, till he touched the very heart of her.

Theo responded, crushing her beneath him. His kisses were savage now, his teeth fastening on her lips, her neck, her breasts. He was an animal clawing its way to satisfaction, and his urgency inflamed her. She became absorbed in him, swallowed up, as nothing compared to his passion and then she felt him convulse, and the wet heat as he spurted his tribute into her.

She lay limply, exhausted by the storm that had raged between them. Theo collapsed, his face buried in the hollow of her shoulder, his cock twitching as it softened inside her. Sylvia needed nothing more, unable to think further than: that was wonderful. When can we do it again?

The spatter of applause rose to a tumult, the audience giving the newly-weds a standing ovation. Theo stirred, propped himself on one elbow, and raised a quizzical eyebrow.

'Well, Lady Aubrey,' he drawled. 'You were a virgin all right. Such hard work, virgins. I had intended to break you in with a lingam, but became carried away, I fear.'

'You had no need to beat me,' she murmured reproachfully, and tightened her internal muscles round his phallus, which started to harden again.

'I did,' he declared. 'I had every reason in the world. You're too impetuous. I'm the one in charge. Now, drink.'

Resting against the pillows, she took the goblet he handed her, placing her lips where his had been. The spectators did not bother her now. Fired by what they had witnessed, they were seeking their own gratification in whatever way they fancied. Farid and Caton were receiving a deal of attention from members of both sexes.

The triangle was constantly occupied and, more than once, Rowena stood before it in a spread-legged stance, a martinet in her high-heeled boots, plying the whip vigorously.

Pleasure splintered through Sylvia as Theo trickled wine over her breasts and licked at the drops, then taunted her labial lips with deft fingers. Pushing her on to her back, he knelt over her and the light slanted across his eyes. They were the colour of sun-filled sherry.

'I'm about to instruct you in the art of fellatio,' he murmured, and brushed her lips with his cock-head.

She tried to pull back, remembering Robert Kelly's abuse of her mouth, but Theo was insistent. As she took him inside she registered desire, not revulsion. His cock tasted of their mingled secretions. Her tongue wrapped round it, enjoying the feel of the velvet-smooth skin. He pressed in further, inch by slippery inch, and then she choked as the clubbed head touched her throat.

Theo stopped, looking pained. 'I hope you aren't going to disappoint me, beloved,' he said. 'This is a skill I insist you acquire. I'll pull out so that you can suck it.'

He slid his penis from between her lips and she instantly missed it, wanting more. He stretched out on his back and his weapon reared upwards, stiff as a lance, a drop of clear liquid hanging like a diamond at its tiny eye.

A whirlpool of desire swirled inside Sylvia. The floodgates of passion had been opened and she wanted more – and more, needing to explore every aspect of this fascinating, terrible, mind-stunningly exciting activity. Now she understood the fever that made even the most respectable woman take the most appalling risks with their reputations. It was sheer insanity, but irresistible.

Oblivious to everything else, she crouched over Theo, her hair brushing his thighs as she put her head between them. He positioned her so that her pudenda was above his face. Even the thought of him looking up at her wide-open cunt did not embarrass her. She longed for him to tongue it, pressing down a little, feeling his warm breath fan the swollen lips. With her back to him, she could not see his face or those piercing eyes, and this encouraged her to be bold.

His penis moved against her mouth, and she grasped it in one hand, then reached below it to cup his testicles, fingers examining the crinkled skin of the sac. He suppressed a groan, but she felt him tremble. Emboldened by this, she ran her tongue up his shaft from base to tip, smelling the musky odour trapped in his pubic bush, sipping the rich brew of his pre-come juice.

She moved the foreskin up then slid it back down, making circles on the glans with the stiff point of her tongue, then washing it in her saliva, taking the jerking organ between her lips again and hollowing her cheeks as she sucked him strongly.

He heaved beneath her, his hands grasping her buttocks, the soreness left by his whip adding to her exaltation. She gave a muffled cry as she felt his tongue on her clitoris, lapping at it, nibbling it, poking into her bruised vagina, returning to her epicentre.

She sucked more wildly, knowing her crisis was near. Her blood throbbed, her heartbeat raced, and she was caught up in a panicky crescendo of sensations that ended in a blur as she spilled over, sighing and sighing against the thickness of his phallus.

He jerked out of her, shouting, 'Enough! Or this will be over before we've begun. I've another way of taking to show you.'

He pushed her from him and rolled her over, facedown among the silks. With a hand under her pelvis he dragged her to her knees and she submitted, his every movement thrilling low in her bud. His hands were on her stripes, fingers running over them as if assessing the damage, and then he spread her buttocks wide, his thumbs pressing on the insides of her thighs. Every one of her treasures was revealed to him – her wet sex-valley, the pink mouth of her vagina, the puckered rose of her anus.

Too limp to protest, Sylvia felt him dip his fingers in her tender, honey-slick core and spread the moisture higher. This was followed by something bigger and harder than a finger. It slid past the hungry vaginal entrance and pressed into the eyelet of her arse. Slowly, painfully, the tight ring opened at his insistence, yielding to the cobra-headed serpent, dilating as he began to take her second virginity.

Sylvia yelled as he suddenly thrust with awful force. She was terrified that she might split asunder. He ground into her pitilessly, past her sphincter till his tool was lodged in the narrowest, most secret part of her body.

He gripped her haunches tightly and reached round to find

her clitoris. He rubbed it, submerging her in a frenzied, blissful convulsion. She could not help shunting her buttocks back and forth, aiding his final victory over her rectum.

The pain was excruciating. So was the overwhelming pleasure.

Shuddering with the shockwaves that ravaged her from head to toe, her muscles closed around his prick, gripping it, feeling it slide into the darkness of her body. She had the sensation of devouring him, taking him into her depths, never to let him go.

Theo groaned with delight, and his cock spasmed as he reached the quintessence of bliss. He cried out and she felt the scalding spurts of his ejaculation. It was as if she had forced it from him, milking him dry, his manhood crushed by her female will.

He slumped against her back, his limp member slipping from her anal ring. Sylvia let her body relax, her legs closing over those secret parts which were once more her own.

She felt his warmth withdrawn, and turned her head to look at him. He was breathing heavily, his hair tousled, his expression baffled, even a touch chagrined. His prick hung slackly, though still enlarged.

'You look surprised, sir,' she said, filled with an afterglow of contentment.

'I am, madam,' he answered, and continued to stare at her while Caton refilled their glasses. 'It seems that far from marrying a shrinking violet, I've taken a man-eater to my bed.'

Theo was not happy. Though his marriage had brought financial security, a large country estate, a stable of thoroughbreds, cotton mills in the North and coal mines in the West, these hardly compensated for a wife who was a shrew.

She was lamentably wilful, despite his frequent use of cane and whip. Balty had just come to him with a long, mournful face. Opening his breeches, he displayed his bandage wrapped phallus.

'What's this?' Theo said, a gleam of amusement in his amber eyes. 'Did a bee sting you? How awkward. You should keep it covered up, my friend, even when swimming. Especially at this time of year.'

Scrope had shown Balty into the smoking den where, amidst oriental splendour, Theo and his intimates indulged in the dreamy, narcotic pleasures of the hookah. He was even dressed the part, in a flowing robe and turban, and his slippers had turned-up toes. Caton sat cross-legged on the floor, playing the flute, the weird cadences of eastern music awakening the echoes. Theo silenced him with a gesture.

'It wasn't a bee,' Balty averred, thoroughly disgruntled as he gingerly lowered himself on to a couch. 'It's that wife of yours. The damned vixen.'

Theo's dark brows winged down in a frown, and his accent was clipped as he said, 'I'll thank you to speak of Lady Aubrey in more gracious terms, sir.'

Balty harrumphed and muttered, 'That's mighty strange, coming from you. Didn't you say I could roger her?'

'Of course. I expected you'd be with her even now, taking your pleasure between her thighs. Didn't you invite her to supper after your visit to the opera last night?'

'I did, and she accepted, though reluctantly, it seemed. Ain't I good enough for her? That's how she makes me feel – inferior, don't-cher-know. She's a hell-cat and don't like me at all,' Balty grumbled, his heavily jowled face suffused with rage.

'I'm sure you're mistaken,' Theo replied, removing the mouthpiece of the pliable tube-like stem from between his lips and handing it to his friend.

Balty sucked at it greedily, the rose water in the bowl bubbling like a miniature kettle. 'I ain't, you know,' he mumbled, relaxing a little as he inhaled the pungent fumes. He ran a finger under his stock and loosened his sky-blue tailcoat. His trousers gaped over his wounded weapon.

Theo nodded towards it, giving a sardonic smile and saying,

'What ails it? I hope you've not got the pox. If so, keep well clear of my lady. My dear fellow, your cock looks like one of those mummified corpses they unearth from the tombs in Egypt, all swaddled in grave wrappings.'

'Ask your wife what happened to it, sir,' Balty fired back at him. 'She did this to me. After supper at my place. I'd been toping well. Was full of lusty feelings towards her. Went in for the kill. I saw how she sucked you on your wedding night and wanted some.'

'Did you force it on her?' Theo asked, his eyes heavy-lidded, his phallus stirring as he imagined Sylvia suffering under Balty's heavy-handed wooing.

'Maybe I was a trifle enthusiastic... got carried away... like a fellow does, you know. I stuffed it in her mouth and the next thing I knew was this blinding agony. She'd sunk her teeth in it! Bloody bitch!' Balty shouted, his face a picture of outraged indignation. 'Could have ruined me for life! And my father's expecting me to marry well and produce an heir. He'll cut me off without a shilling if anything goes wrong with my equipment.'

Theo laid the pipe aside, anger surging through him. He stood up and prowled the floor, his robe billowing behind him. This was too much!

Sylvia had offended one of his oldest and dearest friends. He and Balty had been through Eton together and then Oxford University. They had racketed around the place, got drunk, gambled their allowances away, tumbled whores and generally behaved atrociously as was fully expected of the aristocratic scions of Great Houses.

How dare this upstart from the country refuse to pleasure Balty? Especially when Theo had expressed his wish that she do so.

Two months into marriage and she was becoming increasingly difficult, proving to be an embarrassment. She seemed to have some romantic notion that they should remain faithful to one another. It was ludicrous.

There had been a frightful scene when she found him in bed with Rowena. He had been on the point of releasing his seed and her interruption had infuriated him. She had been soundly whipped for her presumption and made to watch them fornicating. This had not curbed her. Neither had nipple clamps and restraints.

From then on, she seemed to have declared open warfare, even more disobedient and recalcitrant. She refused to allow his friends access to her orifices, made scenes at orgies where everyone else was fully prepared to share their favours and demanded that he made love to her, and her alone.

It was the height of bad manners to say the least, and making him the laughing stock of the town. People were beginning to say that Theo Aubrey was hen-pecked and could not control his wife.

'Where is she now?' he demanded, relieving his feelings by picking up a cane and swishing it viciously, then ordering Caton to bend over a stool and receive half a dozen swipes.

'Don't rightly know. With Rowena, maybe?' Balty answered, his bulging eyes darting to where Caton's bare arse was raised high to receive the strokes, his buttocks wide open, his pouting anus promising fulfilment.

'I think not. They aren't the best of friends. Sylvia has taken a dislike to her, viewing her as a rival for my affections.'

'Not jealous, too!' Balty exclaimed.

'I'm afraid so. I almost wish I'd never married the damn' girl.'

'Got you out of debt though, old chap,' Balty reminded, nursing his cock and adding, 'Lord, but this thumps. It'll be weeks before I can use it. Can't even contemplate giving it a good frigging.'

'I'll whip Sylvia, but I don't think it will profit me,' Theo said, taking to the divan again, legs tucked under him. 'It's time for stronger measures. I'll need you to help me. Here's what we'll do.'

Sylvia tried to ease herself into a more comfortable position on the whipping block. She wanted to speak, but a three-inch long, penis shaped gag had been stuffed into her mouth and fastened securely. The vault was deeply shadowed, the flares casting a lurid glow.

She knew what was coming, half terrified, half warmed by the thought of it. Theo would beat her and then take her, subjecting her to torment and intense pleasure, one feeling overlapping the other.

She could hear him moving behind her, the sound of his footsteps, the rustle of his ballooning shirt sleeves. She caught his smell, too, that familiar, exciting body odour that she would recognise anywhere.

The block was contrived to lift her buttocks high, while her arms were stretched down and manacled to struts on one side, her ankles on the other. She was powerless to move.

She knew why she was about to be punished. She had bitten Balty's cock, and felt no remorse. Let Theo be as cruel as he liked, she still treasured the surge of satisfied revenge as her teeth had clamped down on Balty's small fat phallus. He'd had a job to hold an erection, she recalled, too far gone in his cups. She smiled grimly round the gag. With any luck, he'd never get one again, his self-esteem taking a severe jolt.

Now he was in the vault to witness her chastisement. This was the worst part, and she resolved not to give him the pleasure of seeing her cry, glad the gag had been inserted. It would prevent her from screaming. Whatever happened she would cling to her dignity, neither moan nor writhe or discharge her bladder.

This would be easier thought than done, for she was certain Theo would choose an instrument calculated to cause her the most grief.

She heard him pacing round to the side of the block where her head hung down. She focused on the toes of his highly polished boots as he came to rest before her. His crotch was on a level with her eyes, and he was aroused, the fabric of his skin-tight breeches stretched to capacity over his swollen phallus.

He gripped a handful of her hair and jerked her head up at a painful angle. 'Look, wife,' he grated harshly, and his golden eyes blazed as they pierced hers. 'This is the tool I shall use to punish such a naughty girl. Bite my friend, would you? Let this bite *you*, my dear.'

The thing in his hand rustled as he held it close to her eyes. It was shorter than his usual whip, with a thick stock from which trailed a dozen plaited thongs, each one knotted at the end. Sylvia's sphincter clenched and, like an animal in danger, she needed to empty herself.

She clung on, fixing her thoughts on the serpent in his breeches, hoping he would reward her later, when he had appeased his wrath by flaying her shrinking flesh.

But it was another woman's black-gloved hand that appeared from behind him to cradle his erection. Sylvia caught her seductive perfume and glared up at her.

'Theo, let me beat her, too,' murmured Rowena in honeyed accents. 'After all, I am her guardian.'

'You were, my love, but no longer. I am in sole charge of her,' Theo replied, letting Sylvia's head flop down once more. 'You may watch, however, and help Balty's poor wounded prick to revive. There's no one more skilled in handling a man's tool than you.' He thrust the tawse at Sylvia's gagged lips, adding, 'Kiss the instrument that will bring you to heel.'

She felt the brush of the leather and smelled its strong aroma. It was immediately withdrawn, and Theo left her. A bead of sweat trickled from her hairline and coursed down her face. The tension was terrible, every minute seeming to stretch into an hour.

There was a rushing sound behind and a bolt of lighting seemed to hit her. Despite her resolutions, Sylvia found it impossible to stifle a cry, teeth clamping on the wooden phallus that filled her aching mouth. White-hot waves crashed over her buttocks as the individual lashes bit home. Before she had time to recover, they seared her again, spreading their punishment wide.

Her buttocks contracted and relaxed, quivered and throbbed as Theo trained the tawse on the fatty underhang and the tops of her thighs. The thongs sang as they rose high and crashed down again, and anguish exploded in Sylvia's depths. She flung her head about, although it added to her torment, the binding holding the gag cutting into her mouth.

Somewhere, out of timeless agony, she heard Balty crying triumphantly as Rowena dragged an orgasm from his damaged prick. Then there was only hell, a blazing inferno of pain. Sylvia endured, hanging on to her sanity by a thread. She clenching her inner muscles to hold in her water, concentrating on this achievement, stubbornly determined not to let go and give them the satisfaction of seeing her wet herself.

She relapsed into a blazing world of semi-consciousness, inert, almost lifeless, vaguely aware of the continued hiss and smack of the lashes, hardly realising it when they ceased.

Hands were on her now, Theo's she was sure, coated in fragrant, slippery oil that stung, then cooled her burning flesh. The oil went lower, running between her bottom crease, and his fingers opened her nether hole, easing the fluid round the tight anal ring.

The flame of desire warmed her, the ache of her stripes mingling with lustful passion. His cock slid into her, past that obstructive circle that softened to receive it, plunging into the very depths of her abused body. Theo moved in and out, taking his pleasure slowly, and Sylvia clenched her muscles round that invasive prick, the anointing oil running down to smear his cock-base and mingle with his pubic hair that brushed her avenue.

Her clitoris ached to be rubbed forcefully, the violence done to her exciting her nubbin. Theo held her whole pudenda in the palm of his hand the more to increase his thrust into her anus. His thumb frigged her clit, and Sylvia was lost in sensation. Passion gnawed at her loins and tears ran down her face as he took her to a blinding, obliterating orgasm.

Rowena took Sylvia's head in her hands and removed the gag. Barely recovered from that shattering climax, the convulsions still shaking her, Sylvia stared at the bare pubis that appeared before her, the dark red lips wet and parted between the silken, perfumed folds of Rowena's raised skirt.

The fingers clenched in Sylvia's hair and, as Theo pumped his cock into her fundament, so she opened her mouth and sucked at Rowena's sex. She ran her tongue over the folds, tasting the musky juices, and finding the button of the clitoris, the wellspring of her aunt's pleasure. It was like a cock, yet so much smaller, its very neatness thrilling Sylvia. She sucked and licked and fondled it with her tongue, till Rowena spread her legs wider, thrusting upwards with her hips, gasping with pleasure.

Sylvia's own sex was ablaze.

Behind her, she heard Theo give a single, barking cry as the semen jetted from him into her nether passage. Then both her lovers withdrew, glutted with pleasure, leaving her hanging over the whipping block.

He spoke then, his voice echoing under the vaulted ceiling, 'You'll stay here tonight, Sylvia, to reflect on your disgraceful behaviour.'

She shook her head vigorously and mumbled, 'Free me, sir. I've paid my debt.'

He stared down at her with his vulpine eyes, saying, 'From the block, maybe, but you'll be tethered here till I say you can return to take your place among civilised people.'

Caton loosened her bonds and Sylvia cautiously lowered her naked feet to the cold flagstones, her body weak and trembling, every movement agonising. She leaned an arm against the block, taking her weight and cautiously testing her ability to stand. Theo's rapidly cooling emission slithered from her anus and down her thighs.

Balty sat in a carved chair, his legs astraddle, that pathetic penis limp between them, the indentations made by Sylvia's fangs showing fiery red. He grinned across at her and waggled his prick, shouting, 'You ain't damaged it too much, she-devil! It spat at you while you were receiving your just reward.'

'I should have completed the job and bitten the thing right off!' Sylvia snarled viciously. 'Then thrown it out in the street for dogs to eat!'

'Be silent!' Theo thundered.

He grabbed her arms and chained her to one of the several stone pillars. 'I'm cold,' she muttered, dragging at the manacles on her wrists. 'You have no right to do this.'

'A husband has undisputed control of his wife,' Theo said icily. 'You'd do well to ponder on this, madam.'

'I hate you!' Sylvia hissed, glaring up at him. 'No, you don't,' he said with a mocking laugh. 'You're a hot-arsed strumpet who loves everything I do to her. But you'll have to manage without me, my dear... for a while.'

'What d'you mean?' Sylvia demanded suspiciously, trying to find a comfortable position on the hard floor, her bottom one throbbing ache.

'I'm going away,' he answered, standing before her, balancing himself on wide spread legs.

'Away?' she repeated, unsure whether to be glad or sorry.

'To Greece. I feel the need of warm sunshine, balmy breezes and boys with skin like coppery velvet,' he pronounced, watching her warily.

'And I?'

'You will stay here, until I send for you. Rowena will be in charge and you'll obey her to the letter. Don't think you can cause trouble, for I shall be informed of your behaviour.'

Sylvia managed to give a defiant toss of her head, though the action cost her dear. 'Ha! You think I'll miss you? I shall enjoy the respite from your odious company,' she brought out, adding venomously, 'and your even more odious cock.'

His face tightened, eyes fierce, then he smiled and flicked across one of her nipples. Pleasure stabbed her vitals and she could not repress a gasp. 'You think to queen it here, perhaps, make Burbank Abbey the scene of lustful couplings? Not so, madam. I shall ensure you do not.'

Rowena brought forward a carved box and he took a pair of nipple clamps from its plush depths, then seized one of Sylvia's breasts and pinched the tip hard. She cried out as the metal teeth snapped over her tortured teat. Theo slapped her other breast and repeated his action. Then he drew out a curious purse-like object made of gold. It was the size of a female pudenda, and, with Rowena's assistance, he forced Sylvia's legs apart and slipped it over her shaven mound.

It fitted perfectly, a rigid dome fastened tightly with thin chains around her hips and passing into the crack of her bottom. It contained her sex absolutely, and Theo secured it tightly with a small padlock and gave Rowena the key.

'A chastity belt?' Sylvia whispered.

'That's right. You'll wear it at all times.'

'But what about bodily functions?' she cried, this humiliating object the most shameful thing she had yet experienced.

'Rowena or Nairi will remove it when necessary, and be with you throughout the voiding of bladder or bowels. You'll not be permitted to masturbate, and neither of them will play with your clitoris, no matter how much you plead for relief,' he said, and touched the gold mesh casket that contained her jewels.

The clamps on her nipples seemed to tighten. Tears stung her eyes, glistening like emeralds as she stared into his cruel, beautiful face.

'And how long will this continue?' she asked at last.

'I don't know. It will be my decision as to when you are freed. I shall write to Rowena and have you dispatched to me at Zante. You'll enjoy the Greek islands, but I warrant anything will seem like heaven to you after weeks of enforced celibacy. By that time you'll be in such a ferment of lust that even Balty will seem desirable. Just imagine it, Sylvia... no cocks, no juicy cunts... no chance to caress yourself to climax. You'll be chaste as a nun, my dear.'

Chapter Ten

The deck rose and fell beneath Sylvia's feet, but this persistent motion no longer compelled her to empty the contents of her stomach over the side of the sailing ship.

The *Dover Star* had been travelling for days, negotiating the treacherous Bay of Biscay and rounding Gibraltar into the placid waters of the Mediterranean Sea. That morning, Sylvia and Phoebe crept from their cabin, ashen-faced and debilitated. The sun shone down on them, the azure sea and sky almost dazzling, the white sails billowing overhead as the vessel bore them towards their destination.

The island of Zante, where Theo waited.

Three months had passed since his departure and Sylvia had very nearly forgotten what he looked like. True to his word, he had ordained that she wear the chastity belt constantly during his absence. Then, at last, he had sent instructions that she should join him. Rowena had removed this impediment for good when she went on board to see her off, but Sylvia had proved to be such a bad sailor that she had been unable to relieve the lust that had raged for weeks beneath the little golden dome.

Perhaps tonight, she promised herself, and her vagina ached, the dew of arousal moistening the feathery floss that had grown again on her *mons veneris*. Tonight I can indulge myself in a long, leisurely, solitary frig, or maybe have Phoebe share my bunk. Perhaps both! The prospect was dizzying.

During the wretched illness that had laid her low, she had spent no time with the captain and officers. Now she made note of several likely looking lads among the crew. They were ogling her, while pretending to be about their duties.

The master of the ship, Captain Dabney, came down the

steps from the quarterdeck, a splendid figure in a blue uniform, his face weather-beaten, eyes crinkled at the outer corners as if forever scouring the horizon in search of tempests or enemies.

'Ah, Lady Aubrey. Quite recovered from your indisposition, I trust?' he pronounced in those fruity accents favoured by navy officers. 'A devilish bad business, *mal de mar*. Most passengers suffer from it, particularly in turbulent waters.'

'Thank you, sir, I am much better,' Sylvia replied, glad that she had had the forethought to have Phoebe dress her hair, then help her into a stylish gown and drape a paisley-patterned shawl about her shoulders.

'Delighted to hear it. I hope you'll grace my table at luncheon,' the captain said, bowing gallantly.

'I will, sir. I feel in need of company. Shall we be arriving in Zante soon?'

'Indeed yes, madam. You're eager to see your husband, I dare swear,' he replied with a twinkle. 'Not long a bride, I hear. Too bad he had to go away.'

She nodded and rested her elbows on the rail again, looking out over the sparkling water that separated her from Theo.

Had she missed him? It was a moot point. She had missed his cock, his expert lovemaking, the excitement of his presence, which stirred her into a frenzy. But had she really missed *him*? Who was he, anyway? She did not know.

He had made her suffer, depriving her of freedom. Even when the nipple clamps had been removed and she was permitted to leave the vault, reside in the house and go out with Rowena, she had been constantly aware of the restricting belt beneath her clothes.

It had chafed her tender inner thighs, prevented her from answering the call of nature without assistance and added to the inconvenience of her monthly flux. Forever there, like a firm hand snuggling her mound, it constantly drew her attention to her sex but prevented her from satisfying herself.

Though raging against it and deeply resentful, she had grown accustomed to the belt's confinement. It felt strange without it. Now she was aware of her damp cleft, longing to run her fingers over the freshly sprouting bush and rub her tiny erection till the build up of tension was released.

'This weather, milady! Isn't it grand?' said slum-born Phoebe, in a transport of delight. 'Who'd have thought I'd be journeying to foreign places. And it's all down to you.'

Sylvia smiled. It was more than the sun and sea that was exciting her maid. The plethora of hulking males working on the deck and climbing the rigging had much to do with it. Phoebe had filled out, her bosom shapely, her hips wide enough to accommodate the most well blessed of men. She had recovered her confidence, arch and flirtatious, gathering quite a following among the menservants at Burbank Abbey and Laurel House.

Sylvia was aware of a lightness of heart long absent. When the bell clanged for lunch, she went into the main cabin. The *Dover Star* was a merchantman, but also carried passengers when the need arose. The cabin was large, with windows curving along the stern. The furnishings were of fine quality, the woodwork and metal fittings gleaming.

The oak table in the centre was bolted to the floor to prevent it moving during a storm, and there were chairs on either side. Seated on the captain's right hand, Sylvia studied him and his officers. It seemed that she was the only passenger present, Phoebe taking her meals in the stateroom she shared with her mistress. Sylvia was treated with the greatest courtesy, the crewmembers delighted to have a lady among them.

The remainder of the trip promised to be pleasant, and she cast a speculative eye over the midshipmen in their dark blue jackets ornamented with rows of brass buttons, their tight white breeches displaying muscular thighs with highly provocative bulges between.

She realised that her feelings of late had been ones of acute boredom. Maybe one of these bright young sprigs would help her pass the time till they docked at Zante. It would serve Theo right if she took her pleasure with another man's prick.

Scheming how this could be accomplished, she retired to lie on a daybed under an awning during the afternoon. It was hot and somnolent, and she was tempted to go below to her cabin, there to masturbate, the blood flowing like fire in her veins as she thought of taking a lover. Her nipples rose against the fragile bodice. She fidgeted restlessly, unable to sleep, and then the rocking of the ship lulled her into a half-waking dream.

She came to herself with a start, aware of Captain Dabney's crisp voice issuing orders, feet running, men shouting. Phoebe appeared at her side, yawning and sleepy-eyed, saying,

'What's all the rumpus, milady?'

'I don't know.'

Sylvia got to her feet, and she and Phoebe ran up the steps to the poop where the captain stood, a brass telescope to one eye. He had it trained on a vessel in the distance, under full sail and advancing towards them at a rapid rate of knots.

He lowered the glass when he saw Sylvia, and said, 'You should go below, madam.'

'Why?' she asked, the breeze lifting the curls that wisped on her brow. She, too, stared at the vessel as it came on with ominous speed, tall and black, surging powerfully beneath a mountain of canvas.

'She carries no flag and has ignored my signals to name herself and her business,' he replied, his face set in stern line. 'Frankly, marm, I don't like the cut of her jib. These waters are haunted by corsairs.'

'Corsairs? And what, pray, Captain Dabney, are they?'

'Pirates, Lady Aubrey, sea wolves seeking prey. They use Moorish ports as hideaways, and are thieves and slavers, scum of the earth devoid of honour.'

'Are you going to fight them?' Phoebe squeaked, her face paling under its light dusting of freckles.

'I'm duty bound to protect my cargo and passengers,' he answered. 'The *Dover Star* is not fast enough to make a run for it. Perhaps my fears are groundless and she is an honest vessel in need of assistance.'

Sylvia stared till her eyes ached, watching the steady way in which the sinister black ship bore down on them. Suddenly, a puff of white smoke gusted from the beakhead and a boom reverberated across the water. Spray shot up as a cannonball landed in the sea just beyond the merchantman's prow.

'Sweet Jesus, save us!' Phoebe cried, clasping her hands to her breasts.

'Calm down, girl!' Captain Dabney shouted. 'It was a warning shot. They are telling us to heave to.'

He darted away, giving orders for flags to be raised in answer to the stranger's signal. The black ship came nearer, shortening sail. Every detail was clear in the brilliant sunshine. It was ornate, terrifying, magnificent, so close now that Sylvia could see men leaning from the rails and swarming on the ropes. They were grim-faced and silent, weapons clenched in their fists. Some were black, their gleaming skin contrasting with white turbans, scimitars glittering. Others were European, sun-browned hellions with rat-tailed moustaches and full beards, greasy hair banded by tattered scarves. A few were striplings on their first venture.

Dabney had lined his men up, muskets at the ready. The moment had come. The merchantman shuddered as, with a shattering impact, the two ships ground together. Timbers rent under the bite of grappling irons, making the *Dover Star* a prisoner.

'Lay down your arms!' commanded the corsair leader, a big-built man who swung aboard, a pistol aimed at Dabney's chest. 'Do as I say and no one shall be harmed.'

'This is an outrage!' the captain shouted. 'What do you want?'

The pirate bared his teeth in a wolfish grin. 'Women!' he answered, while his men roared with laughter.

'You're an Englishman, by God!' Dabney blustered. 'You scoundrel, sir, attacking your fellow countrymen!'

'I'm not about to harm a hair of anyone's head, providing you obey me to the letter,' the pirate said smoothly and his eyes lit up as they fastened on Sylvia.

Her knees weakened with terror, but her sex pulsed and throbbed. He was agile and muscular, his clothing splendid but dirty, waist spanned by a silk sash and a whip coiled round him like a snake. He moved with an arrogant swagger, a swashbuckler who cared for no one. His nose curved, set between flashing dark eyes, and he was already aroused, an erection straining his crimson velvet breeches.

He strode towards Sylvia with a clack of black leather top-boots. Gold hoops gleamed in his ears, half concealed by dark, oily hair. She gasped as his hand shot out, gripping one of her breasts and dragging her towards him. Heat flamed from her nipple to her clitoris, and she could smell him, a potent conglomeration of male sweat, salt spray and brandy.

His stubbly chin rasped against her face as he pounced on her mouth, holding her tightly as his tongue dived between her lips. It was big and fleshy, tangling with hers, his saliva strong as dittany. His kiss was ravaging and contemptuous, and his erection rubbed against her thigh. He chuckled deep in his throat, pressing her to his groin, leaving her in no doubt as to his intention.

He was a filthy blackguard, a pirate, a slaver, yet Sylvia was filled with lubricious need, her vulva clenching, her clitoris a bead longing to be threaded on his tongue and suckled by his lips.

He felt her response, even as she struggled, and he lifted his head from hers and smiled into her eyes, triumphant and masterful.

'Captain Dabney! Help! You can't let him take me!' Sylvia shouted, her hands wide-spread as she tried to claw at the pirate's face.

He ducked, caught them, lashed her wrists together firmly, then swung her off her feet and lay her over his shoulder. She yelled with fury, her hair a tumbling mass of curls, falling across his back.

The captain rested a hand on the hilt of his cutlass. 'I can't aid you, Lady Aubrey,' he said, and he refused to meet her eyes. 'Go with them and do as they say. It is for the best, I promise you.'

'You're a coward, captain, and I'll see that my husband hears of this,' she raged, longing to feel a dagger in her hand, wanting to kill the rogue who held her.

'I pray that you'll be reunited with him one day, my lady,' Dabney said, a note of regret in his voice.

Another of the pirates seized Phoebe, though she fought like a cat as he hauled her over his broad shoulder. Sylvia could hear her spitting fury and screaming abuse, but was too winded to do other than endure as her captor strode across the gang-plank linking the ships and set her down on the deck with a force that made her teeth rattle. She attempted to spring away, but he stamped a foot on her hem, bringing her up with a jerk. She was tied to the mast, along with Phoebe, while the ship set sail, the *Dover Star* becoming no more than a dot on the horizon.

Then the leader paced over to Sylvia, bowing mockingly and saying, 'Torr Hearn, at your service, Lady Aubrey.'

'You scoundrel!' she stormed 'How dare you abduct me?' She wanted to weep, but would not allow the tears to come.

On every side she saw grinning, lecherous faces. They laughed, elbowed one another, made rude gestures, panting, waiting.

For what? For *her*? Sylvia shuddered.

'I dare anything,' Torr answered, eyeing his men sternly, the only barrier between her and their low-grade lusts.

'Where are you taking me?'

'To the slave market,' he answered.

Visions of harems and despotic sultans filled her imagination. Rowena had once told her that this is what happened to captive white women, much in demand in Islamic countries. She had made it sound fun, almost a desirable adventure, but the possible reality was appalling.

'You can't do that!' she cried.

Torr bent his dark head and sucked at her right breast through the muslin, his tongue arousing the nipple to a sharp peak. This evoked gales of merriment from his men and a torrent of shameful desire in Sylvia.

'I have plans for you,' he murmured, a faintly cryptic smile forming on his lips.

Sylvia spat full in his face.

He grabbed her by the hair, jerking her head back and banging it against the mast. 'Bitch!' he snarled. 'You shall pay for that!'

'Let me go,' she cried, stars dancing before her eyes. 'I'm a titled Englishwoman.'

He withdrew a little, wiping her spittle from his cheek. 'You want me to untie you?' he asked, with a taunting smile.

'Yes. Deliver me safely to my husband at Zante, and you'll be amply rewarded.'

He shrugged, and loosened her bonds. She stepped away from the mast, but still kept it at her back. His men were watching like a pack of hungry animals, mouths open, saliva running. Several had taken fully erect cocks from their trousers and were rubbing them, others had their hands sunk deep inside their breeches, fingering their balls and cocks.

She heard Phoebe give a frightened sob, and then suddenly Torr unwound the whip from his waist. He flourished it in front of Sylvia, its short handle fitted with a metal joint to allow the lash full play.

With a flick of his wrist, he made it crack against the decking at her feet. She danced away. The ship was in an uproar, his men urging him on, forming a wide circle. They stood on the bulwarks, even hung from the shrouds to obtain a better view.

'You bastard!' Sylvia stormed.

Too late she realised that the whistling in the air was the sound of the lash coming down. With unerring accuracy, Torr wrapped the leather thong round the top of her dress and ripped the material away, leaving her stinging breasts bare. He struck again, the rawhide tangling in the gown, reducing it to ribbons that dangled from her shoulders, her body gleaming through the tatters, breasts, belly and brown pubic floss exposed. Sylvia hunched over, trying to hide herself.

So far the whip had merely caressed her flesh, and in the midst of her distress, a dark heat warmed her womb, the memory of past beatings and past orgasms filling her with strange, voluptuous pleasure. Her welts and bruises had healed long ago, leaving her back, buttocks and thighs smooth and white.

Oh, Theo! Husband – master! she cried within her soul.

The sky, the white sails, the whole unreal scene was fractured across by tears. Then the lash seared her again, and she bit her lip so hard she could taste blood on her tongue. She tried to fly from the strokes, but met a wall of masculine arms that simply flung her back into the circle to meet that avenging whip.

Torr laid it on with slow strokes, and Sylvia fell to her knees amidst hoarse, raucous cheers, completely naked now, save for a few strips of muslin. She fought for breath and tried to steady herself, the new welts burning and throbbing with that well-remembered pain.

Torr threw the whip aside and undid his breeches, then stood, spread-legged, before her. She stared at the hard length of his penis, his testicles two weighty fruits dangling below it. He seemed to tower above her, silhouetted against the blue sky. And his cock was immense from that angle, a solid bar of flesh, the shaft thick veined, the snout clubbed, shining and red, with a crystal tear quivering at its eye.

One of his hands gripped her shoulder, pushing back and back till she sprawled on the deck. Then he parted her legs and stared down at her treasures, the wet fissure, the rosy anus, the swollen clit. He lowered himself on her, his teeth biting at her nipples, his lips sucking and feeding at those hard teats. Raising himself to his knees, he thrust hard, his buttocks powering his cock as he forced it into her till she was sure she could take no more.

Passion shook her – the harshness of the flooring grating

against her weals – the brutal chafing of his cock-base as he worked his weapon in and out, rubbing against her clitoris. She kicked her legs up over his shoulders, drawing him deeper into her core. Her own hips pumped shamelessly, grinding up and down in the same rhythm, and he drove her to an intense climax which left her mindless and shaking.

She clung to him as he reached his own orgasm, his penis twitching as it discharged its load.

His men, worked to a frenzy, had edged closer. They were almost uncontrollable and a great, hairy ruffian leaned over the prone couple, shouting, 'My turn next, Hearn! I'm second-in-command here.'

Torr roused himself, drawing his penis from Sylvia's body and getting to his feet, tucking it inside his breeches and fastening up.

He reached down a hand and offered it to her and, as she rose, clamped an arm about her body possessively.

'You can't have her. No one can. She's mine for the rest of the voyage,' he said tersely. 'Take her Abigail; she looks more than willing. Let the dice decide who wins her,' and, so saying, he guided Sylvia down a short flight of steps and into his cabin.

She took one last, desperate look over her shoulder to where Phoebe was seated on a barrel, watching in round-eyed anticipation. The bosun and first mate crouched on the boards, spitting on their palms and sweating with eagerness as they hovered over the pair of dice, about to throw and let the little ivory cubes settle her fate.

Torr pushed Sylvia down on the tangled, sweat-soaked sheets of the bed, rolled her over and proceeded to push his stiff prick into her nether hole. 'Jesus, you're tight there,' he panted, his voice husky with lust. 'Tight as a virgin, darling.'

She moaned with pain and pleasure mixed, her thighs bruised, her weals throbbing, her love-tunnel sore. Torr seemed obsessed with her, and had given her no rest since he took her to his cabin. Her celibacy seemed a distant dream. In him she had found a virile, tireless, inventive lover. Yet she burned with shame. Here she was, Lady Sylvia Aubrey, delirious with pleasure under the thrusting, lusting body of a pirate!

Yet she could not resist him. He had not raped her; she was more than ready, fascinated by the length and thickness of his member. It reared to touch his navel, twitching and bucking as if it had a life of its own, a truly splendid endowment.

The hours had passed, and she had been hardly aware. Torr had stopped fucking her long enough to light a lantern that swayed on a gimbal overhead, the better to view her swollen, slippery wet parts. He had sucked her to completion, and then thrust his huge, dark-skinned penis into her mouth. Later, he had taken up his belt and amused himself by thrashing her, gaining further arousal by seeing the leather whack down across her already striped buttocks, drawing redness to any skin left untouched.

Now, her knees were drawn under her, touching the underside of her bosom, and he was thrusting his penis into her anus that, due to her position, was as conspicuous as her vaginal orifice. He started to move, and she felt that great mushroom-shaped head penetrating beyond the first ring, and the tense sac of his scrotum tapping against the backs of her thighs.

She was awash with sweat, sticky with the fluid of former copulation. Torr had his hand under her mound, a finger tickling her clitoris. Far from being weary, her bud thrived on the constant stimulation and repeated bursts of orgasm.

I could stay with him forever, Sylvia thought, having entered that timeless, irresponsible state brought about by almost continual coition. Torr's cock, stabbing into her tight interior, seemed like some huge, inhuman bore reaming her. He pinched the head of her clit and she yelled as she came. He echoed her cry, her forceful anal contractions milking him of his seminal fluid.

Later he lay on the bed watching her, an amused smile curving his full, sensual lips. 'What's your name?' he asked, lazy and relaxed as men are after their spunk has been thoroughly drained from their testes.

'Sylvia,' she replied, sinking her teeth into a luscious grape and letting the juice run over her tongue.

A cabin boy had brought in supper, a surprisingly tasty meal as it turned out, consisting of crusty bread baked in the galley, dried beef and an ample supply of fruit and wine.

'Sylvia,' he repeated softly. 'Ah, so sweet a name. It reminds me of forest glades in England during spring, and rippling streams, wild flowers… and peace.'

'But you're a bloodthirsty pirate, aren't you?' she said, running her hands over his copper-hued body, and fondling his limp cock.

'I am now,' he replied, guiding her hand to the tip, his weapon thickening again under her caresses. 'I was a soldier, fought against Bonaparte, but was penniless after the war. The opportunity for profit arose and I gathered a few old comrades around me and became a sailor instead.'

'What are you going to do with me?' she asked, reality impinging on her sensual dreams.

'We're sailing to Marseilles, and there, sweetheart, I shall sell you at the auction block.'

'How brutal and unfeeling!' she cried, rising to her knees at his side, her naked body gleaming in the lamplight, purple in the shadows, gold where the light struck.

He shrugged and tweaked her nipple. It immediately responded. 'You're the most amorous little baggage I've come across in many a moon, but I'm afraid I'll have to part with you. Needs must when the devil drives,' he said a touch regretfully.

'But I have no clothes. Nothing. My trunks were left aboard the *Dover Star*,' she exclaimed, a frown drawing her wing-shaped brows together.

'You won't need clothes where you're going,' he said, and eased down beside her, fingers coiled in the short curls of her pubis, tugging at them gently.

A pang of fear over-rode desire as Sylvia considered the meaning of his words. What lay ahead, and could she cope with it? Would she ever see Theo again?

Torr had said they would be dropping anchor soon, and Sylvia, who had spent the entire time in his cabin, was joined by Phoebe.

They embraced and stood back, examining one another with anxious eyes and, 'How did you fare?' Sylvia asked. 'Was it very terrible?'

'Oh, no, my lady,' Phoebe answered, the morning sunlight falling on her head, her tip-tilted nipples and sparse pussy hair. 'Those poor lads... deprived of female company... forced to fuck one another. 'Tis no fun being at sea, madam.'

'You're positively blooming,' Sylvia observed, smiling.

'And you, too, milady – if you don't mind my saying so.'

The ship dropped anchor in a small, secluded bay just outside the busy port of Marseilles. Torr ducked his tall head under the cabin's lintel when he came to fetch them.

'But we're naked,' Sylvia protested, rising to her feet, fear ripping through her.

Torr gave a smile, fondling her breasts, and saying, 'I've already told you that clothes are unnecessary.'

'Please, Torr. We can't be thus exposed to public eye,' she begged, while her wayward body was urging her to open his breeches and fondle his weapon for one last time.

He shrugged under his wide-sleeved white shirt and found two lengths of gauze, one pink, the other green, saying, 'Drape yourselves in these. In fact, it will serve to make you even more alluring. The buyers will be curious to see what's beneath.'

'You're really going to sell me?' Sylvia asked, as she wound the fragile material around her body like a sari.

'Of course,' he answered, completely without remorse.

It was hot in the bay, making Sylvia fully aware that she was now in an almost tropical climate. Silver sand stretched in a horseshoe curve, and palm trees waved their graceful feathery heads. The air was redolent with the scent of orange trees and olive groves.

The ship had dropped anchor a little way out and she had been brought ashore in a long-boat. Torr had carried her, wading through the wavelets, then setting her down on the sand. The bosun had borne Phoebe in his mighty arms, but now the women were chained together, manacles on their wrists and ankles.

'This isn't necessary,' Sylvia protested.

'I think it is,' Torr replied, testing the security of the links. 'You don't obey orders willingly, and would escape if you could.' He gave the leading chain a jerk and she was forced to move forward, Phoebe behind her.

'I thought we were going to Marseilles,' she said.

'Not into the port proper,' he replied, and gave a lop-sided grin. 'I refuse to give part of my takings to the customs men. Slavery is outlawed, but I have contacts and we meet at this secret rendezvous. There are always those eager to buy from corsairs.'

There was a road ahead, lined with wooden buildings that resembled warehouses. Stevedores heaved barrels and crates of merchandise from the cool, dim interiors and loaded them on to wagons drawn by teams of shire horses.

Several elegant, open-topped chaise were drawn up in the shade, with liveried coachmen, postilians, and sharply dressed 'tigers', black faces gleaming under tricorne hats, awaiting the return of their masters or mistresses.

Sylvia was led under the portico of the biggest building, the sudden coolness making her shiver after the heat outside. She was in a large rectangular room, the floor strewn with sawdust, a clerk seated on a high stool before a desk at the entrance, a raised platform at the opposite end.

Chairs and small round tables were placed around this arena, and these were already occupied by gentlemen, drinking wine or demitasses of strong coffee, taking snuff and chatting with a sprinkling of refined, fashionably dressed ladies.

There were two pens behind the platform, and Sylvia could see one contained women as scantily clad as herself, and the other young, strong, good looking males. They were completely naked. The audience commented on them, rising from their chairs to approach the cages, the ladies perusing the contents as if they were goods on display in a shop window. The gentlemen prodded them, reached through the bars to cup a full breast or fondle silky maidenhair, then passing on to the males, pinching muscles, tweaking phalli and forcing jaws wide so that teeth could be examined.

But there was one women in particular who paid them no heed, her eyes fixed on Sylvia. She was dressed in black from head to foot, a widow's veil thrown back over her bonnet. With her sharp nose and birdlike eyes she reminded Sylvia of a crow. For some reason she could not fathom, this dame frightened her more than all of the rest put together.

'It's like a cattle market!' she challenged Torr, tawny head high, though her legs trembled beneath her. 'You can't seriously suggest I take my place among these unfortunate slaves.'

'There's no question about it,' he replied, stroking her roughly between the legs, the thin green fabric darkening with the juices lubricating her cleft. 'I've arranged with the auctioneer that you shall be the first item of this morning's sale.'

'Pimp!' she hissed, and tugged fruitlessly at the chain. A bespectacled man in a sober grey suit now climbed to the platform, standing at a rostrum to one side. He made an announcement in French, but Sylvia had learned this language at the academy and could understand the gist of it.

'Ladies and gentlemen,' he said, gavel in hand. 'I am delighted to have on offer a selection of slaves to serve you in any way you desire. The men are fit and strong, suitable to be field hands or house servants, or what you will. The women are young and comely. They can be employed as waiting maids or for whatever purpose you desire. The sale will now commence and I am ready to take your bids.'

The buyers murmured, in their seats once more.

Sylvia and Phoebe were dragged forward by Torr, stumbling as they climbed the shallow steps till they reached the centre of the little stage. There the chains were fastened to a ring in the floor.

Sylvia could not believe this was actually happening to her, the horror and shame of it beyond comprehension. On every side were keen, appraising eyes, some of the expressions plain lustful, some speculative. Only the woman in black showed no emotion, seated in a special chair where she had an uninterrupted view.

Torr pushed Sylvia forward and raised her arms on either side so that her breasts lifted, the pink nipples hardening against the gauze. The wrist-cuffs and dangling chains that shackled her shone in the strong rays that poured through the skylights overhead. She felt his boot between her ankles, kicking her legs apart and she struggled to keep her balance, muffling a sob.

'What am I bid for this peerless English rose?' the auctioneer said crisply. 'Her maid will be thrown in for good measure. Thus you'll obtain two for the price of one. A bargain, if ever I saw one. Anyone here give me fifty guineas?'

The bidding commenced, fast and furious, a hundred guineas reached in a few seconds, and Sylvia could see through a blur of tears, that the woman in black did no more than raise the little finger of her gloved right hand.

'One hundred and ten, anywhere?' The auctioneer asked, gimlet eyes raking the crowd through his glasses. They returned to the woman in black and he said, 'What about you, Madame Fedora?'

'Is she accustomed to the cane?' she asked.

'I am informed that she takes her beatings well,' the auctioneer replied. 'Would you like a demonstration?'

Madame Fedora nodded.

Torr forced Sylvia to bow from the waist and then he snatched the cane that one of the auctioneer's helpers offered. She struggled, but he held her firmly and the springy rod smacked down on her buttocks.

The crowd lost some of their reserve, cheering loudly. Even the ladies clapped their mittened hands together, their eyes bright, cheeks flushing.

Sylvia was in hell, her heart pounding, the sweat trickling from beneath her breasts and armpits. It was beyond endurance. She was nothing but a spectacle to amuse a crowd of rich, pleasure-seeking foreigners whose jaded palates were titillated by this sale of human beings.

The rod cracked down for a second time and she writhed in Torr's grip, anticipating and receiving another scalding blow. Then she felt him worming the tip of the rod beneath her draperies, between the crease of her bottom till it finally rested in her labia. She squirmed against this invasive prong, her already wet lips swelling. Unable to help herself, she wriggled her hips, pressing her clit to the cane's smooth surface, fiery pleasure stabbing into that eager little organ.

There was a renewed wave of clapping and shouting, and the auctioneer bawled, 'Such a lovely prize... educated... genteelly reared, but hot as hell, gentlemen... and ladies.'

Madame Fedora's voice rose above the din. 'I'll take her. I bid two hundred guineas.'

The rest muttered amongst themselves, then shrugged. There were plenty more slaves on offer. The auctioneer brought down his gavel on the rostrum and the deal was struck.

'Sold to Madame Fedora!'

Sylvia and Phoebe were rushed down the steps. There they were separated, hands chained behind them. A bit was pushed into Sylvia's mouth and two long leading reins brought round to the back of her head. The fetters between her ankles were shortened so that she could only hobble.

Then the reins were taken from Torr by a large, bald man

wearing livery, and she was led out of the warehouse in the wake of her purchaser, Madame Fedora.

She turned her head to look at the pirate, and he gave a quirky smile and raised his hand in a salute. That was the last she saw of him.

Chapter Eleven

'A letter, my lord,' said the beautiful nude Greek girl as she crawled across the tessellated floor towards Theo, her full breasts swinging, rounded haunches lifted, pouting labia on display, fringed with springy black pubic curls.

'Ah,' he said, holding out an idle hand.

She gave it to him and remained on her knees, head lowered, her long sable hair brushing her nipples. They were like acorns in the dark circle of aureole.

Theo smiled as he read his correspondence. 'So, all goes according to plan,' he murmured, and allowed the letter to fall. He rested among the embroidered cushions on the divan that stood before arches leading to a terrace. This overlooked the private cove belonging to his villa. Chiffon curtains moved in the warm breeze. Outside grapes ripened on the vine, bougainvillaea flaunted crimson and purple flowers, and cypress trees lifted dark green spires to a cloudless blue sky.

It was cool within this garden room. Spring water trickled into a natural pool, and Theo had been swimming. He was naked, his skin an even olive-brown, the muscles of his chest and abdomen perfectly defined.

'Do it,' he commanded, and the Greek girl rose to lean across his lower belly, take the long, hot stalk of his penis into her full-lipped, sultry mouth and suck vigorously.

Theo thrust his hips upwards to push in further. The girl rocked to and fro, his cock sliding out to the glans on the upward stroke, then disappearing again as she sank down. He gasped, his head flung back, the sinews of his throat standing out.

Sylvia! He thought as he lost control and spurted into the girl's mouth. Sylvia...

He visualised her – her honey-coloured hair, and those green eyes sparking defiance. That girl who had bewitched and teased him and who he had taken to wife. This was no use. He had never, ever, permitted himself to fall a victim to that aberration of the heart, body and spirit that poets prated about – sentimental, mawkish, cloying thing called love.

He pushed the Greek woman away almost impatiently, his cock sliding out of her mouth, curving backwards to rest across his belly.

'Go. Fetch your brother,' he barked. 'I would have you both, my lovely pair of slaves... heavenly twins indeed.'

The seat of the coach was deep and comfortable, and Sylvia might have enjoyed its luxury were it not for her aching buttocks and the chains that clinked at every movement.

Madame Fedora sat across from her, making no sound. Sylvia found it unnerving to face the inscrutable, misty-black veil turned towards her. She could feel Phoebe shivering and would have squeezed her hand reassuringly had she been able.

The carriage was splendid, drawn by four high-stepping chestnuts trotting briskly along. The servant who had taken Sylvia's leash from Torr had bundled her into the vehicle, then handed the rein to his mistress. She held it tightly in her gloved hand.

There had been no communication. Sylvia was bubbling with questions but prevented from speaking by the bit that chafed her lips. Phoebe could have done, but awaited Sylvia's prompting. There was nothing else for it: they would have to accept whatever lay ahead.

After an hour's travelling, during which they passed small hamlets, windmills and fields of ripening corn, they came to a high brick wall and drove through an ornate iron gate hastily opened by a keeper who ran from the lodge house.

The coach turned into a poplar-lined avenue at the end of which loomed a mansion dominated by a clock tower. All the windows had grilles on the outside, giving it the disquieting aspect of a prison. The lawns in which it stood were smooth as velvet, the bushes neatly trimmed, the lower walls clothed in vines and creepers, yet it seemed a grim place, and was surrounded by thick, dark woods.

As the carriage halted, the door was opened by a white-wigged footman who assisted Madame Fedora to alight. Soon Sylvia was mounting the front steps where stood a thin, stern looking woman wearing the robes of a Mother Superior, snowy wimple, crucifix, rosary and all.

'Madame,' she said, curtseying.

'My dear Abbess,' Madame Fedora answered from behind her veil. 'I bring you two penitents in need of correction.'

'Ah, yes, I imagine they do,' the Abbess said, casting an eye over Sylvia's scantily clad body. 'This one has a passionate look about her mouth and a bold posture. Those breasts beg for caresses, and her mound is too prominent for modesty.'

'Indeed. I understand she has recently been fornicating with a pirate,' madame continued as they walked through a cloistered area patched with brilliant gold sunlight and deep purple shadows.

Sylvia, towed along behind, began to be suspicious. Why was the Abbess wearing a scarlet silk habit? And what was a nunnery doing with erotic statuary in its many alcoves – those of gods or satyrs with enormous phalli, and couples entangled in the throes of ecstasy?

Now, from the depths of this ivy-shrouded building, sounded occasional bursts of high-pitched feminine laughter. Surely not the noises made by pious, demure novices, or nuns devoted to prayer and charitable works? What was this place?

Her thoughts were answered almost at once. Madame raised her veil and looked directly at her, saying, 'Welcome to Rochecorbon. It was once a convent. Now it is dedicated to Priapus, and the Abbess presides over the rituals. You are to obey her.'

She reached out and loosened the bit, then removed it from Sylvia's mouth. Her lips were sore, her throat bone dry, and it was a moment before she could speak, then, 'I am Lady Sylvia Aubrey, madame,' she said icily. 'Far from being a willing captive of the pirate, I was abducted, then forced to suffer the indignity of being sold as a slave.'

Madame Fedora smiled, and feathered a hand over Sylvia's breast, lingering as she felt the nipple contract. At once her fingers tightened on the swollen tip, and Sylvia could not restrain a moan.

The Abbess was assessing her reaction, nodding as she exclaimed, 'Didn't I say she was lustful? Oh, yes, I shall enjoy training this one.'

'The maidservant, too,' Madame Fedora said firmly, now feeling between Sylvia's legs.

'Why not? She must learn to do more than comb her mistress's hair and care for her clothing. There are many other duties if she is to serve a courtesan,' the Abbess replied.

'A courtesan? What do you mean?' Sylvia asked, fighting to control the little pleasure pulse that thrummed in her clitoris.

'I purchased you for a noble client,' Madame Fedora stated, an alert expression on her sharp features. 'He is a man of the world... a sensualist who enjoys the refined arts of eroticism. You are perhaps the most perfect example of womanhood I've yet seen, and my experience has been legion. Comte Hercule Avenall will be enchanted, and to this end you'll be instructed on how to give him the utmost satisfaction.'

'I desire to return to my husband,' Sylvia said, finding that she did indeed want Theo more than she had ever imagined she would. 'He'll pay any ransom you demand. Permit me to write and tell him I'm staying at Rochecorbon.'

Madame Fedora shook her head, her sombre veils quivering. 'I can't do that,' she answered, and exchanged a glance with the Abbess. 'You must entertain the comte.'

'But, madame, I'm a married woman. I don't wish to become his mistress,' Sylvia cried, and tugged ineffectually at the chains linking her hands behind her. She was on the point of hysteria.

'Not only his mistress, my dear,' Madame Fedora corrected. 'If you please him, he may take you to Paris to become hostess in his chateau, pleasuring poets, writers and politicians. Doesn't this prospect appeal to you?'

'No, it does not!' Sylvia shouted and stamped her foot in frustration.

'Alas, she shows an ungovernable temper,' the Abbess mused, her calm masking any emotion.

'You're right,' Madame Fedora agreed, and then stared at Sylvia as she said, 'You've been punished for your attitude in the past, haven't you?'

'Yes,' Sylvia said sulkily.

'A very naughty girl, I fear,' the Abbess remarked with a sigh. 'Not in the least repentant, by the look of her.'

They had reached a passage flanked by a series of doors. The Abbess opened one and ushered the newcomers inside. The large room was occupied by a dozen young women in various stages of nudity. They lounged on daybeds, preening themselves or, seated at dressing tables, tried out various shades of cosmetic to enhance their complexions. One was having her armpits and pussy shaved. They chattered like parakeets in a variety of languages, though French predominated.

The Abbess clapped her hands and cried, 'Girls! Girls! Here is a fresh votary of Venus for our temple of love. Treat her any way you like, but don't mark her too much. She's intended for Comte Avenall and he will want to put his own seal on her.'

Sylvia found herself standing in the centre of the room, while the women appraised her. One, taller and bolder than the rest, paced forward and examined her closely.

She was auburn-headed and had a wide mouth and light blue eyes, her arrogant posture reminding Sylvia of Rowena. She wore a burgundy leather bustier, her large breasts bulging over the top, her nipples gilded to match her lips and eyelids. Her belly and pubis were naked, and her cleft was swept clean of hair, the lower lips lacquered in gold. Its glittering line drew the eye to the dusky-pink folds between.

She carried a long-handled whip adorned with fluttering black ribbons. With careless insolence, she touched the stock to Sylvia's nipples, then went lower, brushing against her mons veneris. Sylvia flinched, resenting the girl's dominating manner.

'Can I have her?' the girl said to the Abbess, her voice loud and clear.

'You must draw lots, Lisette,' Madame Fedora answered, and it seemed she had the last word on all things.

Lisette glowered, but one of the others, a small, plump girl with pierced nipples and pearls threaded in her pussy hair, opened the drawer of an escritoire. From this she took a pack of playing cards which she handed to Madame Fedora who shuffled them before holding them out, face down. Each woman took one, including herself and the Abbess.

'Ace high!' Lisette cried. 'I win!'

The others voiced their disappointment, but Madame Fedora smiled and said indulgently, 'Never mind, my pets, you'll have your turn. Meanwhile, let me see who has the next highest card, and the winner shall practice using the rod on the maidservant.'

Lisette began to unwind the gauze from Sylvia as if she was undoing a particularly desirable gift. It fell to the floor, pooling at their feet. 'I don't suppose you're a virgin?' she murmured, her tongue tip coming out to lick over her glistening gold lips as her fingers explored Sylvia's labia, parting those full wings, hidden under the thatch of brown fuzz.

'No,' Sylvia answered, her face on fire.

She turned Sylvia around and looked at her rump, still marbled by Torr's lash. She inserted two wet fingers into her victim's anal ring. 'Ah, ha!' she exclaimed, twisting them in to the knuckle, their length seeming to stab Sylvia's vitals. 'She's tight, Madame Fedora... needs stretching.'

'We shall attend to it,' madame replied, watching the proceedings carefully, an expert on preparing female parts for penetration.

Sylvia could smell Lisette's arousal. Moisture shone on the golden painted sex lips and her gilded teats were pebble-hard. She was a handsome creature with the body of an athlete, not very womanly in aspect, reminding Sylvia of a young warrior, fearless and indomitable.

It was a potent combination and her own nipples hardened, a tingling sensation rushing through her core, increasing the dampness between her thighs. She ground her hips against the plundering fingers, wanting more.

Lisette chuckled and took her hand away, 'We'll do it later,' she promised. 'I want to feel you licking my cunt. I can show you delights you'll never find with a man.'

She gestured to a couple of the girls and they hauled Sylvia to where a low platform stood between pillars. It was covered in crimson carpet. Lisette bent and removed the chains, spreading Sylvia's arms wide and clipping the rings in her wrists-cuffs to stronger ones fastened round the columns.

She was now lying across the carpet, her breasts pushed against the rough surface. Lisette pulled her legs apart and clamped her anklets in the same manner. The chains were tightened till she was lifted into the air, suspended there, vulnerable and exposed, her sexual avenue drawn violently open.

Lisette ran a hand up the inside of Sylvia's thighs and tormented the hard, wet bud of her clitoris. Then she stood back and Sylvia, head hanging down, looked through the triangle of her own legs and saw the whip Lisette was holding.

The first cut made her buck with pain, pulling against her bindings. She moaned, and the next strokes were progressively lower, hitting the backs of her thighs, then returning to her blazing rump.

The agony in wrists and ankles was as nothing compared to the sickening heat ravaging her posterior and flanks. Amidst the snapping blows of the whip she heard another sound – that of the watchers counting each lash, a strangely frightening sound.

Lisette was mistress of the whip, moving to the right, then the left, the tip sometimes coiling round one of Sylvia's breasts to flick and sting. She refused to beg to be spared, choking back her sobs, but in the end could not bear it, breaking down into tears and screams.

'A little more, that's all,' said Madame Fedora, caressing Sylvia's face and sweat-drenched hair. Her clothing exuded the perfume of jasmine and carnations, and Sylvia wanted to sink against her bosom like a child in need of comfort.

'Oh… no… please spare me!' she groaned.

'You must become a submissive, my dear,' Madame Fedora continued. 'Haven't your other teachers insisted on this?'

'Ah… they have! Now let me down, for pity's sake!'

'I know how you feel,' Madame Fedora said softly. 'Believe me, I *know*. In time you will appreciate the contradiction between pain and pleasure, and the ambiguity of these sensations.'

'I'll never understand! Oh… ow!' Sylvia yelled as Lisette's whip laid open the tender lips of her cunt. Her body was alive with the hurt inflicted on this most intimate part.

'You will,' Madame Fedora promised. 'You'll bless the person who punishes you, love them as they love you… hate the torment, yet be never more happy and at peace than when it is over, plumbing the depths of emotional extremes.'

Lisette laid the whip aside and Sylvia was lowered. She collapsed on the platform, lying as one dead, and was aware, through the mists of tears and pain, that Lisette was kissing her eyelids while the Abbess applied a soothing lotion to her weals.

The oil slipped lower and Sylvia felt fingers exploring her arsehole. This was followed by something bigger, longer, thicker and she tried to clench her bottom cheeks. Immediately, the chains were tightened, her legs splayed again. The thing penetrated inexorably, and Sylvia shrieked.

'Don't fight it. Relax those inner muscles,' the Abbess said sternly, and slapped Sylvia's bruised buttocks with a remarkably hard hand. 'This is only the beginning. You'll take bigger and bigger dildos, till I consider you to be stretched enough.'

Sylvia's cries diminished to low wails as, gradually, the discomfort of that invasion was transformed into a curious pleasure. Theo had plundered her heartland in similar fashion, not once but many times, and she had begun to appreciate his novel way of taking. But this pseudo phallus was different, so impersonal and completely lacking in the essential warmth and pulsating life of a real one.

She felt it withdrawn, was aware of the coldness and lack, her body bereft and empty. Then she heard Madame Fedora speaking, close to her ear. 'Look, Sylvia. I want you to know exactly what is happening to you.'

She opened her eyes, cheek pressed sideways on the carpet, and saw the woman was holding six large china beads, strung together on a cord.

'On to your hands and knees,' the Abbess ordered from behind.

Sylvia struggled to obey, the chains slackening. Then she felt hands pulling her buttocks apart, and cringed as she begged, 'Oh, no! Not that!'

She wriggled to no avail. The hands were firm and insistent. Something hard and smooth and cold was pushed into her rectum.

'Submit. You must learn to do whatever your dominator desires,' Madame Fedora said, standing where Sylvia could see her calm face and bright, watchful eyes.

Sylvia submitted, tears sticky on her cheeks. And the feelings in her inner core underwent a change. Her vagina was responding to the thing sliding against the membranes of her back passage. Another smooth, chilly object touched her anal ring as a second ball pressed in harder. This time she felt herself opening, swallowing it like some exotic carnivorous flower, the hard round bead slipping in easily to join the first.

Then followed a third, and fourth and fifth.

'I'm full. I can't hold any more!' she yelled.

'Yes, you can,' Madame Fedora insisted, and nodded to the Abbess.

The last ball jostled for place behind its fellows, and Sylvia's muscles fought to expel it. Her love-tunnel was unbearably sensitised by the tumult churning in her bowels, and her clit responded to that inner turmoil, pleasure shocks jangling through the erectile tissue. The balls did not hurt now, their presence causing her to experience wild frustration. Every part of her loins felt congested, heavy and fully aroused.

All around her she could hear gasps and moans as the women masturbated, roused to fever pitch by witnessing Sylvia's schooling.

'On your knees, Sylvia. Don't slump. And don't dare eject those balls!' Madame Fedora ordered, sounding like Nanny Talbot and Mrs Dawson.

Sylvia complied, and as she moved the beads caused her such blissful agony that she could hardly bear it, awash with the most tormentingly exquisite sensations. Her anus had closed greedily over the last ball, the string protruding. There was a hand beneath her, skilfully toying with her clitoris, while others rubbed her nipples in unison.

Her hips jerked with shock as another outsized dildo was thrust into the wet depths of her womanhood, forcing its way in till it touched her cervix. Now she was utterly filled, muscles clenching round the objects invading her rectum and vagina, clit still unrelieved of its burden of need, full to bursting.

Through the haze she became aware of someone standing in front of her. 'I promised you could lick me,' Lisette said, her voice husky with desire.

The fingers manipulating Sylvia's clitoris dipped down into the slippery wetness oozing from her vulva, then spread the juice over the straining head of her nub. She moaned her pleasure and reached out her tongue, the tip exploring the softness of Lisette, inhaling the fragrant odour, so like her own, and curling into the divide of the lips that opened like a ripe peach under her caress.

The finger on her clit teased and played, sometimes concentrating on the head, then leaving it to massage the swollen wings on each side. Sylvia sobbed against Lisette's delta, giving her the pleasure that she herself was being denied. Why was it all so cruel? she wondered. Why did there have to be this mixture of agony and extreme arousal?

Lisette was approaching her crisis. Her hands clutched Sylvia's head and her hips gyrated gently. 'Go on,' she urged, and her juices flowed copiously, smearing Sylvia's lips.

Delight consumed Sylvia. Even the agony of her stripes blended with it, and the finger arousing her with such consummate art was bringing her to the summit of pleasure, yet making her hold off till Lisette had reached her own pinnacle of bliss.

The balls filling Sylvia's rectum shifted. The phallus inside her tunnel discovered her most erogenous spot as the Abbess thrust it in and out.

'Do it harder! Make me come!' Lisette shouted.

Sylvia's tongue worked furiously over that sliver of flesh and Lisette gave a sudden cry, shuddering in ecstasy. Her pelvis jerked and juddered, and her nails dug into Sylvia's scalp.

'Yes… yesss! Oh, yes!' she howled. 'It's here! I'm coming!'

The fingers rubbed fervently now, and Sylvia came in a violent paroxysm that wrenched her whole body and plunged her into an instant of complete blackness.

The convent contained many beautifully furnished bedrooms allocated to these high-class whores, for,

'Make no bones about it, that's what they are, my lady,' Phoebe said later. 'They beat me sore, the bitches, but work me up into such a lather that I come as soon as one of them touches my button. I've chatted to them – there's a few that speak English – and found out that Madame Fedora is a procuress, helped by her lover, the so-called Abbess. She don't belong to no religious order, but runs one of the busiest brothels in Marseilles. This convent's set up to amuse the rich who come here to get their jollies.'

'So I'm to become a whore,' Sylvia answered listlessly.

She was lying on the canopied bed in a room furnished with flair and imagination. Though the outside of Rochecorbon was stark, within was every luxury imaginable, albeit of a decadent, overblown nature. There had been no sign of clients, so far.

'Maybe you are, but there again, maybe you ain't. Cheer up, milady. There's a grand party planned for the weekend,' Phoebe continued, applying gold-flecked paint to her mistress's toenails, as she had been instructed.

She was at home in her wasp-waisted corset and transparent skirt, under which she was bare save for black stockings, garters and neat black pumps. Her bottom was a deep shade of pink through constant paddling, the whores whiling away idle hours in spanking her.

Well fed and cosseted, Sylvia had nothing to complain about on that score. Handsome attendants, both male and female, bathed and massaged her, rubbed scented oils into her skin, shaved her sex, washed her hair, and subjected her to so much pampering that she felt quite boneless. The whores showed no resentment of her sudden arrival in their midst, proving more than helpful as they indulged in the endless pleasure of dressing up in various costumes, rehearsing their performances for the party and making love to one another.

On the minus side, however, Sylvia was daily subjected to rectal plugs, each larger than the last. Sometimes, the Abbess or Madame Fedora strapped one to her so that she could not expel it, making her wear it for hours on end. At others, they tried out different nipple clamps till her teats were red, sore but highly sensitive.

There were creams they used on her delta, aromatic concoctions that burned and irritated and caused deep-seated, throbbing desire. After this excursion into arousal, they would strap her mons into an inflexible metal cup, like the chastity belt, the chains sliding between her anal crease and fastening tightly round her thighs.

She was given wine spiced with aphrodisiacs, and forced to suffer hours of torment when her clit throbbed and her mind was filled with a multitude of wild and obscene images. She pictured massive cocks and splendid erections, felt fingers crawling over her skin and secret parts, thought tongues were lapping at her secretions and mouths sucking her nipples. Then, when she was sure she would go mad with desire, Lisette would come along to set her free and take her to the heights of fulfilment.

It was a most curious establishment in which Sylvia now found herself, a place governed by women. Apart from clients, the only males permitted to pass through its sacred portals were the bodyguards and menservants and these, she quickly discovered, were not interested. Like eunuchs in a harem, they preferred members of their own sex.

Preceded by booted and spurred outriders a massive, elaborately carved and gilded coach rumbled up the white-pebbled drive. Drawn by six bays in glittering harness and guarded by a trio of mounted postilians, the imposing equipage rolled to a halt before the entrance to Rochecorbon.

'Men!' shrieked the whores, rushing to the windows and staring down, jostling for the best view.

'Stupid cows,' Lisette commented scornfully, posing before the pier-glass in the Amazon costume she was to wear that night.

'Who is it?' Sylvia wanted to know, leaning over the stone balustrade.

'Comte Hercule Avenall,' Lisette answered, strolling across to join her. 'He's a tyrant... and Madame Fedora bought you especially for him. Rather you than me.'

Sylvia shivered and looked down at the man who would soon own her. He stepped from the carriage, resplendent in a full-skirted greatcoat of rust wool, trimmed with bottle green. A top hat was set at a jaunty angle on curling iron-grey hair, and he bore himself in a military manner.

Madame Fedora rustled down the steps to meet him and he bowed over her hand.

'The first to arrive and the last to leave – that's him,' remarked one of the girls with a toss of her plumed helmet, already attired for the mock battle they intended to enact.

Sylvia was impressed by his appearance, despite herself. Older than she had anticipated, but supremely confident and elegant. Perhaps her fears were groundless.

Excitement rippled through the convent. The women liked displaying themselves on the stage; vibrant, unconventional creatures who used their assets to make their way in a harsh world.

More carriages began to arrive, disgorging gentlemen in the main, though there were a few members of the demirep, too. Music swelled from the salon, and a wonderful mixture of aromas arose from the kitchen where the chef had been busy for days, preparing for this major event in the convent's calendar: The Feast of Priapus.

'Get down there and take 'em by storm!' Phoebe advised proudly, her eyes sparkling as she looked at her mistress.

Madame Fedora and the Abbess had worked hard to perfect Sylvia's appearance, while Phoebe had done all the fetching and carrying. Standing in front of the mirror in her bedroom, Sylvia hardly recognised herself. Was this alluring being really her?

Her hair had been polished till it resembled corn silk. It flowed freely over her shoulders, fell down her back, and undulated as she moved. Flowerheads had been woven into the several little plaits that trailed on either side of her face. Her body shone through the folds of a white voile chiton, each curve emphasised rather than concealed. Her hairless mons showed a darker triangle of plump flesh that focused the attention. Her breasts were naked, the nipples restrained by jewelled clamps and linked by a thin chain.

'He'll adore you,' Madame Fedora said, hands folded at her waist.

'It's true. He will,' the Abbess agreed. 'You have a virginal quality which will demand that he wrest it from you. The comte likes nothing better than corrupting innocents.'

'I'm no innocent,' Sylvia protested, wishing her gown was a little less revealing.

Madame Fedora placed an arm around her and murmured, 'You are, my dear. Life has barely touched you yet.'

This is hardly true, Sylvia thought. I'm not sure that I've ever been entirely innocent – naive, maybe. But I feel widely experienced, what with Robert Kelly and Mother Challis and her disgusting offspring, and my own husband robbing me of my maidenhead in full view of his friends. Then there was Torr, that likeable rogue, and the beatings I've had since I've been here. An innocent! She gave a smile that contained a trace of cynicism.

Madame Fedora led her protégée into the softly lit room where a quartet played under an arch and the good-looking lackeys and shapely maids drifted about pouring wines and brandy while others deftly replaced guttering candles.

It could have been a respectable gathering, apart from the fact that the theme was Ancient Rome, and the footmen were naked to the waist and wore exceedingly short kilts that showed their wiry pubic hair, stiff cocks and taut balls. The maids, too, were available to be fingered at all times, nipples bare, pussies and anal avenues exposed in their bacchante costumes comprised of brief tunics and strapped sandals with vine leaves in their hair.

The guests had entered into the spirit of it. Many of the men had attired themselves as senators in robes and togas, while the pleasure-hunting ladies pretended to be goddesses and nymphs in drifting, transparent muslin.

Madame Fedora and the Abbess encouraged female clients, catering for the tastes of all-comers and making a fortune in the process. They had long ago decided that there must be male prostitutes, too. Why should men have all the fun? Besides which, many women sought female paramours, and they also provided these. Extra whores had been shipped in from Marseilles. At the Feast of Priapus, anything was acceptable, as long as it concerned the satisfaction of sexual urges.

The wine flowed and Sylvia, who had already downed several glasses in order to steady her nerves, waited to be presented to Comte Avenall.

He arrived when the guests were already loosening up, couples pairing, the chemistry of sexual attraction working like yeast. But when he appeared at the head of the stairs, everything stopped – the music, the chatter, and the gales of laughter. A frisson of excitement, danger, even terror, ripped through the atmosphere, all aware of the aura of aristocracy and power emanating from him.

It lasted for a heartbeat, no more. Then he moved down and all around him people were bowing and scraping. Looking neither right nor left, he strode to where Sylvia knelt between the Abbess and Madame Fedora.

Disobeying orders, she could not resist peeping up at him. He was a big man, his once fine physique running to seed, but impressive nonetheless. His clothing was superb. He had scorned changing into masquerade costume but wore an immaculately tailored tailcoat in peacock blue, with narrow beige trousers that strapped under the instep of his black shoes. Diamonds flashed about his person, on the buttons of his jacket, at his frilled shirtfront, at his cuffs and on his strong fingers.

He came to a halt just in front of her, a smile curving his full, sensual lips as he looked at her with cool grey eyes. They had a remarkable glitter, seeming to penetrate her very vitals. His strong nose and heavy jaw added to the overwhelming strength of his face.

'Ah, beautiful,' he murmured in heavily accented English, his seductive voice stirring Sylvia's loins. 'You have surpassed yourself, Madame Fedora.'

'I'm glad you approve, Comte,' she replied, inclining her head.

He rested a hand against Sylvia's cheek, then moved down

her neck and fastened on the chain linking her nipples. He tugged on it. Instantly fire raced down from the tormented tips to connect with her womb.

He drew on them, forcing her to her feet, dragging her closer to his body. She sensed menace in him, staring up into those steel grey eyes, the irises black pools in which she could see herself reflected. It was as if she was sinking into them, swallowed up, entering a world of dark, ferocious knowledge.

He loosened his hold on the chain, then without warning, slapped the side of her right breast. Sylvia flinched but stood her ground, breathing in the scent of the man, learning to know his touch. Another ringing slap caught her on the left side and she could not help stepping back. At once her calves and thighs met the sting of the Abbess's rod, forcing her close to the comte again.

'Why are you hitting me?' she cried, tears welling up, breasts and legs flooded with heat.

He smiled and slapped her across the face, and she could see he was inflamed by what he was doing, his penis unfurling and thickening behind the immaculate trousers.

Then he thrust one of his perfumed fingers into her mouth, examining her teeth. He caught one of her tears on his fingertip and lifted it to his lips, licking the moisture.

'Your tears are like crystal drops,' he said, his voice melodious, almost caressing. 'The dew of your arousal will taste even sweeter. I want to see you in action. I prefer my croissants well buttered.'

He nodded to Madame Fedora and she conducted him to a chair placed in a prominent position. A space was cleared in the middle of the floor and the crowd surged round it, yet were careful not to obstruct his view.

Sylvia was pushed forward. Her girdle was untied, the single robe whisked from her. She was naked to the gaze of all. In vain she hunched her shoulders in an effort to hide her breasts, one hand dropping down to cover her hairless mons. This was not allowed, her hands held firmly to her sides. Then, to the solemn accompaniment of a snare drum, she was marched down the room to where a pair of heavy wine-red curtains hung, concealing a small stage.

Footmen sprang forward to light candles floating in metal containers in a shallow trough of water set before a row of polished reflectors. At once the curtains came to life, glowing red, and anticipation rippled through the onlookers. Two magnificently muscled Negroes stood close by with arms folded, their skin oiled and shiny. They wore white turbans and baggy emerald green trousers. At a signal, they seized the gold scalloped edge of the drapes in their mighty fists and drew them back, revealing a low platform behind an arched proscenium.

The audible gasp that arose might have come from a single throat. A shiver passed through Sylvia's limbs. She was filled with the dreadful conviction that in some odious way she was about to become the main item of entertainment.

The crowd started to murmur, excited by the prospect of a unique performance. They had learned to expect nothing less at Rochecorbon, the ingenuity of the Abbess and Madame Fedora admired far and wide. The world-weariest debauchee who had thought himself immune to further stimulation experienced a resurgence of sexual power under their roof.

Tonight would prove no exception.

In the centre of the stage stood a tripod consisting of three strong poles that reared to the ceiling. They were painted in red and yellow stripes and fastened securely at the apex. Long ropes hung down from this, supporting a carved chair with a hole in the seat.

The Abbess applied a whippy white paddle vigorously, propelling Sylvia forward as it lashed her naked backside. Swish, swish, it went as she was driven up the steps to the stage. The Negroes lifted her into the chair, clamped her wrists into manacles fixed to the arms, while the Abbess commanded her to sit cross-legged with her arse precisely above the aperture in the seat. Then her ankles were shackled.

The seat was moulded and comfortable, though it sloped towards the opening, thrusting down Sylvia's buttocks and cleft. Her inner lips unfolded like exotic flower petals, protruding and aching to be fondled.

At a gesture from the Abbess, one of the Negroes came nearer. His baggy pantaloons were open over a solid brown prick with a purple cap, glistening with moisture. In the full glare of the footlights, Sylvia realised that this formidable weapon was level with her mouth.

He smiled down at her, a genial giant with luminous black eyes and dazzling white teeth. Raising one shovel-sized hand, he placed it on her head, wound his fingers in her hair, pulled her head towards his hairy crotch and let his stiff prick rub along her lips.

Sylvia gripped the chair arms, possessed of a powerful wantonness that urged her to push her exposed cunt further through the hole, dying to have something touch it – a cock, a finger, a tongue, it did not matter which. She opened her mouth and drew in the black man's plum. His was a mighty weapon indeed. Her jaw ached and her cheeks were stretched wide to take it. Even when it jabbed into the soft membrane of her throat, no more than three-quarters of it had been absorbed. The rest was still exposed, his belly hair nowhere near her chin.

There was a tumult all around the stage, couples inspired by the show, the room throbbing with an intensity that was entirely carnal. But the performance was far from over.

'That's enough, Tarik,' the Abbess shouted.

He withdrew, his cock still rigid, and helped the other Negro revolve the chair till huge knots formed in the sustaining ropes, gradually lifting Sylvia and her throne towards the tripod's apex.

Now another man appeared, a large mulatto naked except for silver manacles. His cock was ready, a sturdy bough, the glans robbed of its foreskin, naked and gleaming, dew running from its slit. Amidst cheers and shouts, he lay beneath the chair, a cushion wedged under his hips. This raised his cock higher, a spear pointing directly at the chair seat and Sylvia's wet and engorged cleft.

'Let her go!' the Abbess cried.

The chair was released and at once started to revolve, faster and faster as the rope unwound, the knots in it magically disappearing as it whirled towards the mulatto's monstrously upright member. His helm pierced her as she corkscrewed over him. The chair was halted in its spin, her vagina acting as a break, rudely and shatteringly impaled on that mighty prong. She opened her mouth and screamed with pain and an equal agony of pleasure.

The mulatto lifted his arms and gripped the chair, his hips rising and falling, pumping, bucking, driving his phallus home. His lips drew back in a snarl as he came in an extravagant flourish, his libation trickling out of Sylvia and running down his shaft, soaking the thicket that sprouted from his lower belly.

'Enough!' The comte's voice crackled as he gave the terse command. 'Bring her to me!'

Sylvia was unbound and lifted from the chair. Dazed, her genitals on fire with need, frustration acute, she was conducted to where the comte was seated, slouched low with his legs spread. A tiny spark smouldered in the dense pupils of his grey eyes. He seemed unaware of the milling revellers, concentrating that flinty gaze on her.

'That was well done,' he said, and licked his lips. 'Now, on your knees and unfasten my trousers.'

His cock sprang forth, an immense weapon ready to spew his seed. It was thick and long and circumcised, the stem embossed with veins, the bulging, naked glans twin-lobed and glossy. Beneath this prong were his balls, no youthful globes these, but heavy fruit filled with sap.

Sylvia, heated to the point of insanity by the attentions of the Negro and the mulatto, wanted him with desperate need. She could not even begin to fathom why a man of his standing should choose to enter a furrow so recently ploughed by another

– did not really want to know or think about it. The mulatto's spunk still dribbled from her vulva, the feel of it quickening her feverish desire.

Everywhere she looked people were engaged in sexual activity. Gentlemen with robes torn open and laurel wreaths awry, dipped their cocks into wine glasses and had girls suck it off. An extremely beautiful youth was being sodomised by an elderly man wearing a toga. Another man was sucking the cock of a burly individual who, in turn, was slurping at the labia of a marvellously lovely blonde while she used her foot to play with a slave-boy's tool. The sounds of paddles and tawse punishing bare flesh, the howls of pain, the cries of ecstasy, rose in a bewildering chorus, and Sylvia wanted to take the comte's cock into her and clench her inner muscles round its erect hardness.

As if reading her thoughts, two of the Abbess's acolytes lifted her, legs held at right angles and spread wide over his lap. Then she was slowly lowered on to his upward curving weapon. The head touched her vulva and, the weight of her own body bearing her down, she felt it penetrating her lower mouth. Her own wet muscles convulsed, drawing it in, further and further till it butted her womb, the feeling deep and visceral.

She wailed, throwing back her head as his coarse pubic bush brushed against her bare mons and agitated her clitoris.

Hercule Avenall did not move, letting his head rest against the carved chair back, his hands clenched on the padded arms, abandoning himself to sensation as the acolytes raised and lowered Sylvia over his engorged cock.

She was absorbing the rhythm now, making it a part of herself, aiding the rise and fall of her hips, revelling in the rock-hard thing within her, even forcing herself down on it to feel the harsh jab of its clubbed head against her cervix. Her vagina made sucking noises, like a hungry mouth. Her swollen clitoris responded to the friction of his cock-base. She lifted her hands and cupped her tingling breasts, thumb-pads gliding over the tense nipples. Hovering on the brink of orgasm, she gave a deep, quivering sigh.

Then lightning struck, searing her buttocks with devilish pain. The Abbess swished her whip and struck again, each blow coinciding with the pumping of Sylvia's pelvis. It was a terrible harmony of contrasts, orchestrated by the Abbess.

Beneath her she could feel the comte lifting his body to meet her, on the edge of losing control. A groan escaped through his clenched jaws, his face that of a mask in a Greek tragedy. Sylvia closed her eyes. Her body felt weightless, her emotions ones of pure sensation.

The whip rose and fell. Sylvia was gasping, sobbing, no longer conscious of anything but exquisite, throbbing pleasure, her vagina contracting on the comte's phallus.

He gave a strangled roar, and his weapon convulsed. She felt his hot essences filling her, and cried out as she came.

Sylvia was the queen of the feast. Comte Avenall's chosen one, his odalisque and beloved.

He had her crouch at his feet while he ate and drank and watched the antics of the crowd. He caressed her intimately, her breasts, vagina and anus his to probe and enjoy as he fancied. At one point, he had her kneel between his thighs and mouth his ever active cock. He seemed tirelessly virile and potent, flaunting his prowess openly.

The whores, wearing feathered *papier-mâché* helmets, tightly laced breastplates, greaves, sandals and the briefest of tunics, mounted the stage and went into their routine. As Amazons, whips at the ready, they marched up to the footlights, amid drunken cheers and thunderous applause.

'Let battle commence!' cried Madame Fedora, and they leapt into action.

Part of the improvised plot was that one of them, pretending to be a prisoner, was caught, chained to a post and flogged. Then there was a fight between those who were supposed to be rescuing her. It was a grand excuse for an exhibition of flashing limbs, flying hair, swirling colours, whips whirling on naked breasts and cunts.

Their screeches of pain inspired the dishevelled audience to hurl obscene advice and encouragement, the bloody and violent show inflaming their lust to an even higher pitch.

The Amazons, prompted into action by the hope of reward, laid about them vigorously till their costumes were reduced to shimmering ribbons and breasts, rumps and thighs ablaze with vivid scarlet stripes. Whenever a lash struck, screams rang out to join the general pandemonium.

Hercule Avenall looked bored, saying, 'I've seen enough of this crudity, Madame Fedora. What else have you on offer?'

Madame gave a tight little smile, accompanied by a shrug. 'You might care to try the paddle on Sylvia?' she suggested. 'Or,' and here her smile deepened, 'she has not yet been pierced and wears no sigil. I was leaving this particular operation until your arrival, my lord comte.'

'Well done,' he answered, and ran a hand down Sylvia's spine till he touched the dimple where her buttocks divided. 'Come, my jewel,' he added. 'It's time you were marked to prove that you now belong to your master.'

Chapter Twelve

Whenever the comte visited Rochecorbon, he occupied the finest suite of rooms. It was there that Sylvia was taken by the Abbess, up the sombrely grand staircase, along a succession of carpeted corridors, till they reached the carved doors which gave entrance to his apartment.

Madame Fedora remained behind to keep a watchful eye on the orgy, though never taking part in it herself, save for the occasional whipping if an influential gentleman, a magistrate or bishop perhaps, demanded more in the way of punishment than the whores could provide.

Sylvia followed where she was led, fearful of yet fascinated by Hercule. He filled her with the same awe she had felt for her father on the rare times she had seen him. Now she watched him covertly, adopting a submissive pose, head down, arms raised, hands clasped at the nape of her neck. This way, naked as she was, she could not protect herself. Gradually, she was beginning to accept this, disoriented by being beaten and pleasured, all at the same moment.

She wished with all her heart that she had learned this lesson when she had been with Theo. Now it was unlikely she would ever see him again. This thought sent scalding tears to her eyes, and she wept silently.

Hercule, with the help of his valet, had changed into an East India robe of purple brocade with a wide sable collar and deep cuffs. It was held together by a sash round the waist, but as he walked across the room it parted at each stride and he wore nothing beneath, his thighs and legs strongly muscled and hairy.

Sylvia peeked from under her lashes, seeing his magnificence, shivering at his lordly air, remembering the thickness and force of his cock buried deep in her vagina, an even more vital organ of generation than the mulatto's.

He nodded to the Abbess, and said, 'Shall we begin?'

'Certainly, my lord. Far be it from me to hesitate when a novice needs instruction,' she replied, piously. She pulled Sylvia's arms down and guided her to the monumental bed where, using thick, silken cords, she tied her by the wrists to the carved foot-post where serpents writhed upwards from acanthus leaves, to be lost in the dense forest of the tester.

Sylvia rested her cheek against the wood, which warmed under contact with her skin. It was hard, solid, the bed centuries old, once owned by kings. Within its dark interior many a virgin bride had been speared by her lord's prick, and many an heir conceived and brought forth.

Had these girls been willing? she wondered. Or had they been forced into marriage? Had the chamber rung with their piteous cries that had been ignored as their dominating husbands thrust their proud cocks into them, rupturing their maidenheads, as Theo had hers?

Given no time for further speculation, she felt Hercule behind her, smelt him, and her loins clenched, lust coiling deep in her womb. Her thighs were sticky with the semen he had already injected into her, and her honeydew trickled down to join the milky substance.

'I am going to give you an example of my mastery, Sylvia,' he said softly, but with a kind of breathy eagerness. 'While you are with me, you will be faithful and obey my commands. At times I may order you to receive selected persons into the divine temple of your body. You may climax only if I say you can, not otherwise. Do you hear me?'

'I hear you, master,' she whispered, and delicious tremors ran through her from nipples to clit.

His hand was on the back of her neck, his fingers soothing and caressing. 'That's right, my dear child,' he murmured. 'They tell me you have been rebellious, denying your husband his will. This is unwise behaviour. A woman must keep to her place and accept the wisdom of her lord.'

'How do you know I was disobedient? Who told you?' she asked, surprised that he could speak of her past so knowledgeably.

'Word travels fast,' he replied casually, running a finger down her spine to touch the dimpled 'V' where her buttocks joined. 'I was distressed to hear of your naughtiness towards Lord Aubrey. This must have distressed him sorely.'

'I'm sorry. I truly am,' she sobbed, shivering in ecstasy as he bent his head and nipped the ivory skin at the side of her throat, leaving indentations which she knew would purple very soon. Love-bites, a stigmata she would wear with pride.

'I believe you,' he whispered in her ear, his breath scented with wine, his greying hair fragrant with pomade. 'Now I shall demonstrate the regard I have for your welfare.'

He gripped a handful of her hair, turned her head a little and held up a riding crop. Its tip was covered by a small wedge of flat rigid leather. This he placed against her lips and she dutifully kissed it.

It was withdrawn. Hercule vanished from her sight. She braced herself. The moment stretched out like a protracted scream. Heat pervaded her, sweat beading her face. She took in the embroidered damasks of the bed, the gilded friezes of the room, the sumptuous carpets and statues and landscape paintings, the roaring fire in the ornamental grate – waiting with baited breath.

The crop's initial bite brought a yelp to her lips. The cords that bound her were carefully fastened, but not painfully so. She tugged on them involuntarily, her cringing flesh seeking to escape the lash, her hands yearning to reach round and rub the injury, but prevented by her restraints.

Hercule added three more strokes, the leather tip slapping and stinging, leaving marks that turned crimson, Sylvia's bottom brighter than before. She was crumbling now, each slash drawing a scream from her as more followed hard on the others. The Abbess observed the ritual impassively, arms folded over her breasts, admiring the comte's skill in laying on the crop, a skill born of long practice.

He brought it down so the tip penetrated Sylvia's buttock crease. She gave a long, ululating cry as that fearsomely stiff triangle caught her between the legs. She scissored her thighs together, trying to comfort her sex lips, but felt a hand on her rear, forcing her legs open. The crop swished and she screamed as the tip kissed the opening to her rectum.

Once she had started screaming she could not stop, her cries echoing under the ornately decorated ceiling. Incited by the sounds of her yells, Hercule beat her faster and harder, fully erect now, his penis jutting through the gap in his robe.

Then he flung the whip aside and rammed his cock into her, his hard body slamming her against the bedpost as he came in long, hot spurts. He withdrew as speedily as he had entered, leaving her unsatisfied, her clit aching, the mouth of her vagina spasming.

He mopped his brow with a monogrammed kerchief and poured himself a brandy from the cut glass decanter on the bedside table. After taking a deep swallow, he turned to the Abbess and said, 'I am ready for the next stage. Are you?'

'Certainly,' she replied, as frigid as a mountain stream.

'But I shall need assistance.'

She lifted a little brass hand bell and rang it. Shortly, two of her menservants stepped into the room. Between them they half led, half carried Sylvia to a scroll-backed *Directoire* couch. They were muscular young men, and her struggles were futile.

Faces impassive, the dark zigzagging on their posteriors betraying their own slavery, they laid her on her back, pushed a bolster under her hips to raise her pubis aloft and then tethered her wrists and ankles to the sofa legs. Her welts stung. Her bruises throbbed. The air on her cleft told her how exposed she was, how open to view and how vulnerable.

Fear beat like a frantic pulse in her viscera.

'What are you going to do to me?' she shouted, twisting her head and staring up at Hercule.

'I shall do nothing. The Abbess is the one who will pierce your outer labia,' he answered, caressing her wet delta. 'I shall merely insert the rings. It won't hurt, dearest. No more than when you had holes punched in your earlobes.'

'It's infamous! Humiliating! I'm a lady, deserving of respect, not some tuppenny trollop. I don't want this done,' Sylvia protested. Never had she felt so alone, not even when she shivered in Mother Challis's rat-infested cellar.

'Haven't you learned by now that your wants aren't important?' he asked, and stood at the foot of the couch where he could glance down the length of her nude body, her mons lifted, legs spread, the avenue between them flushed scarlet, kissed by the crop.

'I'm learning this – fast,' she retorted bitterly.

'Were you a tuppenny trollop, as you so quaintly put it, I would not waste my time on you. I do this because you are a lady... one day to be a very great lady,' he said.

He raised a finger to his lips, wetted it with spittle and touched the tip of her engorged clitoris. She made a mewling sound, a pricking sense of urgency tormenting her bud and, though he stroked it lightly, she pulsed and wriggled and almost came.

'No more, comte,' the Abbess reminded him. 'She'll bleed too freely if she's aroused.'

She dipped a sponge into a bowl of water where ice-cubes floated and squeezed it over Sylvia's pudenda. This drew an anguished gasp from her as the cold water ran in rivulets across her cleft, her swollen clit retreating into its hood. Then the Abbess dried her carefully and took up a curious instrument that resembled pincers.

Sylvia's eyes widened in horror as the Abbess bent over.

'No! No!' she implored.

She felt the coldness of steel, a sharp pinch on her lower lip and then a stab of pain. The comte slipped a gold keeper from a velvet-lined jewel box, opened its hinge and inserted it through the blood-edge puncture in the middle of Sylvia's right labia majora. The Abbess repeated the operation on the other wing, directly opposite the first, and he added a second ring.

Sylvia moaned, praying inside, Oh God, let my ordeal be over!

She thought for a second that her prayer was to be answered when the slaves untied her, but they merely turned her so that she lay on her stomach, the cushion replaced under her belly, the shackles snapped shut again.

Hercule rested a finger on Sylvia's left buttock as if indicating a spot. She could not see what was going on, but heard someone raking at the fire and then the sound of footsteps and the *froufrou* of skirts coming closer. It was the Abbess. She wore a heavy leather gauntlet on one hand in which she grasped a poker. Its end glowed red-hot.

'Is it finely engraved?' the comte enquired.

'Magnificently so,' the Abbess replied. 'Only the most expert craftsman worked on it. Fear not, sir, the result will be superb.'

At the same instant that horrified awareness dawned, Sylvia felt sudden, scorching heat on her shrinking rump followed by excruciating agony and the smell of burning. She screeched in her extremity, fire and ice boring into her skin.

'Keep still!' the Abbess ordered, and the branding iron was held there for several seconds, till it seemed as if it would sear Sylvia to the bone. Then it was removed.

'That's taken well. Neatly done, Abbess,' she heard Hercule remark, through the dizzying fog of agony.

Her bonds were released, but she was unaware, slumping on the couch as if dead, lost in waves of total darkness that folded over her and carried her to merciful oblivion.

The sun slanted through the high windows of the stable, flecked with dust motes and circling flies. These had once been arrow-slits when, in medieval times of war and bloody conflict, the place had been a fortified manor. Now the sweet smell of hay and the gentle movements of Comte Avenall's thoroughbreds were pleasant adjuncts to an atmosphere of warmth and peace.

Sylvia absorbed it into herself as a groom waited to prepare her for the morning trot through the grounds of the Chateau Grecourt, the comte's family seat in the countryside not many miles from Paris.

She had breakfasted with Hercule as usual, one of the more pleasant moments of the day when he read his mail, and talked with her of politics and world affairs, all of which interested him keenly. She had not partaken heavily, needing to be agile and brimming with energy. She had left him reading a newspaper and made her way through the immense house to the stable yard, reached by way of a private door.

On every side she had come across servants who bowed to her deferentially while going about their duties. She was the mistress of this nobleman, his favourite among all women, and treated accordingly.

There were occasions, however, when he ordered that she move among them naked, crawling on hands and knees to serve them. Then she had to abase herself and do whatever they asked of her, be it never so menial and ignominious. Hercule considered that it was character building for her to learn the doctrine of humility.

Thus she could become the vessel for the seed of the lowest man on the estate, or allow any of them to whip her till she bled. The women, some jealous and spiteful, took advantage and had her suck their cunts till they screamed in delight. But when the comte tired of this spectacle, he would put them in their place, stern and wrathful should anyone dare show disrespect to Sylvia.

By now, she had come to accept whatever he commanded, her lot no longer appearing to be strange or unreasonable. They had arrived at the chateau some weeks before, and Hercule had proudly shown her over his beautiful home, filled with treasures and works of art, saved by devious means from the power-crazed peasants of the French Revolution and the long-time war with England. Hercule had survived both, his money and lands intact, his influence considerable.

She was given a magnificent apartment overlooking the gardens, clothes, jewels: anything she desired was hers for the asking, except the thing she longed for above all and which had become no more than a distant dream – freedom.

Had she ever really lived in England? she wondered. Had there been a time when she was a schoolgirl in Bath? Had she married Lord Theo Aubrey, or had she always resided in this glittering, luxurious prison, a plaything for a wealthy despot? She chose to blank her mind to the memory of her stay with Mother Challis, the whole episode too terrible to contemplate.

She could have argued with Hercule, stating that she had already been humbled enough by that ghastly woman, but one look at his stern face dissuaded her.

As time passed, it seemed more and more likely that he intended to keep her by his side. Memories of her former life faded, even her stay at Rochecorbon no more than a distant dream.

The rings in her labia were a constant reminder of her serfdom, sometimes weighted which made walking painful, sometimes encrusted with jewels when Hercule held soirees and exhibited her before his friend – his concubine, hostess and odalisque. He liked to shower her with presents, his favourite piece being a gold collar with diamond insets.

'I prize diamonds highly,' he had said when he gave it to her, clasping it around her neck and fastening it with a small key, his fingers brushing over her soft skin. 'They have such a pure sparkle. And you, my darling, I prize almost as much. Thus it is right that diamonds should grace your swanlike neck. This torque was once worn by a Russian empress.'

The brand seared into Sylvia's buttock had been agonising at first, blisters forming till it healed. It had left a sigil the shape and size of a guinea which she traced with her fingertips. She could not see what it was, even if she squirmed round so that her backside was reflected in a mirror.

'What is it?' she had asked Phoebe impatiently.

'Looks like one of those crest things, same as Lady Rowena

had on her carriage doors,' the maid had answered, puzzling over the mark. 'It's a sort of dragon with words round it, but I can't read, milady, so that's no use to me.'

When Sylvia plagued Hercule to tell her, his lip curled in an ironic smile as he said, 'Your maid's right. It is a crest with a family motto in Latin.'

'Yours?' she had demanded, angry that she was stamped for life as someone's property, and did not know whose.

'No, not mine, but very apt, nonetheless,' he had replied teasingly and refused to elaborate further.

'Madame?' the groom said, rousing her from her daydream.

'Ah, yes... we must proceed,' she replied.

She was acutely aware of him, this pleasant young man in his tight suede breeches and laced waistcoat, worn over a striped cotton shirt. His complexion was ruddy through outdoor work, his hair bleached by the sun, and he had impudent blue eyes that gleamed with admiration for her. She could see his arousal, and longed to take out his thick serpent and caress it till it spat; Hercule had taken his fill of her last night, finding his own resolution but refusing to grant her the same favour. Sometimes it amused him to keep her boiling with frustration.

'Come here, Jacques,' she said softly.

'I can't, madame,' he answered, rubbing the uncomfortable bulge he yearned to release. 'It's forbidden just now. The comte will dismiss me and make sure no one in the district employs me.'

'Oh, Jacques, no one will know,' she pleaded, her mouth red and seductive, her eyelids heavy, senses inflamed by the risk of discovery.

He groaned through his teeth and unbuttoned. His prick escaped, seeking a nest in which to burrow. He reached for Sylvia. Her nipples, instantly aroused, firmed at his touch. Within seconds, he had her backed against a stall, lifting her high in sinewy arms, her legs widespread around his waist. Then he impaled her on to his exposed organ.

Sylvia whimpered her pleasure, one hand diving down to

rub her kernel, the other arm round his neck. He pressed his lips fervently to hers, his tongue darting into her luscious open mouth, his hands cupping the hemispheres of her buttocks, strong labourer's hands that held her firmly, brooking no denial.

She was caught in a wonderful sensual web, oblivious to everything except this crying need for completion. She raised herself on his cock, and then sank slowly down, smelling their mingled juices, feeling the delicious, slippery wetness that made this action so easy.

Her passion mounted. She tangled her tongue with his, rubbing her breasts against the coarseness of his leather jerkin, her finger massaging her nubbin. Jacques grunted, the earthy smell of his sweat tantalising her nostrils, his cock so turgid within her that she thought it might explode at any moment. She came against her finger while he panted and strained, his hips pumping frantically till he climaxed in a great surge.

He laid his curly fair head on her shoulder and rested there, heartbeat slowing, the sweat soaking through the back of his shirt. Sylvia unwound one of her thighs from his body and put her foot on the floor, taking her weight. She felt his limp cock slip from her, sticky against her pubis, and lowered her other leg, freeing herself, and he voiced his protest.

'Don't leave me, madame. I can't get enough of you. I've never seen anyone so beautiful. He don't treat you right, the comte. My God, if I were him I'd wrap you in silks, smother you in furs and jewels and care for you, feed you strawberries and cream every day. You'd not find me whipping and abusing you,' he muttered, his sun-browned face shining with sincerity.

She placed tender fingers over his lips. 'Hush,' she said. 'You must not say such things. Perhaps harsh treatment is what I need and want. Have you given this thought?'

'I don't understand, madame,' he said, shaking his head, his open, honest countenance clouded. 'Who'd want to be shown up in public? And I've seen a common forester use you... and others, besides, poking their cocks in you, the dirty

231

bastards!'

'You should thank your lucky stars that the comte is so generous with my person,' she replied with a crooked little smile. 'Otherwise, we'd not have been together so intimately.' Then, able to think clearly once lust had been appeased, she added briskly, 'It's time to get me ready for him.'

Jacques sighed unhappily, but dared not disobey. It was more than his job was worth. No matter what he felt towards Comte Avenall's mistress, he was in no position to challenge him.

The articles required were already hanging over a trestle and she stood still while Jacques fastened a girth around her waist that covered her from upper pubis to ribs, laced at the back like stays. He added a filly crupper. This passed between her legs, digging into her anal avenue, its central strap dampening from the moisture creeping from her vulva. Every time she moved, she could feel it brushing against the rings and rubbing her bud.

A leather, gold-studded choker was clasped round her throat, her bare breasts emphasised by the thongs passing round and lifting them, crossing her chest. Her nipples were kept erect by silver clamps decorated with bells that jingled as her breasts bounced, and her wrists were banded by deep cuffs to match the collar.

She sat on a stool while Jacques, still sulking, knelt to help her into knee-high boots with flat soles, lacing them tightly round her calves. Then he rose to place an elaborate headdress over her hair. It was adorned with gems and crested with black ostrich plumes.

Next he took up a phallus-shaped object, smooth at the glans but with a long, flowing, chestnut horsetail at the base. Sylvia stood up, presented her back to him, gripped the stall tightly with her hands and spread her legs.

Jacques, aroused once more, dipped the dildo's tip in a jar of oil. Then she felt his hands on her buttocks, parting them gently but firmly. His fingers strayed.

'Jacques!' she cried sharply, controlling her own urge to

have him take her again.

He desisted reluctantly. The mock phallus pressed against her anal ring, and her muscles wanted to eject it, but she controlled them, feeling the large oily thing slide deeper and deeper into her nether orifice. At last the tail tickled her crease and the tops of her thighs and she knew that she was now transformed into the sprightly mare the comte required.

She opened her mouth to allow the passage of the metal bit between her teeth. The bridle and reins were attached to rings on either side. She practised her role for a moment, snorting through her nose, whinnying and pawing the ground, the restraints round her genitals stimulating desire, hot waves of lust rolling through her groin.

'Well done,' Hercule complimented as he strolled through the big arched double doors, totally ignoring Jacques. 'What a charming filly you make, Sylvia. I swear I shall miss our excursions when the weather gets colder. There's already a touch of autumn on the breeze, and I can't risk you developing an ague, my precious one.'

He patted her rump and gave the plug in her fundament a quick jab, making her spasm, her loins ablaze. He was faultlessly attired in riding breeches and boots, a red jacket and silk topper. He flourished a long whip. Sylvia quivered at his touch, and prayed he would not be aware of the odour of Jacques' secretions that lingered between her legs. The comte was shrewd and little escaped his notice. She did not want her bucolic swain to get into trouble on her behalf.

Jacques, glowering resentfully, brought over a lightweight, two-wheeled chariot. It was a strong though dainty vehicle, varnished in cherry-red picked out in gold, its trappings a tribute to the lorimers' art. Sylvia, knowing her part, backed between the curved wooden shafts and took them in her hands. Jacques fastened her cuffs securely, his fingers lingering on her skin, and attached the long straps that linked the girth to the sulky.

It was beautifully balanced, the weight slight even when

Hercule occupied the maroon velvet seat. Sylvia stood motionless, waiting the pull of the reins on the bit. When it came, it was accompanied by the merest whisper of the whip end.

Her head jerked up. She lifted her feet high and trotted out into the yard, the chariot bowling behind her. The phallus jiggled in her anus, the tail swishing realistically, and she set up a rhythm, clopping across the gravel and, responding to a pull on the bridle, turning down the avenue towards the lake.

Her skin was soon lathered in a light sweat, and the whip flicked her haunches, urging her to keep up a steady pace. The splendid formal gardens, the stately trees and velvet sward swept by, and the blue lake stretched ahead, as if a piece of sky had fallen to earth.

Groundsmen glanced up as the sulky passed them. Sylvia blushed scarlet. She had been driven out several times by now but had never got used to the stares of these rough men who tended Hercule's herbaceous borders and flowering shrubs, clipped the privets into the shapes of birds and animals, and rolled and scythed the grass.

Somehow, she felt more naked then ever, the tail swishing against her buttocks, the shaft pushed into her anus. They must be aware of how it was kept in place, those workmen with the sly eyes who touched their forelocks respectfully as their lord drove by, his mistress between the shafts.

To the left lay the chateau, its facade adorned with busts in sheltered niches. There were four large circular turrets and four smaller ones, each with conical tops like witches' hats, and the whole was decorated with scrolled stonework, resembling icing on a wedding cake.

Smoke coiled from a dozen square chimney pots. In the distance stood a dovecote, and the round brick building that housed the comte's pigeons. He was fond of eating the latter baked in delicate puff pastry, a dish in which his chef specialised. In several ways he reminded Sylvia of Theo, priding himself on being a connoisseur – of fine food and wine, art and literature and sexual diversions.

Sylvia's eyes scanned the vista, and she brooded on it.

This was her master's domain where she might be incarcerated for the rest of her existence. There would be no security, of course. He could never marry her, for she was still Theo's wife. One day he would bring an aristocratic lady home as his bride, hoping to breed an heir. And what will happen to me then? Sylvia mused. Shall I be dispatched to Madame Fedora?

The whip walloped her smartly, the dildo shifted and plunged deeper, the tiny bells on her nipples rang as her breasts jounced, and tears ran down her face, were dammed by the straps, then inched onwards to drip off her chin.

They left the formal gardens, circled the lake, and approached a folly built over a grotto, a pretty concept for a rich man's fancy. This was better. It was a private spot with no coarse eyes to watch her. Three tugs on the reins and Sylvia slowed, standing shivering as the wheels ceased turning. Hercule was right. There was a definite nip in the air.

He climbed down between the shafts and, positioning himself with legs astride, withdrew the dildo from Sylvia's rectum and replaced this wooden phallus with the real thing. He cupped her mons and thrust aside the filly crupper, finding her clitoris and moving his cock faster in her arsehole.

'Wonderful... wonderful,' he muttered, his breathing heavy and uneven. 'My gorgeous wild mare.'

She, too, panted from exertion and excitement, her clitoris burning under his finger as he massaged it hard. She needed that harsh friction, feeling the extreme pressure of his cock in her anus, the splitting, in and out sensation, the terrible driving heat as he forced her climax, shouting,

'Do it now! Come for me!'

Sylvia convulsed in her harness, orgasmic shocks tearing through her as Hercule cried out and swamped her with hot spurts of semen.

He held her hard against him for an instant, her back pressed to his belly and chest. She heard him speak and opened her eyes, the world righting itself again, no longer a whirling sphere of star-spangled darkness.

'If only you were mine for all time,' he sighed, his words astonishing her, spoken in so sorrowful a tone.

'But I am, aren't I?' she rejoined.

He shifted then, standing back, then dried his replete penis on the horsetail, hid it in his breeches and buttoned them. 'Of course,' he muttered, recovering himself. 'Mine, until I tell you otherwise.'

He replaced the plug in her anus, took his place on the velvet-upholstered seat and shook the reins. Sylvia leaned into the shafts and moved off, the pull on the bridle indicating that she should return to the chateau.

'I am expecting a visitor this evening,' Hercule said, seated at his desk in the library where he spent much time cataloguing his treasures.

'Yes?' Sylvia replied, looking up from the piece of gros-point in her lap, the needle poised over a half finished damask rose.

'Yes. You will make yourself especially lovely, and appear here nude. On your knees, mind. This is an honoured guest and you are to do everything he desires. Do you understand?'

'Yes, master,' she murmured, and her heart sank.

She stuck the needle through the canvas again, trying to ward off alarm. What now? she thought, and put down the tapestry frame.

The library was filled with warm, golden dimness. The perfume of the exotic flowers tumbling in carefully arranged profusion from an antique Chinese urn mingled with the spice of Morocco leather, printers' ink, old parchments and dusty books.

'May I be permitted to know who this is?' she asked, as she started to rise, a slender figure in an artlessly simple faille gown with a Greek key-pattern around the hem.

'You may not,' he growled, glaring at her through his pince-nez. Some inner worry seemed to be agitating him. 'Get you gone, madame, and have your woman prepare you.'

'Do you know who is expected?' Sylvia questioned Phoebe when she reached her bedchamber, which was beginning to darken as twilight fell.

'No, milady. I haven't any idea,' Phoebe replied, and continued ordering the servants about as they hauled up buckets of hot and cold water for her mistress's bath.

Phoebe was a person of some standing in the backstairs hierarchy, personal maid to the comte's lady. She revelled in this position, a shrill-tongued martinet, now that she had mastered the language, giving no quarter and taking her pick among the footmen, practising her wiles on that other important personage, the comte's valet.

When bathed, fragrant as a lily, her skin soft and smooth, Sylvia added the smallest amount of cosmetic – rouge brushed on with a hare's foot, powder dusting her face. Phoebe sprayed her with a generous cloud of perfume, and then draped a pale pink silk cloak over her shoulders. It was fastened at the neck by a ruby brooch and whispered down to her bare feet. Hercule had ordained that this, coupled with her diamond necklace, was all she should be allowed to wear.

She supped in her room, obeying his orders, then when his manservant came to summon her, walked down the central staircase and entered the library with all the aplomb of a duchess, head held proudly on her slender neck.

It was candlelit, a fire crackling in the carved stone fireplace with its lofty hood. Contrary to Sylvia's expectations, Hercule was alone, glooming in his great chair by the hearth, a large globular wineglass held between both hands.

He looked up as she came in, but did not rise. Instead he indicated that she should kneel. Her robe stretched out behind her, brushing the mosaic tiles, her body bare, nipples erect, the fair down rising on her limbs.

As if suddenly coming to a decision, Hercule jumped to his

feet, saying, sharply, 'Take that off!'

With shaking fingers, she released the clasp and the pink silk puddled around her. He was in an irascible mood and she trembled, waiting obediently on her knees, eyes lowered. Hercule gave an exasperated gesture and two servants jumped to attention.

'Blindfold her!' he snapped.

A silk scarf was placed round her eyes and, plunged into inky blackness, Sylvia felt herself lifted and guided to where the desk stood. Then she was pushed over it, the leather chilly against her breasts, the brass edge digging into her belly, the diamonds stabbing into her throat.

'You've been fucking the groom, haven't you?' Hercule said from somewhere behind her. 'How dare you, without my permission?'

'Don't dismiss him, please, master,' she begged, not caring what happened to her if that innocent youth might be spared. 'The fault was mine. I freely admit it. I seduced him.'

'Wicked, wicked girl!' Hercule shouted. 'You will stay still under the lash, madame. I'll not have you tied. Your obedience as you take your punishment shall be willing and absolute.'

'Yes, master,' she said, her voice unsteady. 'And you'll pardon him?'

'It will cost you dear,' he snarled, and she heard the whistling sound of a whip being tested on the air. 'Twelve strokes, as well as the dozen I intend to inflict on you.'

'I agree,' she sobbed, her body already jerking as if the lash had cut into it.

'Very well.'

There followed a time of such tempestuous agony that she felt she might die of it. Hercule did not spare her, the lash burrowing in, biting, cutting, welting her buttocks and thighs while she clung to the desk, helplessly enduring, till it seemed that she was suddenly divorced from pain. She floated somewhere high up, finding peace in the centre of this hurricane.

Her body still bucked as each merciless blow descended on it, yet now she had the strength to submit to the most rigorous punishment. In a sudden flash of revelation she understood what Madame Fedora had meant about the strange dichotomy of pain and pleasure.

When it seemed that she would be whipped through all eternity, Hercule stopped. Sylvia, fainting, was slapped into consciousness and her blindfold removed. Hercule forced her to the floor, his hand on the back of her neck.

Humbled and submissive, she knelt there with heaving breasts. Slowly, through the thumping of the blood in her ears, she heard the sound of footsteps drawing near. She dared to look through her tear-spiked eyelashes, seeing the vast shiny floor and the tips of a pair of shoes part covered by the bottoms of fawn trousers. There was something else: the end of a Malacca walking stick.

Its owner stepped closer. An odour pervaded Sylvia's nostrils – heady and potent, one she could never forget; cedar and spice, the smell of one special male, overlaid by tincture of opium.

In a flash she threw back her head and looked up.

'Theo!' she gasped.

'Good evening, wife,' he answered, his voice laced with that well remembered and dreaded sarcasm.

'You?' she blurted. 'Here?'

He chuckled, amber eyes slanting with mocking amusement. 'Why not?' he asked, and raising his cane, used the end to lift back one of the curling tresses that had fallen forward over her breast, then trailed it down till it touched the rings in her labia. He nodded in approval, adding, 'The comte is a very old friend of mine. Is that not so, Hercule?'

'But how… why…?' she stammered, staring up at him, drinking in the sight of the fine bone structure of his face, the cruel, pleasure-loving mouth, the wavy black hair.

His skin was much darker through exposure to the sun, swarthy as a gypsy's, and his eyes had a golden glitter that filled her with a delectable mixture of fear and delight. She jumped up, the rush of adrenalin blotting out pain, and fell into his arms.

'Oh, Theo... Theo! You've come for me! Take me home, for God's sake!' she begged through tears and laughter.

He held her off, though she could feel his hands trembling. 'Not so fast, my dear,' he cautioned, but could not resist taking one of her breasts in his palm, his thumb revolving on the nipple.

Emotions chased through her in quick succession – wonder, terror, desire, and anger.

'Don't you want me back?' she cried indignantly.

This was terrible. Supposing he had heard all that had transpired since their last meeting. Could he present her to the world as his lady, when she had been used and abused by so many people? Would he, in fact, feel deeply ashamed of her?

'Not so fast,' he replied, and glanced over at Hercule who was watching them with a strangely sad, cryptic smile. 'Let us consider your present state. Hercule has progress reports, I think.'

'I have, sir, and we'll discuss it later, but I shall relinquish your wife with regret, I must admit,' the comte answered, the harsh grooves each side of his mouth deepening as he looked across at Sylvia. 'During the time we have spent together, I have grown to love you, Lady Aubrey.'

She could not believe her ears, amazed by this unexpected declaration. 'Love, sir?' she murmured. 'I had no idea. You did not treat me as if you loved me.'

'Love comes in many guises,' he demurred, soothing his feelings with a pinch of snuff. 'I have spent much effort in subduing you,' he went on, tucking his lawn kerchief back into his pocket. 'Bringing you to heel, and turning you into a *real* woman.'

'I never asked this of you,' she replied, pithily. 'The matter was entirely out of my hands.'

Shivering with shock and emotion, she reached for the cloudy pink cloak and covered herself. Neither of them stopped her. The soft material enfolded her body, her whipped bottom showing through it, the colour of crushed roses. Thus clad, she drew herself to her full height, recovering her dignity, though in pieces inside.

'You may stay with me if you wish, Sylvia,' the comte expounded, the candlelight sparkling on the silver in his hair. 'If you go, I shall miss you more than I care to admit.' He switched his gaze to Theo, continuing, 'I am prepared to reimburse you for all the expenses you've incurred during this exercise and more besides, if you'll sell your wife to me. What do you say, Sylvia?'

'She has no choice in the matter,' Theo snapped, a black scowl bringing his strongly marked brows together. 'This was not the arrangement we made, Avenall.'

In a trice his arms folded about Sylvia and she closed her eyes and gave a rapturous sigh, relaxing against him, aware of the animal magnetism he exuded from every pore. Yet as his words penetrated her mind, she suddenly pushed him away, beating at his chest with her clenched fists.

'Arrangement? What are you talking about, Theo?'

His eyes narrowed to feline slits and his upper lip curled, even as he grabbed her back into the heat and hardness of his body.

'You think everything that has taken place was pure chance?' he said, and she could feel a movement in his groin as he trapped one of her thighs between his muscular legs, letting her know his cock was erect, ready to drive into her core and repossess her.

'Of course… a series of unfortunate accidents,' she answered, her wayward desires threatening to swamp reason. She writhed against him as if he was already whipping her.

'Oh, no. That is not so,' Theo brought out, and she was thrilled by the fierce light in his sherry-gold eyes. 'The whole thing was planned by me, down to the last detail. I had you

241

abducted by pirates. Torr Hearn is in my pay. Captain Dabney had been instructed not to resist him. I own the merchantman and the pirate ship, though Torr is mostly a smuggler, working for me. I've known Madame Fedora for years – she'll do anything for money. And Comte Avenall owed me a favour.'

Sylvia was dumbstruck, then, 'You knew your orders had been carried out? How?'

'I had my informants. Letters reached me in Zante and Torr anchored in my cove for a while. He found the whole thing highly amusing. When it seemed you had been suitably tamed and subdued, I sailed for France with him… to collect you.'

'Lady Rowena had a hand in this dastardly plot?' she hissed, furious at their deception. She was angry with Torr for frightening her, disappointed in the seemingly honourable Captain Dabney, and thoroughly disgusted with the instigator of the whole charade – her satanic husband.

'Naturally. We discussed it at length after you had bitten Balty's tool. You were too defiant and wilful. Strict training was necessary for your own good. It was an interesting experiment and has brought the desired result. You took Hercule's latest beating with style. It was a pleasure to watch.'

'You watched me being thrashed?'

'Of course,' he answered carelessly, swinging his cane. 'There are many useful peepholes in the chateau. I wanted to see how you responded, and if our plan had worked.'

Sylvia wanted to slap his arrogant face, but did not quite dare.

'What a horrible, despicable scheme! How could you do that to anyone, let alone your own wife!' she shouted, her eyes flashing with rage. Her very hair seemed to spark with it. 'To inflict such degradation on me! You're a monster, sir!'

'Tush, my dear! Such language, and to your lord and master, too,' Theo reproved with mock gentleness, then he added as his fingers tightened on her arm like talons ready to rend and maim. 'You should go down on your knees and thank me for taking the trouble to provide you with such severe discipline.

Come, confess that you've known more pleasure than you ever expected to have in your whole life.'

Sylvia hung her head. She could not conceal the blush that spread a rosy glow over her breasts, throat and face. Her entire body seemed to be heated by it. Should she tell him that, yes, she had known voluptuous satisfaction beyond her wildest of wild dreams – situations filled with painful ecstasy – orgasms that had carried her to heaven and back – agony that had plunged her into the deepest, fiery pits of hell?

Above all, through all, and to her everlasting shame, she ached for Theo's phallus. The heat between their bodies interacted. Her breasts throbbed with the urgent need to feel his fingers on her nipples, her clitoris was a hard pearl eager for his tongue, her rectum spasmed with longing for his invasion, and her love-tunnel yearned to have him sheath his weapon in its velvety depths.

And the cane in his hand! Oh, bliss!

To think of him raising it, testing it, bringing it slashing down across her buttocks set the nectar flowing from her lower mouth.

'You want me to confess my sins to you?' she asked with a catch in her voice.

He took fire from her, sensing her capitulation, and his cock twitched against her imprisoned hip. 'I command it,' he grated.

'And I am to come with you, not remain with the comte?' she breathed, staring up into the slumbering fire of his eyes.

'Yes, until I tire of you,' he said. 'The future is in your hands. Please me, obey me, entertain me with fresh delights and, who knows, we may stay together till death us do part.'

Sylvia hung on the triangle in the torture chamber that lay in the bowels of Chateau Grecourt. No longer used to wrest information from unlucky prisoners, it was Hercule's punishment place for those of specialised tastes, in great demand when he held weekend frolics. His guests hunted and fished, rode and danced, gambled and fucked, but the high spot was a visit to the dungeon.

Coals smouldered in a brazier. Candles blazed in sconces on the walls and in flambeaux standing on the stone floor, illuminating the whipping blocks, gags, blindfolds and chains, ferrules and rods, arsehole plugs, dildos, clips, cuffs and shackles that provided a range of amusements for deviants.

She trembled, eager for the pain to be over so that the pleasure could begin. Theo made her wait, deliberately refraining from touching her once she had been firmly tied to the cross. Before that, she had reached for his mouth, and sought the dark male nipples under his shirt, longing to tweak then tongue them, and all in vain. With callous deliberation he had kept her hands away from his crotch.

He faced her now, stripped to breeches, thigh-length black boots and a full-sleeved white shirt, the neck thrown open over his hirsute, deeply tanned chest. He braced the Malacca cane between his hands, and looked so devilish that fear shot along her nerves and quivered in her epicentre.

'You have disgraced the name of Aubrey,' he said in clipped tones. 'Firstly, by your defiance and insolence towards myself. Secondly, by your loose and bawdy behaviour during your travels. Thirdly, by accepting diamonds from Comte Avenall, which I have already taken from you. You're a lascivious, greedy slut, and I shall beat you for it. But before I commence, I order you to describe in detail your dirty, filthy fornications.'

'I submitted to Torr Hearn, the pirate,' she whispered in a strangled voice, entering into the game. 'He beat me and used me in front of his crew, making me come. Then we stayed in his cabin for hours, fucking. He tupped and buggered me and I sucked his cock, and he feasted on my juices, tonguing my cunt and bringing me off over and over again.'

'A pirate's doxy. How foul. Next!' Theo shouted, and brought the stick sharply across her thighs.

She clenched her muscles, took the white-hot pain, and whimpered, 'I was caned at the slave auction and sold to a procuress and became an inmate of her brothel.'

'Did many men use you?' Theo asked, his fingertips flicking over the tight buds of her nipples. Desire flared from the hard tips to her clitoris, and her vagina convulsed.

'No, my lord, but women did. There was one called Lisette, a handsome girl who liked me to lick her quim. She had such clever fingers and an artful tongue, bringing me to thunderous orgasms. The Abbess and Madame Fedora examined my arse, inserted their fingers and said I was tight. My rectum was stretched and plugged. I was forced to wear larger and larger dildos in my rectum,' Sylvia cried, the shame and secret pleasure of her adventures making her hot within.

'Go on,' Theo commanded, a mighty erection rising under his tight breeches from gusset to waistband.

'I was whipped by all who felt inclined and then given to the comte who had me pierced and branded and then brought here,' Sylvia went on, fascinated by the effect her words were having on his bulge. 'He has taken me in every orifice, made me dress as a horse and pull his chariot, and sodomised me regularly.'

'What a lewd tale! You're promiscuous, madam. A woman of easy virtue. A harlot. A whore. Do you repent?' Theo roared and brought the cane down across her belly, knocking the breath from her.

'I repent,' she gasped, jerking at the cuffs that bound her to the wooden frame, the wellspring of her being opening in the aftershocks of pain, hungry for the reward of pleasure.

'And now you will submit only to me, your lord?' He sounded so angry that her bowels churned.

'Yes… yes… I submit. I am yours,' she sobbed, and knew that this was true.

She *was* his for evermore. No more rebellion – well only a soupcon to give him an excuse to beat her, not that he needed one.

'This is as it should be,' he said, and gave himself over to the furious delight of wielding the cane.

Each blow was a separate source of pain that gradually

changed to sexual heat. Determined to please him, she screamed at each swipe and, looking into his set face, was satisfied to see he was so aroused from asserting his mastery over her that it would not be long before he lost control, flung the whip away and penetrated her violently with his rampant cock.

He beat her thighs, her belly, the undersides of her breasts, and she bore it stoically, her mind streaking ahead to the time to come. For as surely as dawn follows night, so Theo would free her from bondage and bear her away to his bed, there to perform the magical act, that blend of passion, fierceness and divine unity that she craved.

They lay amidst the sweaty, tangled sheets of the four-poster. Sylvia's body smarted, and her juices smeared Theo's skin as she straddled his legs and took his phallus into her mouth. Her fingers trailed between his thighs, caressing his balls, and he groaned.

She ran her tongue over the glans, tasting the salty emission, smelling and tasting herself on it, for her vagina had known it repeatedly since they left the torture chamber. Using all the skill she had acquired under Hercule's tutelage, she held the thick stem in one hand, caressing the satin-smooth skin, while Theo pushed upwards, pumping against the roof of her mouth.

He was nearing pleasure's critical point, but she showed no mercy. Then he suddenly pushed her off.

'I want you to watch me come,' he panted. 'I'd have you see it spurt from me.'

Sylvia ran her fingers down her belly and found her pubis, parting the swollen lips and smoothing the mingled fluids of their intercourse over her clitoris, excitement heavy within her. Theo was frowning and wincing, his penis held in his hand, the flushed head protruding between his fingers. Then it gave a final jerk and like a volcano spitting lava, its tribute shot from him, hitting Sylvia's breasts.

She gasped, caught some of it and spread it over her body as her orgasm flared and exploded within her. Theo kept spurting and spurting, as if it rained semen, until the pleasure had drained out of him and he was truly spent. Then he slumped back against the pillows and she fell across him, lying on his chest.

She felt his lips on her forehead as he eased her down till she rested with her head cradled in the hollow of his bronzed shoulder. One of the candles guttered and went out in a puddle of wax, a thread of smoke coiling upwards. Dawn smudged the windows and somewhere outside a blackbird began to sing.

'But, Theo,' Sylvia said, following a dreamy train of thought. 'I still don't quite understand how you could have treated me so shabbily.'

He sighed and stroked her hair, then circled her nipples, her navel, the swell of her mound, finally running a finger round the rim of her labia with a touch like slippery satin.

'It was a test, a jest, a prank, if you like. Balty was all for it and several fellows laid wagers that it couldn't be done,' he said casually, leaving her cleft and tapping her thighs lightly at first, then increasing the pressure to stinging slaps.

'A wager? Is that all, my lord? You did it to amuse yourself and your friends?' she demanded, squirming under his hard hand.

'Not only that. Doesn't it prove anything to you?' he asked indulgently, turning his attention to her breasts, striking one and watching it bounce, then rubbing her labia again.

'No. What?' she questioned, her lower lips responding to his fingers like flowers opening to the sun.

'Well, my sweet, I should hardly have taken so much trouble unless I cared for you, should I?' he said, continuing to massage her bud with his thumb while he slipped two fingers into the lush folds of her vagina.

'You care for me?' she whispered, wonderingly, giving a little gasp as he withdrew his wet digits and began to probe into her anus.

'Of course, my witch. I didn't intend to let you fasten your claws into my heart, but you've done it, nonetheless. I'm pleased with you, my dear. I watched you pulling the comte in his little chariot and the sight of it delighted me.'

'When did you arrive? How could you have seen me?' she asked, not knowing whether to laugh or cry because he had witnessed her in the guise of a mare.

'Early this morning, but secretly. Only Hercule knew I was here,' he whispered. 'He told me about his habit of driving the sulky with you between the shafts and said I would get a fine view from the battlements. When we get back to England I shall take you to Monk's Park and have my own gig made so that I, too, can be your driver. My God, the thought of seeing your haunches rise and fall, and flicking at them with my whip makes me hot as Hades.'

Sylvia went quiet, listening to the soft, lapping intimacy of his voice as he stopped playing with her and, filled with a superabundance of sexual energy, entered her again. He moved in a leisurely fashion and his shaft, sinking into her molten depths, created a dark, secret heat.

She stilled the rising tide of desire that threatened to engulf her, needing to speak with him. Could it be true that he loved her, was intrigued by her, felt his life incomplete if she was not there?

Joy gathered like a great bubble in the region of her heart.

'That's all very well, and I want to go home with you, but you ordered that I should be branded with someone's crest,' she argued, and her hands clenched about his buttocks to quell that deep, slow pumping action. It was essential that he listen to her. 'How can you love me and how can I be truly yours if I bear another man's mark?'

She heard him chuckling, low in his chest. Then he withdrew his penis from her and rolled her over on to her stomach. He sat up, his swarthy face in shadow but his eyes shining like polished amber. She felt his fingers feathering across her weals, making her skin smart. It was as if he was reading her pain as a blind person will read the shape of objects. Then he touched the scar made by the hot iron, fingering the edge of it, and the pattern within.

'My dear Lady Aubrey,' he said with teasing formality. 'The sigil you bear is my family crest. It's a pity you can't see it, for it was skilfully executed. The heraldic beast is a wyvern, winged and two-legged, a cross between a dragon and a griffin.'

'And the motto?' she asked, stretching a hand across the pillow to reach him, Theo Aubrey, rake, profligate and rumoured devil worshipper, who might – just *might* – need her.

'It has been ours since my ancestors invaded England... Norman knights... robber barons no less,' he replied, with his sardonic, cynical smile. 'It says: *Nosce teipsum*. "Know thyself". It is most suitable for you, don't you think? Have you learned to know yourself, Sylvia?'

More exciting titles available from Chimera

* * *

All **Chimera** titles are available from your local bookshop or newsagent, or direct from our mail order department. Please send your order with a cheque or postal order (made payable to *Chimera Publishing Ltd*) to: **Chimera Publishing Ltd., Readers' Services, PO Box 152, Waterlooville, Hants, PO8 9FS**. Or call our **24 hour telephone/fax credit card hotline: +44 (0)23 92 783037** (Visa, Mastercard, Switch, JCB and Solo only).

To order, send: Title, author, ISBN number and price for each book ordered, your full name and address, cheque or postal order for the total amount, and include the following for postage and packing:
UK and BFPO: £1.00 for the first book, and 50p for each additional book to a maximum of £3.50.
Overseas and Eire: £2.00 for the first book, £1.00 for the second and 50p for each additional book.

*Titles £5.99. All others £4.99

For a copy of our free catalogue please write to:

Chimera Publishing Ltd
Readers' Services
PO Box 152
Waterlooville
Hants
PO8 9FS

or email us at:
sales@chimerabooks.co.uk

or purchase from our range of superb titles at:
www.chimerabooks.co.uk

Sales and Distribution in the USA and Canada

LPC Group
1436 West Randolph Street
Chicago
IL 60607
(800) 626-4330

* * *